# CRIME IN RETIREMENT

A fiercely addictive mystery

# CATHERINE MOLONEY

*Detective Markham Mystery Book 17*

JOFFE BOOKS

Joffe Books, London
www.joffebooks.com

First published in Great Britain in 2022

Cover art by Dee Dee Book Covers


ISBN: 978-1-80405-496-3

# PROLOGUE

Normally Chloe Finch felt very drained after Christmas. Too many mince pies. Too much enforced jollity. Too much everything, including the in-laws.

But on the morning of Saturday 22 January, she felt her spirits lift.

Perhaps it had something to do with the clear blue skies and glorious sunshine after days of unrelenting grey drizzle. In such conditions, the Rosemount Retirement Home always looked its best.

As she sipped her coffee in the staff room, Chloe told herself that all things considered, this was a cushy berth and she had been lucky to get it. Healthcare assistant at Rosemount was a cut above working for Bromgrove General Hospital or any of the local authority providers thanks to the home's 'celebrity' cachet, with just a dozen rooms available for illustrious citizens who had distinguished themselves in some field or other and those who possessed the financial resources to spend their twilight years cushioned by comfort that most could only dream of.

Situated on the town's outskirts, with a commanding view over Bromgrove Clough, the home was a two-storeyed white stucco Georgian mansion with gently curving wings either side of a portico entrance. Mantled in ivy, the building's aspect was modestly unpretentious, but on closer inspection there was no mistaking the air of exclusivity and quiet luxury.

The long winding driveway to the house, bordered by tall pines and cypresses, was dotted with quaint pergolas and latticed arbours, affording a vista onto banks of crocuses and fragrant narcissi in spring, changing to vibrant bougainvillea in summer.

In front of the house, down a flight of shallow steps, was a simple knot garden, its old-fashioned box hedges, symmetrical flower beds and classical lines in keeping with the restrained elegance of the main façade.

At the rear, however, things were more lavish. To the right was a rose garden, its concentric circles separated by low hedges of dwarf myrtle and gravelled walkways. The central area comprised a courtyard whose granite flags formed an interlocking pattern of grey and white, dominated by a three-tiered baroque sculpture, rather like a wedding cake, topped by a semi-nude Venus combing her hair. On the left, through an archway, a walled herb garden soothed and charmed even in January with its ranks of dainty snowdrops, cyclamens and Butcher's Broom. Steps from the courtyard led to a red sandstone path, bordered by well-established topiary, which meandered gracefully down past manicured lawns on either side to a lake surrounding a small island with a willow oak in the middle. Beyond that, was a wildflower meadow at the boundary of the home's grounds.

Rosemount's brochure said that its setting held 'the suspended stillness of a Constable landscape'. All very la-di-dah, but after looking at some of the painter's pictures online, Chloe got the point. It was the kind of magical countryside setting — all beautiful and calm — that made you just want to sit and stare.

Sitting and staring was pretty much all that most of the residents could do these days, since virtually all were elderly with varying medical issues and levels of dependency.

But there was no sense inside Rosemount of physical unpleasantness or the indignities of age and infirmity. The place had the feel of an ultra-genteel private members' club, with the faded elegance of tea-stained chintz and worn Aubusson carpets. 'None of those awful Modernist prints and everything decorated to the nines,' as Mrs Clark was wont to say with a contemptuous sniff.

Chloe's expression softened at the thought of Andrée Clark OBE, former ballerina, television personality and *grande dame* of Bromgrove's cultural scene. She knew Mrs Clark had been head judge on some sort of TV competition and a big noise in the Arts once upon a time. One of the nurses said she'd even been on *The South Bank Show* with Melvyn Bragg, and all kinds of folk were always wanting her to do stuff, but these days she preferred to take it easy.

Chloe liked Mrs Clark with her bottle-black hair coiled into a dancer's chignon, green eyes, false eyelashes, over made-up features and smoker's rasp. She had to be in her sixties, but there was something very youthful about her energy and high spirits. 'Like Tennyson's Mariana, I'm surrounded by dilapidation and decay,' she was in the habit of proclaiming theatrically, but there was nothing pitiable about her, even though illness now forced her to use a wheelchair increasingly often.

The only thing about Mrs Clark that did creep Chloe out was those weird dolls in her room. What the heck was that all about?

Apparently, Mrs Clark was a serious collector, but how many dolls did one person need? Her bedroom was always a nightmare to dust, but that wasn't what unnerved Chloe. No, what spooked her were the figurines in bisque porcelain wearing velvet, lace and taffeta ballet costumes, some with their limbs extended in unnatural-looking positions while others perched atop musical box contraptions which you wound up to make them dance. Chloe hated their pebble-flat black eyes and pursed-up prissy little mouths painted rosebud pink. 'They're by Jumeau, and some even have musical recordings inside,' Mrs Frost the home's manager said reverentially, but then 'Frostie' was mad about ballet and all that jazz so no wonder she lapped it all up. Personally, Chloe didn't care if they were worth millions, she just couldn't get rid of the feeling that the dolls were somehow *evil*. Equally strange was Mrs Clark's toy theatre for which she was always ordering miniature stage sets and accessories — right down to figures in the orchestra pit — as though by this means she could somehow recapture the glories of yesteryear.

'She's got to have autism or Asperger's,' Chloe's daughter Margaret, a nurse at Bromgrove General, insisted. 'Some kind of mental health thing.' But Chloe didn't think that was it. Mrs Clark was just unique . . . eccentric, a one-off.

To be honest, for all that she was freaked out by Rosemount's very own 'Valley of the Dolls', Chloe felt somehow obscurely proud that most of these residents who passed through the home weren't your common or garden patients, with many having led fascinating lives out in the world, so there was some truth in Mrs Frost's oft-repeated mantra that it was a 'privilege to look after them'.

Of course, now Chloe came to think of it, not everyone at Rosemount was seriously loaded or famous. She knew there were a few publicly funded patients who had passed through the home over the years under various arrangements with the local authority, but they blended in so seamlessly that she and the other staff had no idea which residents were fee-paying and which were what Mrs Clark called 'nonpukka'. Despite Mrs Frost being in thrall to her Dancing Queen (as the staff called Andrée when the manager was well out of earshot), she didn't gossip about such matters, so Chloe was willing to bet Mrs Clark was as much in the dark as everyone else.

She was relieved that it was Hafsah Peri's day off, since she didn't particularly care for the nurse who had overall responsibility for Bluebell Corridor's three residents: Mrs Clark, Mrs Linda Merryweather (well-known author of romantic fiction) and Mr Nicholas Gower (theologian and biblical scholar).

It wasn't racism or anything like that which made her uncomfortable around Hafsah. It's just that the woman was so starchy and such a Goody Two-Shoes, as though she considered herself far superior to the likes of Chloe. On the other hand, Mrs Clark loved her, so there had to be something special about the woman. She had found it difficult to stifle giggles when Hafsah came out of her patient's room one day clutching a velvety black doll with large gold earrings, a stiff cotton petticoat and pantaloons. 'She's called Belinda,' the nurse had confided rapturously. 'Very special . . . from Egypt, so Mrs Clark wanted me to have her as a reminder of home.' There wasn't a ban on gifts — not that Andrée Clark would have taken the slightest notice of any such prohibition — but in this case Chloe suspected that it was more a question of paring down the doll menagerie (most likely to make room for further purchases) than any particular mark of favour.

Linda Merryweather wasn't too bad — at least provided her sciatica wasn't playing up and nobody challenged her pre-eminence as chair of the Residents' Committee. Short, plump and bespectacled, with her white hair styled in a symmetrical perm like the queen's ('circa 1950', as Mrs Clark acidly observed), there was nothing in her appearance to suggest she was the best-selling author of steamy bodice-rippers, but so it was. Chloe had never read any — it just wouldn't feel right somehow — but Margaret said they 'weren't bad', which was high praise coming from an avid consumer of Penny Vincenzi and Danielle Steel.

Nicholas Gower was a total sweetie, just like someone's grandad even though he too was a writer — 'an expert on the Turin Shroud', as Mrs Frost had explained in an awed whisper. Chloe wasn't too sure what that was. Something to do with Jesus leaving his face on a tea towel, Margaret explained later, which sounded even freakier than Mrs Clark's dolls. But Mr Gower had a string of letters after his name and priest types writing to him from all over, so it was dead high-powered and respectable. Chloe thought Mr Gower looked a bit like Pope Benedict — the one before the bloke they had now . . . something about his shy lopsided smile and the way he looked too holy for words.

The large high-ceilinged staff room with its two bay windows overlooked the grounds at the back of the building. It was comfortable, albeit somewhat lacking in character when compared with the rest of the home ('very Trusthouse Forte', according to Mrs Clark). On the other hand, since visitors rarely saw it, there wasn't the same need for lavishness. Even so, it was a pleasant place to catch a breather, though the armchairs ranged in a semicircle in front of the ornate marble fireplace gave it the feel of being in a prayer meeting. Chloe always preferred to perch on one of the cushioned window seats from where she had a view of the outdoors and could tuck herself behind the heavy green damask curtains, the better to observe without being observed.

Mrs Frost's office was separate from the staff quarters (for which Chloe was devoutly thankful), so there was none of the usual paraphernalia of a business room, the rolltop Chippendale desk and chair over by the right-hand wall rarely used except for letter-writing and the like. The glass-fronted bookcases with assorted leather-bound volumes (never consulted by anyone in living memory), various small oil paintings of Bromgrove Clough, herringbone patterned red Axminster carpet, low oak coffee table and a few high-backed leather chairs ranged round the walls, all contributed to the impression that this was the reading room of some modest country house hotel. Above the fireplace hung a head and shoulders portrait of a moustachioed man incongruously sporting a fez and a sort of quilted Nehru jacket festooned with blue sash and an array of military decorations.

'General Charles Gordon,' Mr Gower had confided when she asked him about the picture. 'Victorian hero killed at Khartoum,' which left her none the wiser. 'They said he always went into battle with a cheroot, his cane and Christ,' he added with a twinkle. 'Bit of a matinée idol in his day.' With that face and whiskers, Chloe couldn't imagine him being anybody's pin-up, but she didn't like to say so for fear of sounding rude. One reason why she preferred a window seat to any of the armchairs, was the way General Gordon's eyes seemed to follow you round the room. He was worse than Mrs Clark's dolls when it came to that.

Enjoying the morning sunshine, Chloe stretched languorously, feeling curiously disinclined to move. She glanced at her watch. Nearly eight o'clock, so time to go and relieve the night shift.

Suppressing a groan, she made her way through to the tiny staff kitchen cunningly hidden behind a door in the wood-panelled wall that opened on a spring when the right spot was touched. Chloe always felt a childish thrill — as though she was the heroine of an Agatha Christie story — when she passed through the concealed door.

Not that there was anything mysterious or glamorous about the kitchen, which held all the basic conveniences but was at least immaculately clean and tidy; Mrs Frost insisted on that, though it caused some grumbling in the ranks — 'like we're always on bleeding parade'. Given the brooding presence of General Gordon in his gilt frame next door, it wasn't an inappropriate analogy.

Chloe rinsed her mug and returned it to the cupboard, then headed for the hall and the stairs to the first floor. There was a lift with art deco cast iron grille, but this was strictly for moving patients and, anyway, she needed to fight the flab. Margaret had given her a fancy Fitbit tracker for Christmas, but she felt self-conscious about using it until she'd shifted a few pounds, otherwise God only knew what unflattering statistics the gadget might reveal.

The house was very peaceful, all sound muffled as though it lay under an enchanted spell, waiting for the day's machinery to be set in motion.

The beautiful oak staircase was treacherously slippery without its plain mint-green stair runner, but in any event, residents rarely descended the stairs unattended. There was no trace of disinfectant or stale food or any of the other odours traditionally associated with a nursing home. Just the subtle scent of an old country house, vast ceramic bowls of potpourri on an antique dresser in the hallway and in the window recess halfway up the staircase contributing to the delightfully old-fashioned ambience.

Chloe vastly preferred the jewel-coloured medieval knights and ladies in the stained-glass window to gloomy old General Gordon of Khartoum. They all looked like they were having a high old time and not sitting in judgement on other people.

On the Bluebell Corridor, to the right at the top of the staircase, she made her way to the nursing station at the far end. Bearing little resemblance to the usual hospital nursing station, this was a comfortably appointed bedroom-cum-office with a monitoring console tastefully recessed within a walnut desk.

'Nothing to report,' was the laconic greeting from stocky Nurse Barbara Callaghan, obviously eager to take her leave. 'Claire should be along any minute,' she added, referring to the weekend agency nurse, 'but I can hang on if you like.'

'No, that's alright,' Chloe replied to the other's evident relief. 'I'll just check on them and let the kitchen know about breakfast.'

Padding along to Mrs Clark's room, she wondered ruefully if her patient had made any more auction purchases lately. Another troupe of flipping munchkins with their beady peepers would be the giddy limit . . .

The room was in darkness as she slipped in and went straight over to draw back the heavy maroon blackout curtains that the patient insisted on 'for her beauty sleep'.

Turning back towards the bed, Chloe's cheery greeting died in her throat at the sight before her.

Andrée Clark lay on her back with her hands fastened on the counterpane like claws. The former ballerina's gamine features were twisted in a grotesque grimace that seemed like a horrible parody of the geisha-like glance she had once flicked towards adoring fans. Staring at the congested features on the swansdown pillow, with bloodshot eyes protruding from their sockets, the dazed healthcare assistant wondered if her patient had suffered a fit or stroke.

Then her eyes wandered down to a livid weal around the neck and the appalling truth began to sink in.

This was no natural death.

*Andrée Clark had been strangled.*

On the bedside table stood Mrs Clark's favourite doll, a figurine in white porcelain with candyfloss blond hair to its shoulders, wearing a tutu with a crimson bodice and pink ballet slippers. The jointed arms were always extended high above its head in a ballet pose. But with a shock, Chloe saw that this time something was different.

One arm was lowered, a dainty finger pointed towards the woman in the bed.

As if the doll had come to life.

Hardly breathing, never taking her eyes off the taffeta-clad toy, Chloe backed towards the door.

## 1. NEW BEGINNINGS

As DI Gilbert 'Gil' Markham lounged on his favourite bench in the graveyard of St Chad's Parish Church overlooking the police station, according to his invariable habit at the start of a new investigation, he kept a wary eye out lest the new vicar ambush him for a spot of pastoral 'outreach', by way of building bridges with the local constabulary.

The Reverend Dodsworth, St Chad's previous incumbent, was a retiring individual who had instinctively understood the DI's need for reflective solitude. However, his successor — a former bank manager before he 'received the call' — had none of the same finesse, being in no way put off by Markham's aloofness and apparently determined to bring the handsome detective out of his shell (if not into his flock).

'Whass all that he said about a call?' Markham's former wingman, DS George Noakes had muttered after their last encounter with the vicar. 'Makes him sound like the Avon Lady.'

'He means his vocation,' the DI replied patiently. 'As in the call from God.'

'The last geezer was much better,' was Noakes's nostalgic verdict. 'Doddy always knew not to get in your face.' In fact, the Reverend Dodsworth giving Noakes a wide birth owed much to his nervousness at the other's jokes about 'sky pilots' and his decided preference for calling a spade a blunt instrument. However, Markham chose not to disillusion his sergeant, who continued to bewilder the unfortunate clergymen with witticisms such as 'Fighting's against my religion cos I'm a devout coward, *geddit*.' The Yorkshireman's psychological makeup was as much a source of mystification to the holy old man as it was to DCI Sidney ('Slimy Sid' to the troops), their boss in CID. Markham's hawkish features relaxed into a reminiscent grin as he recalled Noakes's memorable retirement party, when the DS had produced notes for a speech and regaled the room with jokes specially chosen to enhance the occasion.

"'Crime doesn't pay." "No, but the hours are attractive." . . . "Do you know one man is murdered every six hours in Manchester?" "I'll bet he's getting ruddy fed up with it."'

There were anecdotes too. And since, as DI Chris Carstairs observed sarcastically, there was nobody like Noakesy for cutting a long story to pieces, the expressions on the faces of the top brass grew increasingly frigid as the evening wore on. The high point as far as Markham was concerned arrived when his wingman — well refreshed at this stage — jovially hailed a senior late arrival, who sported a somewhat savage new haircut, with the immortal words, 'You can sue him you know'.

God, he was going to miss Noakes. The worst dresser in CID. The man whose verbal atrocities and malapropisms were legend. The man who never ate on an empty stomach.

The man who, ultimately, always had his back.

And now instead of Noakes he had recently been saddled with an anaemic protégé of Sidney's, DS Roger Carruthers, who had been greeted with a notable lack of enthusiasm by the other two members of the team, both wearing expressions of the 'Hell, they've landed' variety. At least DI Kate Burton and DS Doyle had been scrupulously polite. If Noakes had been there, no doubt he'd have scanned the newcomer's face and then essayed an opening

11

gambit such as, 'How long were you on the operating table?' All in the interests of breaking the ice, of course.

That was the best thing about George Noakes. He was refreshingly un-PC in a world concerned with wokeness, and utterly undeferential in the backstabbing careerist atmosphere of CID. Kowtowing to no one, his loyalty to Markham was absolute.

Which wasn't to say that Markham understood the half of what went on in Noakes's mind, nor in his marriage to overbearing, snobbish Muriel Noakes ('the missus') whom he had met, of all places, on the ballroom dancing circuit. There had been a crisis, both professional and personal, during the Bluebell investigation when he discovered that perma-tanned beautician Natalie — the apple of his eye — was not his biological daughter, but the Noakeses had made it through and his partnership with Markham had weathered the storm.

But there were hidden depths to the porky bulldog-featured detective who, by some mysterious alchemy, was in tune with Markham's mystical, poetic streak (or 'Markham's fey side', as the DCI called it) and understood, without the need for words, the scars left by childhood abuse that had eventually seen Markham's brother die young from drink and drugs.

Most surprising of all, Markham's highly strung English teacher partner Olivia Mullen adored Noakes whose chivalrous devotion to the willowy redhead, along with his tendency to regard her as a star which shone high above the world, was a source of considerable irritation to his redoubtable wife.

*Olivia.*

She had moved out just before Christmas in the wake of a quarrel whose origins he barely understood.

Markham knew that Olivia resented his affection for DI Kate Burton, the earnest, politically correct DI who had been his protégé and was superficially everything that Noakes was not — a university-educated, ambitious 'intelleckshual' — but yet who, like Noakes, stuck to him through thick and thin (thanks to DCI Sidney, there was always plenty of the latter) and with whom he shared a largely unspoken telepathy that made them as comfortable with each other as an old pair of slippers. Burton's engagement — to Nathan Finlayson, professor in clinical psychology at the university — hadn't defused Olivia's jealous fears, and her resentment of his job only intensified with each investigation, resulting in their pre-Christmas bust-up.

It had been a lonely holiday and Markham badly missed his sparky, albeit acerbic and neurotic girlfriend, not least the sexual compatibility that made them a perfect fit. He didn't know how to bridge the impasse short of, God forbid, deploying Noakes as some kind of go-between. His former wingman's desolation at the split was little short of Markham's own, but he had told the other firmly: 'Liv will come round in her own good time, Noakesy.' One thing in favour of an eventual reconciliation was the fact that George Noakes had lodged himself in both their hearts. Each knew that the other liked Noakes, and that he loved both of them; so he was what no one else could be — a link between them. Which wasn't to say that Markham wanted to encourage any overt Sancho Panza-style meddling by his ex-sergeant, not least as Olivia in her current frame of mind was likely to resent it.

And besides, there was an investigation waiting for him to get stuck into.

The timing was unfortuitous, given that it was barely a fortnight since Noakes had taken up his new job as security manager at Rosemount, resplendent in a new suit chosen by Muriel to reflect his 'executive' status — a Harris Tweed number that made him look like a rubicund farmer, but undoubtedly a vast improvement on the down-at-heel combinations (reminiscent of a bookies runner) that he had sported in CID. Whatever the implications of this murder for the longevity of Noakes's position at Rosemount, at least it comforted Markham to have his old ally on the spot as a pair of eyes and ears.

Markham's thoughts travelled back to the events of the previous day.

The retirement home had struck him as a pleasant place in which to see out one's declining years, from the entrance hall with its remarkable stained glass and a striking old red tapestry depicting Saint George slaying the dragon to the elegant comfort of the residents' suites upstairs. Not a single discordant note . . . his lips twitched . . . apart from moustachioed General Gordon in the staff room where he and Noakes met with the pathologist Doug 'Dimples' Davidson after he had conducted his preliminary examination and overseen the removal of Andrée Clark's birdlike corpse.

Normally a great fan of the army, Noakes didn't initially seem at all keen on the general. 'Reckon if folk saw *him* hanging up in the hall, they'd take one look and take their old mum right back home again,' was his verdict. 'Fricking creepy . . . Mr Gower says he were one of them Born-Agains. Charging round all over Egypt with his bible asking where he could find the Garden of Eden an' giving folk the heebie-jeebies . . .'

'If God is for us, who can be against us,' the bluff pathologist Doug 'Dimples' Davidson quoted mischievously.

'There were all these boys he kept having round to his house after he'd done stuff in China an' came home for his holidays,' Noakes bulldozed on. 'Called them his "Wangs", like he were this Victorian Jimmy Savile.'

'A dreadful thing to have one's motives misunderstood,' Dimples said, winking at Markham. 'And anyway, I seem to remember that Gordon died a hero in the Sudan, helping to fight against the slave trade and some native despot who had twenty-three wives.'

'Yeah, the Mahdi an' his dervishes,' Noakes replied eagerly, infinitely more comfortable with the subject of battles than Gordon's personal proclivities. 'They jus' kept coming while soft lad sat on a rooftop reciting his bible at the camels an' yammering about God's plan for the universe . . . managed to get his head cut off.' Which presumably put an end to the bible-bashing.

It occurred to Markham that Noakes had a sneaking sympathy with the gallant general's opponents. With a wry smile, the DI suggested, 'Perhaps Rosemount hung Gordon's portrait in the common room to remind staff about the values of service and self-sacrifice.'

'*Nah.*' Noakes was having none of it. 'Frosticles jus' wanted to put everyone off their coffee an' snacks.' Mere weeks into the new job, his ex-wingman was gleefully ringing the changes on the manager's nickname.

It was an odd conversation to be having in the wake of a violent death but, though he deprecated gallows humour and could be savage towards subordinates who displayed any want of respect towards the dead, Markham knew that the other two were badly rattled by this murder and a sense of something uncanny in the air. Something that defied ready explanation. Something quite out of the normal run of homicide investigations.

'It's the same with them dolls upstairs,' Noakes commented uneasily. 'Like that poor lass Chloe said, their eyes follow you round the room.' He shuddered. 'Mrs C seemed like a nice normal woman . . . arty farty an' head in the clouds like all them ballet types, but not the kind to go in for voodoo or owt like that.'

'She was a serious collector apparently,' Dimples mused. 'Plus, the memorabilia were a reminder of her glory days.'

'Nothing was stolen,' Markham put in. 'So they didn't come for the dolls.'

'When that young lady — the healthcare assistant, was it? — found Mrs Clark, she hadn't been dead long,' Dimples told them. 'The trickle of blood under her nostrils wasn't dry. Given the warmth inside that bedroom, it would only have taken around thirty minutes to coagulate . . .'

'Yeah, it were like Centre Parcs in there,' Noakes said, 'or the Amazon or summat. Don' know how she could stand it like that.'

'It's not uncommon for the infirm to have a heightened sensitivity to cold,' Dimples observed. 'And her health was precarious, remember.'

Noakes's expression darkened.

'Cowardly scum knocking off a helpless old woman,' he rumbled. Then, anxiously, 'They do half hour checks here . . . The nurse on the night shift said she looked in on Mrs C about twenty minutes before Chloe rocked up—'

'Which means there was a narrow window of opportunity for the killer to make their move,' Markham finished sombrely. 'And they seized it.'

'I'd say you're looking for someone familiar with the home's routines,' Dimples said quietly.

The words 'an inside job' hung in the air.

'A cool customer too,' the medic continued. 'Even with well-established patterns, there was no guarantee they wouldn't be interrupted . . . or Mrs Clark might've screamed and raised the alarm that way.'

'Do you reckon she fought back?' Markham asked.

'No, I don't,' Dimples said decisively. 'One small mercy is that it was all over in minutes. She wouldn't even have had time to be afraid.'

Recalling the ghastly countenance on that pillow, Markham could only hope it was so.

'A cool customer or desperate,' he mused. 'Someone who needed to kill her for some reason.'

'Cos they're loony tunes?' Noakes speculated.

'Possibly, but I doubt we're looking at some random act of madness,' the DI replied. 'An act of revenge seems more likely, or the removal of a threat . . . maybe both.'

'Chloe's positive that dancer doll next to the bed always had its arms above the head . . . fifth position thingy.' It was surprising how much lore Noakes had retained from their previous investigation into Bromgrove Ballet. 'But when she came into the bedroom this morning, one arm was stretched out pointing at Mrs C,' he shuddered again, 'like it was gloating or summat . . . *horrible.*'

If it was true, then that interference with the doll spoke of malice.

*If it was true.*

The administrator Maureen Frost, a plain high-coloured woman with an unbecoming cropped hair cut, had been anxious to downplay that side of it, insisting that no one else had noticed anything unusual. Chloe must have been mistaken about the doll pointing, she told them. Though the healthcare assistant had looked pretty sure from where Markham was standing.

Looking back now, as he savoured the quiet of St Chad's terraced graveyard, Markham supposed he could understand Maureen Frost wishing to control the narrative. The retirement home had an exclusive clientele, and its reputation was hardly likely to be enhanced by a murder which took place literally in the interval between shift handovers.

He had scheduled a tour of the home tomorrow with DS Doyle while Kate and the new recruit, on whom Noakes had bestowed the sobriquet 'Roger the Dodger', set to work researching the residents and staff. Ideally, they could do with having an incident room on the premises, but he would play that by ear. Hopefully 'Frosticles' would at least be amenable to the police presence.

Markham grimaced as he thought of the DCI's likely reaction to hearing that this latest homicide had taken place practically on Noakesy's doorstep. Sidney's ecstasy at the retirement of his bête noire had been embarrassingly obvious, so he was unlikely to be enthralled at the news that George Noakes was back on the scene so soon. Doyle, by contrast, would be delighted to have his mentor close at hand. Markham had been worried about the easy-going, gangling 'ginger ninja' whose fiancée Paula had forced him to choose between a future with her and his career in CID, leading to a period of dejection that not even the drink-a-thons and heart-to-hearts with Noakes seemed able to assuage.

When the youngster had temporarily lost interest in their beloved Bromgrove Rovers, the older man had become truly alarmed, devoting himself wholeheartedly to a campaign of regeneration. It would appear to have paid off judging by Doyle's cheerier demeanour these days. The proud possessor of a criminal law degree, with ambition to equal Burton's, Markham hoped to find him once more on top form. Besides, he was counting on the sergeant's good looks, frankness and a certain boyish vulnerability to work their magic on Mrs Frost. 'You need to soften her up', as Noakes had put it, confiding to his former boss that the administrator had more than a touch of fire and brimstone about her and entertained (in which she resembled General Gordon) startling notions about taking Christianity literally.

Leaving aside thoughts of DS Doyle and the likelihood of his lethal charm scoring a hit with Maureen Frost, Markham returned to his impressions of Rosemount . . .

Mr Nicholas Gower, whom Markham had met briefly since his room was next door to Andrée Clark's, was certainly a devoutly religious individual, though his gentle bespectacled manner, with its quizzical half-effeminate diffidence, made him a far more congenial character than Maureen Frost. The elderly man, with ascetic features that were both shrewd and kind, had heard nothing unusual, and the same was true of Mrs Clark's neighbour on the other side, Linda Merryweather or 'Mrs Fifty Shades of Grey' as Noakes persisted in calling her. Like Chloe, Markham discerned a distinct resemblance between the romantic novelist and the queen, and there was something undeniably regal in her testy insistence that she too had been aware of nothing 'untoward'.

Their rooms at first glance, like Mrs Clark's, were generously appointed and expensively furnished with large en suites, though a closer inspection would have to wait until his tour of Rosemount on the morrow.

The former dancer's room, however, was characterised by a striking individuality and the lavishness of a stage set, the wall behind her bed being covered in golden silk damask and the rest of the room wallpapered in delicate chinoiserie patterned with oriental trees and birds. Antique prints and lithographs of romantic ballerinas, in costumes that floated like clouds, mist and dew, adorned the walls. Portraying sylphs, undines and other supernatural creatures, their unearthly and ethereal beauty made it seem as though the room was thronged with fairy godmothers keeping watch like sentinels over one of their own.

The dolls, ranged in two glass cabinets and along the dressing table, were another matter and Markham had found them distinctly sinister. Noakes too shared his discomfort. 'They're like them little trolls that folk used to have on key rings . . . all stumpy with weirdy hair like candyfloss,' was his verdict. The dolls' blond mohair wigs were more sophisticated than the retro trolls' strange backcombed bouffants, but Noakes was right about their shapes, oddly robust and stocky under the tulle petticoats and sticky-out costumes. And the glazed porcelain faces with their fixed glass paperweight eyes possessed an inscrutability that he found unnerving.

'Reckon we could be looking for a leotard chaser, guv?' Noakes asked, falling naturally back into the groove of their former professional relations. 'Some sicko with a thing for ballet dancers?'

'A fixated stalker might be more feasible if Mrs Clark were younger,' he replied. 'But she's a middle-aged woman with intermittent MS in the twilight of her life.'

'Yeah, but that wouldn't matter if they're some kind of fetishist who used to go and watch her dance,' the other persisted. 'Y'know, hung up about how she looked onstage. Burton said back in olden times you got poshos taking their binoculars to the theatre so they could look up the dancers' tutus . . . He could be one of them pervs who never grew out of it.'

Markham was amused to hear Noakes quoting Kate Burton's history lessons from the Baranov murder investigation at Bromgrove Royal Court. An unhinged celebrity chaser was obviously a possibility, but he sensed darker, less easily fathomable undercurrents at play.

The toy theatre was an amazing affair which had intrigued both men. 'Mrs Clark was focused on every detail, however minute,' Maureen Frost told them. 'She was incredibly meticulous about it and liked to move the figures through different ballet productions, changing the backdrops and accessories to suit . . . The latest one was La Bayadere. It's an Indian-inspired setting, so she wanted to get the sets and little costumes just right.' As she said this, their eyes wandered to the tiny outfits hanging like roosting bats along a sort of clothesline hooked to either end of the dressing table's newel posts.

Out of earshot of the administrator, Noakes ventured the hypothesis that Andrée Clark might have 'gone a bit cuckoo', escaping into a fantasy world through an inability to cope with real life.

Now Markham found himself wondering if that was true — if the former ballerina had been some sort of modern-day "Boo" Radley, retreating from a world that had the power to hurt. And if so, did the clue to her murder lie in an experience that had scarred her? Or was this simply a case of a woman whose artistic sensibilities sought a fresh outlet? Could the obsession with dolls and her toy theatre be connected with some obscure sexual kink?

As his head buzzed with possibilities, the DI realised he would have to put the woman's life under the microscope. Luckily this was the kind of exercise at which Kate Burton excelled. No doubt his fellow DI was even now busily building a profile of their victim along with a roster of suspects.

Thinking about Burton, his well-moulded lips curved upwards in the rare, charming smile that the station's junior ranks rarely glimpsed.

He knew she secretly missed Noakes, her old sparring partner, more than she cared to admit — even with his disparagement of her beloved *Diagnostic and Statistical Manual of Mental Disorders* (which, as a psychology graduate, was her go-to for any case that threw up behavioural conundrums) and habit of calling her fiancé 'Shippers' on account of his startling resemblance to the serial killer Dr Harold Shipman. A protective avuncularity had gradually crept into Noakes's attitude towards her and, having come through various tight spots together, she was used to the grizzled veteran, right down to the anti-woke pronouncements which brought senior management out in hives.

Yes, Burton missed Noakes alright, and Markham was able to detect that, for all her impeccable courtesy towards Roger Carruthers, she did not care for the newcomer one bit. He felt pretty much the same, feeling fairly sure that part of Carruthers's brief was to act as the DCI's spy. Even though 'Markham's Fab Four' had been reduced to three, and even though Sidney had mellowed somewhat in recent times, his prickly jealousy of CID's wunderkind giving way to a more congenial working relationship, the DI knew that many of the top brass resented his meteoric rise and high profile and would not, in short, mind if he fell flat on his face. Which meant that the stakes with Rosemount were high.

Time to make a move. He would feel more confident about Monday's operations once he had a preliminary briefing with the team under his belt. He had already managed to liaise with Burton and Doyle, and suspected they would be pleased to have the advantage over Carruthers, whom DI Chris Carstairs had temporarily 'borrowed'.

'You owe me, Gil,' his colleague said resignedly on hearing that Markham wanted Carruthers back.

Before he left the graveyard, Markham wandered over to a grotto with a statue of the Madonna that had been created in a leafy corner of the cemetery. Touched to see the little posies and tealights that decorated it, and suspecting these adornments had little to do with St Chad's low-church successor to the Reverend Dodsworth, he paused to say a prayer for Andrée Clark's soul, trusting that the former dancer now enjoyed the exhilaration of something even more wonderful than the magic of her earth-bound performances.

A launch into ballerina space.

## 2. SCOPING THE TERRITORY

CID felt staler than ever after Markham's early-morning sojourn in St Chad's, its tired scuffed workstations and poky glassed-in cubicles a reminder of the council's indifference to the comfort of those who kept Bromgrove's citizenry safe.

The DI felt a sharp pang as he passed Noakes's old desk, transformed by DS Roger Carruthers from a frowsy lair into something altogether neater courtesy of what looked like a raid on the local branch of Ryman, with colour-coordinated stationery, letter trays and pen holders dominating the space formerly covered by Curly Wurly wrappers, takeaway containers and unwashed crockery.

Needless to say, Carruthers was already lurking by the water cooler next to Markham's corner office with its unrivalled view of the carpark.

'Come in, Sergeant,' he said, making an effort to sound cordial. Hopefully Burton and Doyle would be along any minute, sparing him the necessity of protracted conversational feints.

On the face of it, he and Carruthers should have had plenty in common — both grammar school boys who made it to Oxbridge, joined the police and ended by being fast-tracked into CID. Unlike Kate Burton who had overcome stiff parental opposition ('No job for a woman,' her father had said), Carruthers enjoyed the advantage of being a super-intendent's nephew, though Markham somehow doubted that being related to 'blithering Bretherton' had endeared the newcomer to the rank and file.

He supposed Carruthers could be described as persona-ble, but the almost albino pallor, prissy horn-rimmed specta-cles and black leather trench coat put him irresistibly in mind of that comedy Gestapo officer Herr Flick in *'Allo 'Allo*! There was also something profoundly disconcerting about the young man's sibilant, carefully modulated vowels, which added to the impression of foreignness.

'He can brown-nose for England that one,' was Noakes's uncompromising verdict when he heard about his replace-ment. 'Always sucking up to Slimy Sid an' he'd stab you in the back soon as look at you. The get-up's well creepy too. I reckon them specs are clear glass an' he wants folk to think he's MI5 or summat. All he needs is a bleeding homburg.' Pithy and prejudiced as ever, it wasn't a reassuring prognosis.

There followed a few minutes of polite small talk, which merely had the effect of making Markham even more nostal-gic for Noakes's unabashed authenticity, the product of what felt like a lifetime of familiarity with each other's habits. The DI reminded himself to give Carruthers a chance and not be constantly measuring him against the Noakesian bench-mark, since this was hardly fair in the circumstances. There was bound to be awkwardness when someone joined such a tight-knit unit, though Carruthers was perfectly self-pos-sessed, almost irritatingly so.

Then Burton and Doyle arrived, and the DI felt easier, as if they were the blotting paper that absorbed his tension around the newcomer.

Though casually dressed in off-duty garb of jeans and sweatshirt, Burton had a glow about her — a kind of lumi-nosity which gave Markham his second pang of the morn-ing. It wasn't just the fact that she sported a new sleek club cut, with subtle highlights, that had superseded the chestnut brown pageboy. Nor was it the skilfully applied makeup that enhanced her retroussé features. It was the perception that his sober little colleague looked as though, romantically speaking, she had the wind in her sails. Happy and replete, while he felt achingly empty and rudderless after the split from Olivia.

Inwardly reproaching himself for mean-spiritedly grudging Burton her contentment, he was reassured by her gently deferential 'Ready when you are, guv' and the warmth in those intelligent brown eyes.

Was it his imagination, or was Doyle's regard also warmer than usual, as though the youngster sensed how keenly his boss mourned the passing of the old order? Toting a paper bag and a tray of hot drinks from McDonald's rather than his usual breakfast from Costa, it seemed almost like an obscure homage to Noakes and the grease-fests of yore.

Carruthers managed to decline a bacon roll without shuddering, though Burton loyally tucked in while no doubt secretly pining for granola or what Noakes liked to term 'that birdseed crap'. Markham also declined breakfast but readily accepted a coffee, being only too familiar with the watery brew masquerading as the real thing in the vending machine outside. Besides, it gave him a chance to compose himself and attempt to banish the ghost of George Noakes before the briefing began. Carruthers was watching him closely, and it wouldn't do for him to report that CID's wunderkind was having a personal crisis. As he rearranged papers and files, Markham wondered whether news of the rupture with Olivia had got out. If so, the leak certainly hadn't come from Noakes who he knew was desperate for a reconciliation.

Putting these thoughts to one side, he surveyed his team. Finally, it was time to start.

Quietly, Markham summarised the facts and then asked Burton — who had passed round a crib sheet — to start them off on potential suspects.

Whipping on a pair of smart new glasses and with notebook at the ready, she did so.

'Andrée Clark was a well-known ballerina with Bromgrove Ballet and English National Ballet, before going on to guest with other companies and becoming a TV pundit,' she told them. 'There was a messy divorce from the conductor Frederic March at around the time when she began to show the first symptoms of MS in her early forties.'

Burton was always generous when it came to sharing the professional limelight, and now nodded to Doyle who was visibly champing at the bit.

'March played the field while they were still married and there was a fight over money,' he said. 'The *Gazette* couldn't get enough of it. Their Arts editor back then kept stirring the pot . . . name of Honor Calthorpe.'

Doyle cast an apprehensive glance at the DI. 'She was Ned Chester's boss, guv.' Chester being an old friend of Markham's whose involvement in a previous murder investigation had ended in tragedy. But the DI's face was impassive. 'Go on, Doyle,' was all he said.

'Calthorpe always seemed to have it in for Clark . . . had an axe to grind because her niece was a dancer but dropped out because of bullying and then went abroad—'

'Was Andrée the one who bullied Calthorpe's niece?' Carruthers interrupted.

'We haven't got to the bottom of what happened yet,' Doyle answered, with an unconscious emphasis on 'we' that amused Markham, as though the DS was asserting an axis that excluded Carruthers. 'According to the rumour mill and gossip in the press, there *were* complaints about abusive behaviour — stories about "fat shaming" — and Clark might have been mixed up in it.'

Now Burton picked up the baton again.

'After Mrs Clark retired, quite a few people came out of the woodwork to have a go,' she continued. 'Her former professional partner Toby Lavenham dished the dirt big style about how she threw him over for Vadim Montgomery . . . said it was because Montgomery was box office gold whereas *he* was yesterday's man. Lavenham was very bitter about the way she treated him. Then after she moved into teaching, there was trouble with a former pupil Rosa Maitland who attacked her teaching methods on the grounds that they were physically and emotionally abusive,' Burton pulled a face, 'whatever that's supposed to mean. Maitland also hinted that Clark turned a blind eye to her husband's inappropriate behaviour.'

'Sexual abuse?' Carruthers asked.

'The police investigated Frederic March, but nothing came of it,' Burton replied. 'He threatened to sue Maitland but eventually backed off when Andrée wouldn't support him . . . There was a deafening silence from her side, and the word on the street is that he never forgave her for that because it cast a cloud over his career.'

'Yeah, his reputation took a real battering,' Doyle added.

Markham took stock. 'Okay, in the mix so far there's a mischief-making journalist, disgruntled professional partner, aggrieved former student and embittered ex-husband.'

'That's right, sir.' Despite being his equal in rank, Burton was as ever punctilious when it came to affording Markham proper respect. If anything, she was even more scrupulous about it these days as though reminding Carruthers where her loyalty lay. 'Actually, Rosa Maitland wasn't the only person who kicked up a stink about Mrs Clark's teaching methods. One of the coaches at Bromgrove Ballet — a bloke name of Ray Franzoni — also made waves but the ballet trustees basically told him to get back in his box.'

'So, she was well in with management then?' the DI asked.

'It wasn't all hearts and flowers, guv,' Doyle chipped in. 'There were stories that she was planning a Kiss 'N Tell memoir that might've been embarrassing for Sir Edward Hamling, the trust's chairman. She knew where the bodies were buried . . . had all kinds on him.'

'Anyone else?' Markham enquired, with a comically resigned expression.

'A guy called Richard Buckfast,' Doyle said promptly. 'Resident choreographer at Bromgrove Ballet . . . that's the person who works out the movements and stuff,' he explained to Carruthers who didn't look best pleased at the assumption that he was a cultural philistine.

'Buckfast's going through a dry patch right now,' the DS continued happily. 'Andrée had sheaves of notes and designs that he wanted to take a look at, but she kept everything close and wouldn't let him have so much as a peek.' Doyle once again consulted the briefing sheet. 'That's pretty much it, guv . . . Oh yeah. Plus there's two women who were ballerinas alongside Andrée. Lemme see, yeah . . . Clara Kentish and Tania Sullivan They coach at Bromgrove Dance Academy and Sullivan has her own little studio in town.'

'No rifts or ruptures with Mrs Clark?' Markham asked.

'Not that we know of, sir,' Doyle replied. 'Though if you believe what the local papers said, the three of them were at daggers drawn back in the day. Load of moonshine,' he added, assuming a languidly knowledgeable air which amused Markham immensely. The DS showed every sign of turning into a dance aficionado, which was bound to please Kate Burton who had taken lessons as a child and enjoyed every minute of her exposure to the ballet world during the Baranov investigation.

It seemed to Markham that Burton and Doyle had somehow become allies, and that the old quartet including George Noakes survived intact even in that worthy's absence. Certainly the body language of both, as they sat slightly turned in towards each other, suggested a wish to maintain the former dynamic and exclude interlopers, specifically Roger Carruthers. Despite being touched, the DI knew that it was his responsibility to weld them into a team. The trouble being, at the moment he had precious little enthusiasm for the task.

Now Carruthers joined the discussion. 'What about the staff at Rosemount?' he asked. 'Surely *they're* the people who had the most opportunity, seeing as they knew the home's shift patterns and that kind of thing.'

'It wouldn't have been difficult for other people to find out the timetable,' Burton objected. 'The regime's very relaxed . . . more like a top-end hotel than a nursing home. Plus, there were always visitors in and out, so pretty much everyone would know the score.'

'Hmm.' Carruthers didn't appear convinced. 'What about security, CCTV?'

'They only have that on at night,' she said. 'It gets switched off in the morning along with the alarms, so the murderer won't have been caught on camera.' She frowned. 'Again, that's the kind of information staff might've let slip.'

'How about entrances?' Carruthers pressed. 'Some way of getting in without being spotted?'

Markham took over. 'There's a kind of tradesman's entrance round the side of the building which the staff sometimes use. It's got a cloakroom and backstairs which go straight up to the bedrooms.'

Like Dimples Davidson the previous day, Carruthers seemed struck by the killer's sheer audacity. 'Someone could easily have seen them,' he mused.

'The administrator Maureen Frost said weekends are always very quiet,' Markham countered. 'They could've been straight in and out, and nobody any the wiser.' He paused. 'But I agree with you . . . If this was someone from outside, then unlike staff, they wouldn't have had an excuse for prowling around the building at that time of the morning. In which case, they must have been very confident of pulling it off.'

'Either that or they were *desperate*,' Burton put in quietly, echoing Markham's previous conclusions.

'What did you make of the staff, sir?' Carruthers persisted.

'Maureen Frost's short on charm,' Markham replied, 'but married to the job, apparently, and a byword for efficiency.'

'Not that efficient seeing as how one of her residents wound up strangled,' Doyle blurted out. Under Markham's cool regard, he shuffled in his chair. 'Sorry sir, but their security's gotta be *pants* for that to happen.'

'The previous caretaker was past it,' the DI told them. 'He'd been there for donkey's years but they had to let him go on health grounds.' With a wry smile, he added, 'Mrs

Frost wanted to beef up security, which was why they hired DS Noakes.'

'Bad luck it happening when he'd just started there,' Carruthers murmured in apparent sympathy.

'Rosemount was just about to implement Noakes's security audit,' Markham said. 'If our killer got wind that the new broom planned to tighten things up, it might have pushed them into making a move.'

He paused and recalled how Noakes had been upset over the notion that his appointment might have signed Andrée Clark's death warrant.

'How about the nursing staff?' Carruthers's question broke the silence.

'Well, technically Maureen's the administrator as opposed to being the clinical lead,' Markham continued. 'But she appears to be in overall charge of the nurses and health-care assistants.' The DI turned to Burton. 'We're going to need CVs and profiles for all of them,' he said. 'Though, in terms of people likely to have wished Mrs Clark harm, her enemies appear to come from her personal and professional life as opposed to anyone at Rosemount.'

Markham leaned back in his chair. His stuffy office was giving him a headache, even though he had yanked the sash window up as far as it would go. Needless to say, the radiator which never functioned properly in winter was now burning hot despite the mild weather and stubbornly resistant to any twiddling or thumping of valves. He wanted to get out of CID and go for a walk to clear his head. Not back to his apartment at the Sweepstakes, though . . . nor anywhere else haunted by Olivia's presence. The primroses were out early on Bromgrove Rise. He could go there . . .

Markham became aware that Carruthers was watching him. There was something decidedly catlike and stealthy about the man's expression. In that instant, he found himself missing Noakes more than ever.

'I've made an appointment with Mrs Frost to have her show me round the home tomorrow,' he said, endeavouring to sound upbeat and positive. 'I'll take Doyle along for that . . . you and Carruthers can crack on with those staff profiles, Kate.'

It was difficult to say whether Burton or Carruthers was the more dismayed on hearing this proposal, but they put their best face on it.

'Then I want you to arrange interviews with everyone on the list of suspects . . . okay, so it's probably a forlorn hope that we'll get anywhere with alibis—'

'They'll all say they were having a weekend lie-in,' Doyle concluded.

The DI nodded. 'Indeed, but I want everyone's movements accounted for. And I want to know about visitors to Rosemount . . . any contact they may have had with Mrs Clark or any of the other residents.'

Carruthers was struck by this reference to the OAPs. '*Hey*, we never considered whether any of *them* could've had it in for Andrée Clark,' he exclaimed.

Doyle, who was devoted to his nan, looked queasy at the thought.

'They're old and frail,' he said uneasily. 'Wouldn't have had the strength to strangle her.'

'It wouldn't have required excessive force,' Markham pointed out gently. 'Not given the element of surprise.'

The DS looked sick.

'I think it's unlikely,' the DI told him, 'though Carruthers is right: we can't rule anything out.' He consulted his pocket-book. 'I'd like to speak to Mrs Clark's day nurse Hafsah Peri. She spent the most time with her and knew her better than anyone else.'

Carruthers's head came up as though *here* was something interesting.

'There's stuff like undue influence . . . abuse of trust,' he speculated. 'If Andrée was dependent on her day nurse, maybe there was something fishy going on.'

'Like what?' Doyle demanded rudely, evidently finding the notion of a rogue nurse even more unpalatable than a homicidal OAP.

'Like the nurse had extorted money or gifts from her,' Carruthers said patiently, ignoring Doyle's tone. 'But then the old lady threatened to blow the whistle, so this Hafsah woman decided to shut her up.'

'Judging by what staff said, I don't think Mrs Clark was easily cowed or mentally confused,' Markham said. 'Eccentric yes, but easily manipulated no. The healthcare assistant who found her — Chloe Finch — called her "sharp as a tack", and Mrs Frost said she could be "formidable". Which doesn't sound as though she was a likely target for extortion. On the other hand,' he added, with an encouraging smile, 'it's certainly something to be investigated. Do some discreet digging and see if anything like that has ever come up in connection with Rosemount . . . check out CQC inspection reports, that kind of thing.'

The DI had a feeling that 'discreet digging' would be right up the newcomer's street.

'Even if one of the residents didn't have the strength to finish her off, maybe they could've arranged for someone else to do it,' Carruthers said, continuing with his train of thought.

Doyle snorted.

'What, as in they hired a hitman . . . like a *contract killing*?' he burst out. 'Get real, mate. We're talking an old people's home here, not *The Sopranos*.'

Carruthers's lips tightened at this.

Burton looked equally askance at Carruthers's suggestion but was quick to smooth ruffled feathers. 'I suppose it's possible,' she conceded cautiously. 'A bit of a stretch, though.'

Despite her scepticism, Markham was willing to bet that before the day was very much older, his fellow DI would be boning up on geropsychiatric symptoms in her trusty *Diagnostic and Statistical Manual of Mental Disorders*. Just as well Noakes wasn't around to chime in with deeply un-PC observations about 'crackpot coffin dodgers'.

Carruthers noted Markham's wry smile, as though the DI was enjoying some private joke.

Unusually for him, he couldn't get a handle on the famously chilly, enigmatic inspector whose bizarre bromance with that 'neanderthal' DS George Noakes baffled the top brass. Of course, it merely served to stoke the Markham legend and make him a talking point.

Well, the DS told himself, Noakes was history and now there was a vacancy for a talented detective to hitch his wagon to Markham's star.

As far as he could tell, Doyle was a lightweight. Plus, the friendship with Noakes was bound to count against him. So, no reason why *he* shouldn't be the one to step into the former wingman's shoes. Kate Burton might require some work before he managed to get her onside. Word had it she and Noakes were quite chummy towards the end — God knows why, given that the old horror was beyond the pale and didn't seem to have the gene for shame — which meant he would have to take it slowly.

Markham wasn't exactly Mister Popular with the higher ups, Carruthers knew. Too austere and hoity toity. On the other hand, the inspector achieved results and commanded respect, as well as being a pseudo-celebrity in the community. Carruthers decided he would just have to 'play both sides against the middle' and see how far that got him. Of course, there was the matter of keeping Sidney sweet too. The DCI would require careful handling but had shown himself susceptible to a judicious mix of respectful subservience and flattery, spiced with the occasional barb about Markham whose lustre rather cast his boss into the shade.

Kate Burton brought Carruthers out of his agreeable speculations.

'Are you okay to set up interviews?' she asked him. 'We can come into the dance school and the arts centre if that's what people prefer.'

Carruthers knew the earnest DI had the reputation of a culture vulture and liked nothing better than boring the bejesus out of folk about ballet and all that jazz. Personally, he'd never found having your feet up round your ears particularly normal, but at least dancers were easy on the eye. A hell of a lot better than trailing round the desiccated specimens in Rosemount at any rate. As far as *that* went, Doyle was welcome to it.

'No problem,' he said easily. Then, 'Maybe, if you've got the time, you could give me the gen on elder homicide, ma'am. I know your background's psychology.' A self-deprecating shrug of the shoulders and diffident smile. 'My politics and economics degree isn't going to be much use here.'

For a moment, he wondered if he wasn't laying it on a bit thick, but then Burton smiled at him. 'Excellent,' she said approvingly. 'We can start working on a profile.'

\* \* \*

'Honestly, sarge, you should have heard Roger the Dodger,' Doyle said to Noakes the following morning over coffee and biscuits in the staff common room at Rosemount. 'He was buttering Burton up good-o. Came out with some bollocks about Einstein calling dancers athletes of God . . . And she just lapped it up.'

'I ain't your sarge anymore,' Noakes replied gruffly, with a sheepish glance at Markham.

'It's alright,' the DI said resignedly. 'Old habits die hard.'

It was a beautiful Monday morning outside, with the home's landscaped grounds showing to great advantage. As the sunlight struck Markham's finely etched features, Noakes decided the guvnor (as he always thought of him) was looking haggard. The sooner him and Olivia made it up the better. Maybe he could fix it so they both came round for a meal . . . Muriel had told him not to interfere, but it was somehow against nature, the guvnor brooding in that block of flats while Olivia rented a poxy one-bed in town. *Someone* had to make them see sense, so why not him . . .

But in the meantime, there was a murder investigation underway, and *he* was Markham's man on the inside.

'What did you make of old Periwinkle then?' he enquired, keen to know their impression of Andrée Clark's day nurse.

'I wouldn't let Mrs Frost hear you use nicknames like that,' the DI advised. 'She might find it disrespectful.'

'Oh, I can manage *her*, guv. Bark's worse than her bite. Got quite a good sense of humour underneath all that starch.'

'Hmm.'

Markham cast his mind back to the encounter with Hafsah Peri.

The Egyptian nurse was a compact woman with glittering dark eyes and luxuriant black hair streaked with grey. She had an air of quiet dignity which he imagined was well suited to an exclusive facility such as Rosemount. There was a certain possessiveness in the way she spoke about Andrée Clark — referring to her as 'Madame' — along with undeniable pride in her patient's illustrious background. There was no overt demonstration of grief, but Markham guessed that such self-containment was part of her professional persona so no inferences could be drawn from the lack of visible emotion. The nurse was clearly highly regarded by Maureen Frost, though their manner towards each other appeared formally correct as opposed to manifesting any great cordiality.

At least it had been possible to rule out personnel and residents on the home's Daffodil and Honeysuckle Corridors, since the patients in those bedrooms received 'ambulatory' as opposed to 'intermittent' monitoring. The administrator explained it meant that whereas Mrs Clark and her two neighbours were checked at half hourly intervals, the home's frailer occupants received more or less constant attention.

'Mrs Clark, Mr Gower and Mrs Merryweather are, and were, our less clinically vulnerable residents and can still do a great deal for themselves,' Maureen Frost explained. 'Our other residents are equally distinguished . . . leading lights in the arts and sciences,' she positively bridled as she mentioned their exalted pedigree, 'but mobility and other issues mean they require more intensive clinical care. There are two nurses covering those rooms at all times.'

Now the DI said slowly, 'I'm reserving judgment on Ms Peri for now. As regards the rest, going by what Mrs

Frost said, unless the intensive care personnel have cooked up some kind of conspiracy, allowing one of them to nip downstairs and murder Mrs Clark, then those staff and their charges are in the clear.'

Unwillingly recalling Roger the Dodger's hypotheses from the previous day, Doyle ventured, 'There's no chance any of those critical patients could be *pretending* they're not able to walk?'

Noakes boggled at him. '*Get out of it*! They're absolutely kosher. Old mother Frost's right about that. No way, no how.'

Doyle was transparently relieved. 'It's just that Carruthers wondered about it.'

A harrumph of contempt. 'He bleeding well would.' Then, 'Whatcha reckon to Holy Joe and Mrs Fifty Shades of Grey?'

Noakes was incorrigible, the DI reflected, only grateful that Burton was back at base bonding with Carruthers over psychology.

'Mr Gower is certainly a very interesting man—'

'A dead ringer for Pope Benedict, ain't he? All scholarly an' dreamy.'

'I'm not sure about the dreaminess, Noakes,' Markham mused. 'I remembered him from a BBC documentary on the Turin Shroud a few years back. He did a scorching demolition job on the so-called experts who bungled the carbon dating. Not at all your usual talking head.'

''S a bit creepy when he wears them funny bifocals. Says the lenses are light-sensitive cos he buggered his eyes doing so much reading. You can't see where he's looking . . . like he's Blind Pew or summat . . . y'know the geezer in *Treasure Island.*'

'Indeed,' Markham replied gravely, trying not to laugh. Only Noakesy could compare someone simultaneously to Pope Benedict and a notorious pirate.

'Mrs Merryweather doesn't exactly look like she writes bonkbusters,' Doyle opined.

'I believe they're more Jean Plaidy than Jilly Cooper,' the DI said. 'But according to Mrs Frost, the lady has a huge following and made a lot of money.'

'She looks all sweet and harmless,' Doyle continued. 'Said all the right things too. But you could tell she didn't really like Mrs Clark. There was . . . oh, I dunno . . . kind of like an *undercurrent* . . . When she talked about her being an "acquired taste" and having a "colourful career",' air quoting for emphasis. 'It makes you wonder.' The youngster tried to sum up his misgivings. 'Steel underneath the marshmallow, if you see what I mean.'

Noakes wasn't sure that he did.

'She's a diva, same as dancing girl,' he grunted. 'They were always going to clash. Prob'ly Gower had to keep the peace between 'em.'

All in all, thought Markham, it didn't add up to the proverbial hill of beans.

'My Nat comes in here now an' again,' Noakes said unexpectedly. 'Reiki an' reflexology an' stuff.'

Natalie Noakes had trained as a beautician straight from school, since her A levels weren't enough to get her into university. Her mother Muriel affected disdain for the benefits of higher education ('vastly overrated'), but Markham guessed that she and Noakes were secretly disappointed their pride and joy had opted out of academe. She had recently become engaged to the son of a local entrepreneur who owned the Harmony Spa, however Markham suspected the course of true love had hit some obstacles recently, chief amongst these being Natalie's bolshie temperament and the fact that her prospective mother-in-law ruled both her business and her son's life with a rod of iron. Noakes hadn't said anything about it directly — Muriel would have a coronary at the idea of him giving his former boss an inkling that life was anything less than idyllic at Chateau Noakes — but Markham hadn't missed the shadow that crossed his friend's face when he asked after Natalie.

Now, all he said courteously was, 'I remember how useful Natalie was to us in the Carton Hall investigation, Noakesy. I'll be interested to learn her impressions of the setup at Rosemount.'

The other's expression brightened.

There was a knock at the door and Maureen Frost's face appeared.

'Sir Edward Hamling is here, Inspector — one of our most generous donors.' Which Markham knew translated as 'mind your Ps and Qs'. 'He wonders if it might be convenient to have a word.'

'Certainly, Mrs Frost.'

Markham had only the sketchiest recollections of Hamling from the occasional civic event and found himself curious to see the man who rumour had it was the subject of Andrée Clark's potentially explosive Kiss 'N Tell memoir.

Their suspects were stacking up.

## 3. SCHOOL FOR SCANDAL

Sir Edward Hamling was an imposing man in late middle age with iron grey hair swept back from a broad forehead, aquiline nose, high cheekbones, penetrating blue eyes and a strong jaw. Heavier than Markham remembered, he carried the extra poundage easily, while the newly cultivated sideburns and five o'clock shadow hinted at a persona more complex than the usual corporate patron.

Maureen Frost certainly seemed suitably overawed as she served the distinguished visitor coffee before sidling out of the common room.

After the conventional platitudes, Markham got down to business, establishing that Hamling was chair of the Bromgrove Ballet Trust in addition to serving on Rosemount's board of directors. Having made his fortune as a venture capitalist, and being without wife or family, he devoted himself to a wide range of philanthropic activities foremost amongst which were ballet and the arts.

The deep, resonant baritone, with its attractive hint of Irish brogue, fell agreeably on Markham's ears. He could easily imagine an audience falling readily under Hamling's sway, primed to open their wallets for any number of worthy causes.

He gave the man credit for refraining from fulsome insincerity. Instead, Hamling confined himself to a brief and apparently sincere expression of regret that a distinguished resident should have met a violent end.

Noakes as ever went for the jugular. 'You an' her didn't always get on,' he said bluntly.

'That's correct.' If Hamling was surprised to find Rosemount's new security manager turning detective for the occasion, he didn't show it, though Markham thought he could detect a slight hardening of his tone.

'I followed Andrée's career almost from the beginning,' he continued. 'She was a standout from the word go . . . It was obvious she was never going to stay long in the corps de ballet playing a jolly peasant or blade of grass.'

Noakes grinned at this, remembering the daft plotlines they'd come across during the Baranov investigation, the *Nutcracker* and all that stuff with the magical mice and gingerbread soldiers. Mind you, it should really have been called *Nutbuster* given the blood, sweat and tears that went on behind the scenes . . .

'She was fiercely ambitious,' Hamling elaborated. 'Came from an impoverished background. Her mother was a tartar. Andrée told me that once when she wouldn't eat her dinner, her mum said, "Well you can wear it then" and slapped the whole lot over her head.' A craggy smile of genuine amusement. 'It was tripe and onions, so you can just imagine . . .'

Indeed, Noakes could, taking it all in wide-eyed. *Tripe*!

Hamling's smile faded. 'That tough start left its mark. Let's just say, she wasn't the type to tell a rival, "May the odds be ever in your favour".' He held his hands palms upwards in a curious gesture, almost as though inviting them to understand. 'There was an eating disorder and outbursts of rage that made her career a minefield of emotion.'

'She were probl'y jus' hungry,' Noakes said sympathetically. Despite the circumstances, Markham briefly struggled to hide a smile.

'Quite possibly. Certainly she found it difficult to shift from dancing back into civilian mode.' A careful pause. 'It took a toll on her marriage.'

'Didn't her husband, er, sleep around?' Doyle asked.

'There were lapses on both sides, but her volatile temperament didn't help.'

*Lapses.*

Markham probed further. 'Did Mrs Clark turn to you for comfort, sir?'

The other's mouth twisted. 'Tactfully put, Inspector. We had a brief fling, but I was too staid for Andrée, too . . . tame.'

'How do you mean, *too tame*?' Noakes wondered what the chuff Hamling was getting at. Did he mean S&M or kinky stuff like that?

'When you do something so intensely physical for a living, there are barriers that go down,' Hamling said elliptically. 'Not everyone can match that level of disinhibition. With the benefit of hindsight, her MS could have been a factor.'

The man was suave, thought Markham, but nonetheless skilful in suggesting that Andrée Clark had been unbalanced and sexually voracious with a side order of Miss Havisham. The DI wasn't sure that he bought it.

'And then Mrs Clark reinvented herself later on as a teacher and pundit,' Markham prompted.

'That's right. The balletic equivalent of Judge Judy. There were masterclasses for the BBC, and she was a consultant on some high-profile documentaries about ballet companies. *Agony and Ecstasy: A Year with English National Ballet* was one.'

Noakes and Doyle looked blank, but Markham remembered. 'Ah yes, the one with the bullying ballet master who told an older ballerina she was "too old, too knackered, past hope".'

'I'm impressed, Inspector.'

'It was quite an eye-opener.' Markham didn't say it had been Olivia's fascination with the world behind the greasepaint that had drawn him in despite himself. But he felt the now familiar tightening of his throat and a stab of pain deep inside as he recalled his partner's pithy running commentary on the series.

'The performing arts can be a brutal world,' Hamling said slowly, 'and ballet in particular. Onstage, graceful and ethereal as mist, but once the pointe shoes and tutus come off, it's a whole different story. Downright Darwinian. If you've seen the film *Black Swan*, you'll know what I mean.'

Olivia had raved about that too, but Markham forced himself to suppress the remembrance.

'I had the impression *Black Swan* focused on misogyny and *male* objectification of female dancers,' he said.

'Oh, there's definitely always been plenty of *that* around.' Hamling's voice held increased respect as he considered the inspector's ascetic features. 'I mean, George Balanchine gave each of his ballerinas a specific perfume to wear so he could smell them coming or going . . . definitely crossing over into a grey area there.'

'But was *Mrs Clark* abusive?' the DI pressed.

'As I say, ballet's a world where so-called "normal" values are reversed. Brutality is seen as a gift, fear as devotion . . . sadism as love. Touch is a special language, if you like.' A pause. 'What might seem dangerously close to abusive behaviour is par for the course. *Look*,' another expressive gesture of the large solid white hands, 'Bromgrove Ballet Trust investigated two complaints about Andrée, but in the end, there was insufficient evidence to corroborate the allegations. I recused myself from the HR proceedings due to our friendship.'

Noakes's expression said *very convenient*.

'There were stories about inappropriate behaviour by Frederic March,' the DI said evenly. 'Also, reports that Mrs Clark turned a blind eye . . . Were you aware of anything like that?'

The finely moulded mouth twisted with distaste.

'If anything *did* go on, I doubt it went further than lingering glances or clumsy admiration, that sort of stuff. There are lots of men with a thing for adolescent girls who never do anything about it . . . They see them as half dolls who will never rebuff them or criticise, as opposed to adult women who are too threatening . . . It's a kind of arrested development.'

Noakes's ears pricked up at the mention of dolls.

'D'you reckon that's why Mrs C collected them weird toys an' fussed over that little theatre then?' he asked. 'Cos *she* had a thing about being in control . . . kind of all-powerful?'

Hamling considered this. 'I think she saw the dolls as protective talismans. There to ward off evil spirits.'

'They weren't much cop at that,' Noakes grunted.

'It could've been a kind of escapism,' Hamling said uncomfortably. 'Or born of some acquisitive instinct — the dolls are valuable, after all . . . Or perhaps it was down to loneliness?'

'But Mrs Clark had visitors here, didn't she?' Doyle put in. 'I mean, *you* kept in touch, sir,' he added pointedly.

'Oh yes. Rosemount isn't just a gilded cage. It hosts talks and various events throughout the year, though these have dwindled lately . . . deaths and sickness have taken their toll, but there's a waiting list for admissions.'

'So you think Mrs C was happy enough, right?' Noakes pressed.

'Well, she seemed to have come to terms with her situation. She had the relapsing form of MS, so there were periods of remission when she could do a great deal for herself . . . And all kinds of people from the arts world sought her out.'

'Including a choreographer who wanted to get his hands on her private papers,' Markham slipped in. 'Dance notations, designs, that kind of thing.'

'Richard Buckfast,' Doyle added helpfully.

Hamling looked wary. 'I'd heard something about that,' he said. 'But I'm sure he would have accepted any decision of Andrée's with good grace.'

'What about the ones who hoofed it with Mrs C?' Noakes demanded. 'Did they swing by?'

Hamling looked taken aback at the reference to 'hoofers' but answered readily enough. 'Oh yes, she certainly had callers.'

'Including her ex?' Doyle asked.

'I believe he came to see her . . . once the dust had settled on their divorce.' And now a hint of testiness crept into his voice. 'Rosemount isn't a prison, you know. There's a very comfortable sitting room on the ground floor if residents want to meet their visitors downstairs. It's used for lectures and cultural gatherings too. That's very much at the heart of the company's ethos. Talking of the company,' he assumed a brisker tone, 'the CEO, Lord Howth, is away in Singapore at the moment on a fact-finding trip — healthcare models, plans for expansion, donor development, that sort of thing. Mrs Frost has contact details for his deputy who can fill you in on the organisational side.'

Markham nodded politely, though he felt reasonably certain the answer to Andrée Clark's death had nothing to do with Rosemount's command structure.

Hamling was starting to look restive, but the DI hadn't finished.

'I understand Mrs Clark was contemplating a new career as a writer,' he said.

'Oh, yes?' Hamling was politely non-committal, waiting for the DI to spell it out.

'An account of her life, warts and all.'

The other's expression was unreadable, but he spoke calmly enough.

'That type of misery memoir is distinctly passé, Inspector. Old hat. After Gelsey Kirkland brought out *Dancing on My Grave* — blaming all her addictions on an abusive patriarchy — the next thing you know, every little ballerina in town jumped on the bandwagon. Nothing left to say really.'

Noakes leaned forward intently, his prize-fighter's appearance comically incongruous against the armchair's chintz upholstery. 'What about *you*, though?' he demanded.

'Reckon it could've been embarrassing . . . stuff about the two of you swinging from the chandeliers back in the day, especially if things were a bit, well, *unconventional.*'

Noakes hadn't said 'pervy', but there was no doubting his meaning.

A faint crimson streak stained the high cheekbones, but Hamling answered levelly, 'No doubt a publisher would want to ramp up the sensationalism, but I don't imagine our youthful exploits would raise many eyebrows these days. Her husband's double life, and the way he abandoned her when she contracted MS, makes a far better story. Shades of Daniel Baremboim and Jacqueline du Pré . . .'

'My Nat saw a film about them two,' Noakes said slowly. 'He were a conductor an' she played the cello. They got up to all sorts, including her messing about with her brother-in-law. Fell out then moved back together, only she took ill an' never played again.' He frowned. 'Later on, he had this secret family in Paris an' poor old Jackie never had a clue.'

Hamling's urbanity was firmly back in place. 'Well remembered, Mr Noakes. Yes, they were the golden couple who had it all . . . and then everything turned to ashes when Jackie developed MS. Later on, her sister Hilary spilled the beans about the sexual high jinks, and it was turned into a film.' A brittle laugh. 'It's always the Eternal Triangle that pulls in the punters . . . Throw Frederic March's interest in young girls into the mix and you might have something saleable. But, as I say, when it comes to lifting the lid on what goes on in artistic circles, that path's well-trodden . . . hardly a serious commercial proposition.' He shrugged nonchalantly.

*Unless there was something potentially explosive,* Markham thought, not entirely believing Hamling's blasé attitude.

'Given the fuss that blew up that time when March threatened legal action, publishers would be afraid of getting their fingers burned,' Hamling pointed out. 'Andrée would have had to be sure she could make it all stand up.'

Shortly after that, having exchanged some perfunctory pleasantries about the residents, Markham decided to terminate the interview. The whole experience had felt vaguely unsatisfactory, though on the face of it Hamling had been amenable and reasonable. Polite but cool, he only became animated on the subject of Nicholas Gower's scholarship and had little of any interest to say about anyone else.

At the door of the common room, the philanthropist turned back. 'Her real name was *Andrea*,' he said lightly. 'But she thought it sounded too ordinary and working class. That's why she Frenchified it. If you scratched the surface, she was just a small-town girl made good.'

'No chance of scratching *his* surface,' Noakes groused as the door closed behind Hamling. '*He* weren't giving anything away.' He tugged at the startling maroon tie which, as was customary with his neckwear, had the appearance of being permanently askew and knotted somewhere under his left ear. 'An' that about Mrs C's name were dead *sneery*. Like deep down she were really a jumped up nobody.'

'Hamling was on the defensive because of the Kiss 'N Tell stuff,' Doyle pointed out. 'Didn't like you mentioning that one bit.'

Noakes looked pleased at having 'put one over'.

'Did any of the staff say anything about Mrs Clark writing a book, Noakesy?' the DI asked.

'Nah,' he shook his head. Then, not unkindly, 'I reckon she prob'ly jus' dropped hints to visitors to make herself feel important . . . like she had this steamy past an' could tell all kinds of secrets.' Compassionately, he added, 'She looked like a waxwork gone off, with that yellowish face under all the dyed hair an' her lips painted purple, croaked something terrible thanks to all the fags . . . But she were a game old bird.'

'Hamling seemed quite fond of Nicholas Gower,' Doyle observed.

Noakes gave a prodigious yawn. 'God, for a moment back there he turned into Burton . . . yakking on about "botanical breakthroughs in biblical archaeology",' he air quoted viciously, 'like that shroud thingy were some kind of detective story.'

Markham smiled. 'Well, in a sense it is,' he demurred. 'Quite possibly the most important detective story of all time.'

'Don' get me wrong, guv, I understand about *relics*.' In a recent investigation, Noakes had latched on to that aspect of religious faith with a tenacity that had surprised and amused Markham. 'But the way Hamling told it, the old fella's spent half his life squinting at slides with pollen samples an' still not solved it. An' another thing,' with a portentous sniff, '*Jesus* never said anything about us needing microscopes or carbon dating an' all that jazz. He jus' said you gotta have *faith*.'

Doyle grinned. 'It's an academic challenge for blokes like Gower,' he pointed out. 'Gives them a chance to get high on Hebrew and Aramaic.'

'Chuffing intelleckshuals.' But then Noakes's voice softened. 'He's a nice old git, even if he does live on Planet Zog. Miles better than Mrs Fifty Shades of Grey at any rate. She's a proper bossy boots an' no mistake. Wanted to queen it over Mrs C, only she weren't in the same league.'

'What did they fall out over?' Doyle asked curiously.

Noakes yawned again. 'Stuff about the Residents' Committee. Nowt important 'cept to them.'

'What's your impression of this place, Noakes?' Markham genuinely wanted to know, given his former sergeant's infallible 'nose' for when things weren't quite right.

'Nursing care for rich folk,' was the blunt response. 'Apparently they've taken in the occasional ordinary type over the years, but this ain't your usual bedpan motel, no sirree.'

Notwithstanding that her exposure to unadulterated Noakes over the years had inured his fellow DI to un-PC colloquialisms, Markham felt grateful that Kate Burton wasn't around for such gems as 'bedpan motel'.

'According to Sir Edward, Rosemount has a long waiting list,' Markham mused. 'To say nothing of its connections to the great and the good.'

Noakes flashed him an evil grin.

'You know Sidney, guv . . . He'll want this one pinned on some oddball gardener. Deffo not any of the nicey-nice crowd.'

'Do *you* have any such useful "misfit" in mind, Noakes?'

'Well, I ain't been here long enough to suss which ones are screwy.' A shrug. 'So far, they all seem okay to me.'

'What about the nurse, Hafsah Peri? The one who was close to Mrs Clark?' Doyle asked. 'Hamling seemed to rate her, but maybe it was an act.'

Noakes considered this. 'She came across as kind and devoted. Besides, I don' reckon it'd be easy to fool Frosticles . . . If there were any funny business going on, she'd have clocked it.'

Markham agreed that this was a fair assessment but decided to have a final word with Andrée Clark's day nurse. In heavily accented English, Hafsah Peri insisted that the patient knew her own mind and was no pushover. 'Madame was maybe a little eccentric, but nobody could make her do anything she didn't want to do. "Yes" meant yes, and "no" meant no.'

Questioned again, Chloe Finch disclosed something of interest. 'Mrs Clark was nervous the last time I saw her,' the healthcare assistant told them. 'I took her down to the residents' sitting room and she was jittery . . . kept looking around as though she expected someone to jump out at her. About a week before that, I saw her upstairs ripping some paper into tiny pieces. She looked angry and scared at the same time.'

Doyle leaned forward eagerly. 'What did you think it was, this paper?'

'It looked like a letter. I'm pretty sure there was an envelope with a stamp.'

Markham's antennae twitched. 'Did you ask her about it?'

'Yes, but she brushed me off, said she'd always had to deal with jealousy . . . people resenting her for being famous. I just assumed it was some crank. Celebrities get used to poison pen types, don't they?' She looked uncertain. 'I didn't connect it with her being all jumpy that day she was downstairs. But now . . . maybe she was afraid of someone.' Chloe bit her lip. 'Perhaps if I'd reported it . . .' Her voice trailed off.

'No point crying over spilt milk,' Noakes said philosophically as she left. 'Them bits of paper went out with the recycling an' the lass could be reading too much into it. No one else mentioned Mrs C getting spooked.'

Markham nodded slowly, though he had a niggling sense that the incident was significant.

After despatching Doyle back into town to see if he could round up the various dance professionals ('They'll know she was strangled but stick with "suspicious death" for now'), Markham lingered a while, having noticed that his former wingman looked decidedly down in the dumps at the prospect of being outside the investigation with his nose pressed up against the glass.

'You landed on your feet with this job, Noakesy. It's a beautiful place.'

And indeed, the graciously proportioned parquet-floored rooms — including a Jacobean style panelled library, airy dining room with William Morris wallpaper and music room where a Bechstein baby grand piano held pride of place — possessed an indefinable charm that placed Rosemount far outside the usual run of care homes.

'Money talks,' Noakes acknowledged sagely. He wrestled briefly with his tie before admitting. 'The place runs like clockwork, though, so it don' seem like there's all that much for me to do.'

'There is *now*,' Markham assured him.

Noakes brightened considerably on hearing this.

'We could've managed at home on my pension,' he confided, 'but I'm not past it yet . . . Plus me an' the missus need our own space.'

Markham had no doubt about that, Muriel Noakes being one of those women about whom it might be justly said that she married for better or worse but not for lunch.

'Keep your ear to the ground and I'll hook up with you tomorrow once I've tracked down Honor Calthorpe from the *Gazette*,' he said. 'She's got a flat in town, so if you fancy a coffee in Waterstones, that gives us a chance to talk away from here . . . Think of yourself as my civilian consultant on this one.'

'Sidney won't like it.'

Markham gave a wry smile. *Then he'll just have to lump it.*

'How're you getting along with General Gordon?' the DI asked mischievously, gesturing at the framed portrait as Noakes rose to see him off.

'There's this book about him in the library,' the other replied. 'Reckon I came down a bit hard . . . The politicians hung him out to dry an' he just had to make the best of it. They were all jealous, see, on account of him being glamorous an' full of hisself.' He cast a beady look at the picture. 'Jealousy's one of the seven deadly sins an' that's what did for soldier boy in the end.'

* * *

As he manoeuvred himself into a bay in Bromgrove Dance Academy's car park, Markham felt a guilty relief that there were no next-of-kin to be visited, Andrée Clark's sister and parents having predeceased her. He never shirked such tasks nor shuffled them off onto his subordinates, but he invariably felt wrung out after bereavement visits and was glad to conserve his energies for interviewing suspects.

*Suspects.*

So far, there was what he thought of as the Rosemount contingent: Maureen Frost, Hafsah Peri and Sir Edward Hamling from the management side, then — however improbably — Nicholas Gower and Linda Merryweather on residential, it being pretty much a given that he could rule out other personnel and patients (though he had asked Noakes to track their movements).

And now there were Mrs Clark's former fellow 'hoofers' to consider.

*The ghosts from her past.*

Ghosts because ballet was somehow not 'real life'. As he remembered from the Baranov investigation, this was the most ephemeral and rarefied of the arts, with a language all its own.

Meeting Doyle in one of the smaller studios, he inhaled the unforgettable aroma that he recalled from the Baranov investigation: warm, damp air smelling of resin, sweat and soggy leotards.

But this time there were no students sprawled on the floor in geometrically impossible poses, hammering the shanks for their pointe shoes or wadding their toes with lambswool to cushion blisters and bunions. There was just a man who looked to be in his early sixties standing with three women, two middle-aged and the other in her late twenties.

Doyle lost no time in rattling off introductions.

The man was introduced as Andrée Clark's former partner Toby Lavenham, now ballet master at the Academy and Artistic Director of Bromgrove Ballet. He must have been very handsome in his day, Markham thought, taking in the height, excellent bone structure, sensual lips and thick silver hair that curled over the back of his collar, giving him a faintly raffish air that contrasted with the all-white outfit that made him look like Mr Clean: white stonewashed jeans, white sweater, white trainers. Even now, he exuded the commanding presence of one used to instant compliance. Markham noticed that he frequently checked himself in the huge mirror covering one wall, but this appeared curiously without vanity, merely the reflex of an artist focused on visual perfection. He had surprisingly large hands and feet which contributed to the impression of latent power, with tinted glasses completing the enigmatic look.

The youngest woman was Rosa Maitland, a willowy dancer in leotard and practice skirt whose delicate features, soft full lips, unmade-up alabaster skin and chestnut ponytail gave her an air of vulnerability that was accentuated by a slightly pouting overbite and huge pale blue eyes.

So here was the girl who had made allegations about Andrée and her husband Frederic March, Markham thought, appraising her carefully. The limpid gaze held a candour that belied his preconceptions about a spoiled theatre child — an innocent unselfconsciousness about her beauty that was like the freshness of springtime.

The taller of the other two women wore a soft cashmere cardigan in fawn and a pleated skirt of the same colour, with low-heeled sandals completing the look. This was Clara Kentish the ballet mistress and a former contemporary of Andrée at ENB. She had a fine-boned face dominated by enormous dark eyes and prominent cheekbones, though her appearance was somewhat parched, as though from a lifetime of watching what she ate. Slim as a sapling and very erect, with her silvery hair parted in the centre and drawn onto the nape of her neck in glossy wings, she retained the allure of the old-fashioned Romantic soloist she had once been. To his surprise, he saw that she held what looked like a geometric-patterned art deco cigarette lighter.

'It's a prop, Inspector,' she laughed, catching his look. 'I don't smoke these days, but still like having something to hold. People call it my fidget toy because I'm always flicking it on and off.'

The other woman, Tania Sullivan, was also a former contemporary of Andrée. Equally striking, with dyed jet-black hair and the same beautiful carriage, she had a stockier, curvier physique, which made it a surprise to learn she had risen higher up the ranks than her colleague, eventually attaining the coveted position of ballerina with Bromgrove Ballet where she and Andrée vied for top honours. Now working as a freelance dance coach, she gave private lessons at the Academy from time to time. Attired in a black practice leotard and skirt, fishnet tights and soft unblocked ballet shoes, there was something vibrantly carnal about her which contrasted with the nun-like sexlessness of Clara Kentish. However, it was clear the two women got on well, exhibiting an almost maternal solicitude for Rosa Maitland whom they were coaching in preparation for her debut in *Giselle* later that season. From the way Sullivan continually rubbed her thumb against the index and middle fingers of her right hand, Markham guessed that she too must have been a smoker. When the two ballerinas had been starting out, he imagined it was almost *de rigueur* as a means of suppressing healthy teenage appetites.

The three older members of the quartet spoke affectionately of Andrée, with Toby Lavenham insisting that the brouhaha over her chucking him as a partner in favour of the Romanian dancer Vadim Montgomery — currently based in Australia — was 'all in the past' and 'blown up by the local media'. Chuckling over her having nicknamed him 'spaghetti arms' for allegedly deficient *port de bras*, he displayed little resentment.

'Sure, it stung back then,' he told Markham, 'but we were just kids, and anyway I went on to forge partnerships with other top-flight ballerinas which helped me get over it.'

Clara Kentish and Tania Sullivan were likewise scornful of the local media for making mischief. 'Of course we were all in competition with each other,' Sullivan laughed in her throaty contralto. 'But there were lots of incredible people around and we needed the rivalry to spur each other on. The way some of the press people carried on — calling us "the School for Scandal" — was ridiculous.'

'Why *did* the papers get so hung up on all of that?' Doyle asked. 'No offence,' he added hastily, 'but ballet's a bit *niche*, right?'

'Like I said, it was always more the local rags who zeroed in on any hint of backstage brouhaha,' Lavenham said easily. 'Especially when they were having a slow news day.'

'They loved the idea of dancers having diva-style spats, but competition is perfectly healthy,' Kentish insisted, her voice lighter and more refined than her friend's northern twang. 'And anyway, we had our own styles . . . Certain choreographers have a preferred physical type, so that's a factor too. Andrée and I specialised in classical, romantic roles. Actually, we alternated in Coppélia at the end of her final season with ENB.'

Seeing their blank looks, she laughed. 'It's all about this mad inventor and a life-sized mechanical toy.'

'Pure escapism,' her colleague interjected with a grin.

'What about you, miss?' Doyle enquired politely. 'Did you do the, er, classical and romantic stuff too?'

Tania Sullivan smiled at him. 'I'm what they call a soubrette,' she said. 'Better suited to character parts because of my physique. No hard feelings . . . I practically cornered the market in flamenco and folk. Left Andrée and Clara to battle it out over the traditional roles.'

Beneath her breezy charm, Markham detected a faint wistfulness which made him wonder . . . How happy had she really been to relinquish those roles which were practically synonymous with the ballet?

'Really, Inspector, there's room for everyone,' her friend continued earnestly. 'And it's not all about favouritism or dancers sleeping their way to the top.'

Which was an interesting turn of phrase, thought Markham, since no one had so far accused Andrée Clark directly of sexual machinations —though Edward Hamling had hinted at some such shadowy backstory.

Rosa Maitland was composed when Markham raised the issue of abuse. 'I've put all that behind me,' she said softly. 'And anyway, I was just a teenager . . . I didn't know how to handle myself when Mrs Clark kept whacking me with her cane and pulling me about every which way, as well as always telling me I was too fat and needed to go on a diet.'

The older women exchanged looks.

'It's very much in the Russian tradition to give dancers physical correction, but we rather frown on it these days,' Clara Kentish said quietly.

'Cos this ain't the bleeding Bolshoi,' her friend added more loudly.

Markham had the feeling Noakes would have warmed to the diminutive ballerina if he could have heard her, though her fellow teacher looked somewhat askance.

He decided to hold off mentioning Frederic March until he had done further research, something warning him it would be unprofitable to press Rosa Maitland further at this juncture.

They struck him as a tight little group who seemed banded together against outsiders, but he could detect no unusual undercurrents or anxiety. None had an alibi, but this was hardly surprising given that the murder took place early on a Saturday morning. Doyle had taken details of visits to Rosemount, most recently when Lavenham and his teacher colleagues had paid a New Year call. It occurred to him that whatever their past differences, the trio had been reasonably assiduous in maintaining contact. Perhaps the bonds forged during their arduous career were indissoluble. Or was there some other reason why it might have been important to keep the former ballerina sweet? His reference to a possible writing project had merely elicited blank looks, but this might all be artifice. It was important to remember that these were *performers* and, even though they weren't actors, they were still skilled at manipulating their audience.

Clara Kentish volunteered to see him out, pausing in the lobby at his mention of a previous visit during the Baranov investigation.

'Toby and I only joined the staff recently, but it's still a talking point,' she said with a shy smile. 'When I tell people where I work, they always ask about it.'

Markham admired the vast collage of famous dancers and choreographers down the centuries which took over the whole of one wall.

'I see the notorious Mr Balanchine is up there,' he said, smiling back at her.

She gazed reverentially at the picture of a middle-aged man with swept back thinning hair, a hawklike profile and penetrating eyes, his wiry, lithe body folded in on itself, knees crossed, elbow on knee and head in hand, as he watched a group of dancers.

'He's the one who said, "Don't think, just do",' she breathed. 'After that, it was like a mantra for everyone.'

It struck Markham that there might be a message there for him. As in a warning to stop brooding over Olivia and immerse himself in the job.

Almost as though she had seen into his mind, the teacher continued in the gentle silvery voice that matched her hair, 'Balanchine fell in love with one of his muses and wanted to marry her, even though there was a big age difference. When she married another man, he was devastated . . . lost his creativity for a time. But they made it up in the end and he went on to make marvellous ballets for her.'

'What about the man she married?'

'He never made it back into the fold,' she replied, still gazing at the photo, 'banished to the performing equivalent of Siberia.'

'Didn't Balanchine have a number of wives?' Markham enquired.

'Oh yes, the last one was struck down with polio and ended up in a wheelchair. Balanchine felt terribly guilty about that because early in her career he'd cast her in the starring role of a child paralysed by polio. He was a superstitious man and never got over the feeling that he had doomed her by creating that role.'

Encouraged by Markham's obvious interest, she continued, 'It was a ballet called Resurgence and he danced the role of the Threat of Polio himself, wearing a large black cape that he used to cover her. She dropped to the floor when he touched her and reappeared, later in the dance, in a wheelchair using her arms and upper body to respond to the music.' Clara Kentish sighed. 'She was run down and overworked and skipped having a polio shot. Later on, Balanchine divorced her to marry his new infatuation, which is why he was hit so hard when the girl *he* was infatuated with chose someone else.'

The woman fell silent, and he guessed she felt suddenly uncomfortable at the parallels with Andrée Clark, another wheelchair-bound woman whose husband had abandoned her.

'It's a strange world, Inspector,' she said, echoing Edward Hamling's observations. 'You might say it's littered with damaged souls whose lives never worked out the way they planned.'

'Do you think Andrée was damaged?'

'She fought hard to make it to the top and, once there, one's shelf-life is so very short . . .' Her voice was sad, and he had the sense of a repressed sisterhood prepared to tolerate untold miseries in the furtherance of a beautiful illusion.

They moved towards the foyer doors.

'Ballet is a woman and man the gardener,' she quoted lightly as he turned to go.

*Who cut Andrée Clark off at the stem?*

That question hammered in his brain as though on an anvil all the way back to the station.

## 4. HOLDING ONTO AIR

A storm whipped up overnight, so Markham slept badly, getting up very early on Tuesday 25 January.

Brewing a pot of strong black coffee, he took the drink into his study, watching as dawn gradually crept over the neighbouring municipal cemetery.

He had chosen his apartment in the upmarket complex known as the Sweepstakes for its proximity to the expanse of lichen-veined slabs, monuments and headstones which somehow felt like a memorial to the murdered dead he sought to avenge.

Gazing out as the dawn touched the graves with grey fingers, he wondered fancifully what awaited dancers like Andrée Clark on the other side of death. If the Lord's Prayer was correct and eternity meant 'on earth as it is in heaven', then a ballerina's afterlife had to be a very beautiful place indeed.

Now he recalled the dream from which he had abruptly awoken in the small hours. It had been so vivid that he had been unable to distinguish between sleeping and waking.

He had been clambering over some sort of rooftop made out of tall spires. There was organ music in the background — a cacophony of sound — and the pinnacles vibrated as he moved from one to another. A black-haired dancer in a floating gauze skirt was just ahead of him, gliding on pointe, delicate as thistledown. He could not see her face, but one slight transparent finger was raised in warning. The light got steadily brighter and whiter, and they ascended higher and higher as though summoned inexorably upwards. *Come up and be dead.*

Then suddenly the scene changed, and he was in the gardens at Rosemount watching a strange conga wend its way along the red sandstone path that led down to the lake, faceless grey-haired figures in dense black robes, with little girls in black dresses and pink ballet slippers weaving in and out between them. The procession did not stop at the lakeside but descended into the water until it had disappeared from sight. Maureen Frost and Hafsah Peri came up and laughed at his bewilderment, saying, 'Don't look so frightened, it's Paradise.' They beckoned to him, still laughing. 'Come on . . . There are some people here who have died to meet you.'

At these words, a breeze blew across the gardens, and he felt suddenly curiously buoyant as if some phantom had tapped him on the shoulder. There was no one there, but he heard a sibilant whisper. 'Don't worry, I'm not dead. I'm just lying low for a while.' He knew without being told that it was the voice of Andrée Clark . . .

Sipping his strong black coffee, Markham wondered about the raven-haired ballerina who had floated before him in that strange spiral vision. He supposed his mind had been running on the dead woman in all her youthful promise, hence her appearance as a romantic sylph.

There was no mystery about the fantastical procession, which obviously represented his jumbled impressions of the retirement home and its elderly residents in the twilight of their years. The dancing children were more of a puzzle, but it suddenly came to him that they resembled Andrée Clark's spooky dolls come to life. The mohaired porcelain figures must subconsciously have been preying on his mind, which was hardly surprising given the surreal nature of the crime scene.

Markham decided that Rosemount and the ballet dancers had somehow all become tumbled up in his mind. He remembered having experienced a similar phenomenon during the Baranov investigation. Only back then, Olivia was there at his side when the inner cry rose in his throat: What did it all mean?

He paused. *He would not think of her now.*

At least there had been some comfort in feeling that the dead ballerina's heaven might not be unrelieved blackness but rather a mysterious beginning — a lightness past imagining, where the promise of spires which reached up to heaven was answered.

Markham's gaze travelled out to one of his favourite tombs, enclosed by a low iron railing, which featured two angels posed either side of a cross, their curved wings tracing sweeping parabolas against the lightening sky. The statues' graceful attitude and appearance of great calm and authority felt obscurely reassuring, like a guarantee against intrusive images of watery graves and spectral infants.

Another slug of coffee and then he padded through to the bathroom to shave and face the day ahead.

Wherever Andrée Clark now resided, it was down to *him* to bring her killer to justice.

\* \* \*

The wind had died down somewhat by the time he reached the station, though the building looked dreary enough, framed by rain-soaked leylandii which tossed uneasily as though infected by his own restless mood.

Despite the grey day, the team seemed cheery, Doyle having updated his colleagues about the previous day's recce of Rosemount and interviews at the academy.

'No one particularly stood out,' the DI said as they hunched over coffee and paperwork in his office, 'though Sir Edward Hamling was very much on the defensive when it came to the subject of Mrs Clark's memoirs.'

'We couldn't get under his skin, though,' Doyle observed. 'He had an answer for everything.'

Carruthers was much struck by Chloe Finch's account of seeing Andrée shred the mysterious letter. 'Was someone blackmailing her?' he wondered. 'Someone she'd bullied . . . someone with a grudge? Or maybe she'd attracted a stalker — random nutter with a fixation.'

'Sidney'd *like* it to be a stalker,' Doyle grunted. 'All nice and *anonymous* . . . No pointing the finger at anyone important.'

But the newcomer was reluctant to relinquish his previous theory about undue influence. 'The CQC did look into a story about a nurse alleged to have accepted gifts from patients at Rosemount,' he said.

'Historic or recent?' Markham asked.

'Six years ago . . .' There was a sardonic edge to his voice as he added, 'Not Hafsah Peri, just some trainee who claimed she missed the induction where they covered policies about professional boundaries and accepting gifts. But something like that would have put the wind up all of them at Rosemount. So later on, if Hafsah *was* up to anything, she'd make sure to cover her tracks. She's been there for more than ten years, so she's bound to know every trick in the book. Either that or her and the administrator woman could *both* be in on it.'

'Whatever "it" is,' Markham interjected sharply, before adding in a kindlier tone, 'There's no evidence of any malpractice or unethical behaviour at Rosemount.'

'No red flags in any of the HR stuff they scanned across,' Burton confirmed, gesturing to the manila file she had placed on Markham's desk. 'Plus, nothing out of the ordinary occurred during visits . . . at least not according to the visitors' log and staff write-ups.'

'I'm going to pay a call on Honor Calthorpe,' the DI said, postponing his analysis of Burton's manila file. 'Her flat's minutes away in Orrell Lane round the back of Central Library.'

'That *Gazette* woman?' Doyle asked.

'The very same,' Markham confirmed. 'We could do with some more background, and I have a hunch that an hour or so with her will be time well spent.'

'I've got interviews lined up for you at the Arts Centre this afternoon, sir,' Burton told him. 'Frederic March, Ray Franzoni and Richard Buckfast.'

Ex-husband, disgruntled coach and choreographer.

'Excellent, Kate.' Markham knew he could trust her not to mention Noakes's involvement to Roger Carruthers. 'I'll grab a coffee in Waterstones once I've finished with Ms Calthorpe, so why don't you come and meet me there.'

Seeing the rosy glow of delight spread across her face, he reminded himself for the umpteenth time not to take Burton for granted and treat her as an equal.

Doyle, somewhat disappointed at missing out on risqué ballet gossip, put a brave face on it when the DI assigned him to the incident room with Carruthers. Interviews were more fun than slogging over a briefing note for Sidney, but golden boy would most likely seize the chance to shine and do the lion's share of it.

With some final brief instructions, the DI left them to it, deciding he would leave his car at the station and walk to Orrell Lane.

Ten minutes later found him sitting in Honor Calthorpe's cluttered but comfortable living room, every square surface of which seemed taken up by memorabilia from the performing arts. There was an impression of ribbons and roses everywhere — in highly romantic paintings, china and chintz — along with a sense of organised chaos in the shape of plastic carrier bags bursting with ballet and opera programmes. The scent of cigarette smoke was heavy in the air, and Markham imagined the former arts correspondent spending long nostalgic afternoons chain-smoking and chain-drinking thimble glasses of sweet sherry, the Amontillado and tray standing to attention on a quaint Victorian sideboard. Yes, he decided, a diet of cigarettes and alcohol was probably what kept her going. He accepted the offer of coffee which

she served in vintage flowered cups accompanied by chocolate Bath Olivers. It felt like stepping back in time. The
former journalist herself, dyed grey-black pageboy hanging
lankly in zebra stripes and a trail of ash down the front of
her shapeless tunic, struck a somewhat anachronistic note in
such Edwardian surroundings.

They reminisced about Ned Chester for a time, Calthorpe
regaling him with previously unknown anecdotes about his
reporter friend that recalled happier times when Chester had
been practically co-opted into CID. As they talked, Markham
remembered how much he liked this woman and found himself hoping Doyle might be wrong about her having 'had it
in for' Andrée Clark.

To his profound relief, it transpired that Calthorpe had a
rock-solid alibi for the murder, having been in Birmingham on
Saturday morning at a journalistic reunion. 'The Wynfrey will
be able to confirm I was there tucking into the full English,'
she told him laconically between puffs on her cigarette.

It was also reassuring to learn that her niece — on whose
behalf she had apparently taken up the cudgels against Andrée
Clark — was currently pursuing her career in Canada. Which
meant both women could be ruled out as suspects.

During the course of the conversation, it became apparent that Calthorpe's position vis-à-vis Andrée was far more
nuanced than reports of their "feud" had led him to suspect.

By way of leading into the subject, he mentioned his
visit to Bromgrove Dance Academy and encounter with
Andrée's former colleagues. As he had hoped, the former
journalist became expansive.

'Clara Kentish was a highly respected soloist and then
went into teaching,' Calthorpe told him. 'I remember we did
a feature on her when she joined the Academy . . . a vision
in floaty pastels, smelling of lilacs . . . with this incredible
elegant carriage. She told me it was down to keeping her
shoulder blades drawn back and squeezed together, because
it brought her torso and head up.' A wheezy chuckle. 'You
wouldn't get *Andrée* giving away state secrets, but Clara and

Tania were unpretentious. Tania had to work even harder with her solid physique, not your standard swan queen like Andrée with those quick-twitch muscles and thin bones. I can still see Andrée now leaping and flitting all over the stage. She really *flew*, as if she was gravity-less.' A long drag at her cigarette. 'That must have made it even harder when she got MS and came back down to earth.'

As though she guessed his reaction, the journalist added wryly. 'Don't get me wrong. Andrée could be a twenty-carat bitch. Picking fights right left and centre when she wanted to get her adrenaline up. Nobody was safe, not even the stage-hands . . . But she channelled it all into the most riveting performances and never held back, never played it safe.'. She continued smoking greedily before reluctantly extinguishing the stub in the enamelled ashtray at her elbow.

'Don't mind me if you want to have another,' Markham said, noting the way she eyed her packet of Dunhills, grateful that he hadn't brought clean-living Kate Burton along to witness the tobacco fest.

'No, you're alright,' she rasped. 'I've already got through today's allowance.' She suddenly looked wizened and vulnerable. 'Maybe it's all this talking about the past when everybody smoked like chimneys . . .'

Markham waited patiently.

'Andrée was a talented coach too,' she said finally. 'Whenever she gave one of her masterclasses, it made great copy. There'd always be some quote that stuck in your mind . . . like how a teacher was the equivalent of Michelangelo releasing figures from a slab of marble.' Another hoarse chuckle. 'No false modesty *there* . . . And she'd play the big star up to the hilt. Come in wearing a stunning mink or fur or some such over her practice clothes and then casually drop it on the floor, trailing in the resin box, as if there was plenty more where that came from . . .'

Markham pulled her back from these nostalgic reminiscences. 'What about physical abuse towards students?' he asked. 'Did *that* ever happen?'

'It's a tradition inherited from Russia,' she said, echoing Clara Kentish's observation. 'Sure, Andrée moved kids' legs around into the positions she wanted . . . dug her hands into their shoulder blades to make them stand taller and straighter . . . poking and prodding, that kind of thing. It's nowhere near the way they carry on in places like the Kirov or Perm State . . . *That* lot think nothing of dishing out slaps and kicks, and their pupils have the bruises to prove it! It's a cultural thing. They're far more obsessive about weight too.' She sighed. '*Look*, over there if a teacher shouts and hits you, it means they're paying attention to you . . . *care* about your professional development.' All flippancy gone from her voice, she added, 'It's such a specialised craft that there's generally great respect for teachers, because they've "been there, done that, got the T shirt". There's a bond of tradition that links students and instructors . . . the older generation passing their secrets on to the younger.'

'Sounds like the apostolic succession,' Markham said drily, then, 'What about the verbal side — insults, bullying?'

'Again, it's all a matter of perception, Inspector. There's such a machine-age aesthetic these days and the technical demands are so much greater . . . which translates into pretty robust teaching methods. Dancers have to sink or swim. Survival of the fittest.'

And now he heard an echo of Edward Hamling's description of ballet as Darwinian.

Calthorpe waxed earnest. 'If Andrée called someone a two-legged donkey or screamed at them for being a fat cow — Raquel Welch instead of Twiggy — it was all in a day's work. Plenty of male directors fire dancers for not being fit or thin enough — and don't get me started on the ageism! Most of them are on a mission to put ballerinas in their place, and that place is *under* them. So Andrée was actually doing the kids a *favour* by building up their resilience.'

Markham wasn't sure that everyone would see it like that but maintained an inscrutable expression.

Calthorpe regarded him quizzically. 'It's an alien culture to you, but ballet's pretty much *always* been that way,

Inspector. Dating back to when dancers were drawn from the ranks of courtesans. "Gutter sylphs", they called them in Paris, or *les petits rats* because they were seen as trying to gnaw their way out of poverty . . . The management used some fairly barbaric practices to turn them from scraggly rats into airborne ballerinas. Kids today don't know they're born!'

*Rats.*

He found the term disconcertingly repellent.

'Everyone goes all dewy-eyed over Degas's *Little Dancer, Aged Fourteen*,' Calthorpe continued scornfully. 'But his statuette was sculpted on one of those wizened little street urchins. He said any smaller and you'd be tempted to pickle her in a jar of formaldehyde.' The image was as shocking as it was callous. Then, sensing his distaste, she said quickly, 'Things have evolved since then, obviously.'

'What about fat-shaming?' he enquired, making sure to keep his voice even.

'Well, we all know the ideal female body for ballet is one like a toothpick, Inspector, so most budding ballerinas subsist on coffee, lettuce and amphetamines. But Andrée wasn't one of those teachers who wanted to see students' bones. Obviously, she warned the girls not to gain weight — ballet's a visual art which demands a certain look, plus the boys need to be able to lift you like you're a feather — but she was upfront about her own eating disorders and the health problems that created.' She paused for a moment, lost in thought. 'To be honest, some of the ballet mothers were a lot worse than Andrée . . . a real cabal . . . always obsessing about how much attention their daughters received in class and how their "line" was developing, which was really a euphemism for whether or not they were putting on weight.'

It was an interesting glimpse into a fiercely competitive world.

'*I* never saw any really serious emotional abuse,' she continued almost defiantly. 'Tactless and in your face maybe, but no way was Andrée sadistic.'

'And yet you did those feature spreads on the Rosa Maitland controversy.'

'It was a great story. Divas at loggerheads and all that. The bosses *loved* it, and we got our biggest ever postbag.' Her eyes narrowed. 'Which isn't to say that the paper just quoted Maitland chapter and verse. Andrée got a right of reply and explained it from the teacher's point of view. *Hell*, Inspector, if you think about it, there's nothing natural or normal about something designed to contort the body so that it achieves a ninety-degree turnout from the hips. I thought she got that across very well. Taken from that point of view, then calling a kid "dumpling" now and again ain't the worst.' She crossed then recrossed her legs, suddenly self-conscious. 'I admit it, when I wrote those pieces about Andrée I was biased. When she taught my niece, the experiment wasn't exactly a roaring success, so Caro hightailed it to Canada. Looking back, it was probably the best thing that ever happened to her. She needed the edges knocking off. Needed to grow up a bit.'

So that disposed of the reports that there had been an 'axe to grind'.

'Young people are vulnerable, so I can understand you feeling protective towards your niece,' he said easily. Then, 'What was your opinion of Rosa Maitland?'

'Do you want me to be frank?' she shot back, titling her head to one side.

He was amused. 'Can I stop you?'

'Back then she was a neurotic pinhead. Whiny and self-obsessed.'

*Don't hold back*, Markham thought.

And she didn't. 'I never fell for all that soft, wispy, feminine persona. Underneath, I think she's a tough cookie. Knows how to deal with the likes of Toby Lavenham.'

'Oh?'

'He's one of those who treat dancers like children. Very domineering too and he can be vindictive if dancers have outside tuition or skip his classes. Tries to control female dancers' relationships. But Rosa's so chaste and demure — the perfect snow maiden — and gives nothing away.'

'What about the . . . issues with Andrée's husband?'

'The Frederic March stuff was something and nothing really. He was a bit of a ballet groupie.' She imitated a languid drawl. 'Always telling Andrée's students they were "*marvellous* and *shimmering* and *extraordinary*", that they floated or looked like angels. All kinds of guff.' She gave an impatient snap of her fingers. 'They'd widen their eyes, tilt their heads on one side, look modest and pout a bit . . . like a hot and cold faucet. It was all a *game* to them, plus March was big on the arts scene, so it didn't hurt to flirt with him.'

Clearly Calthorpe had little patience with the MeToo movement, Markham thought, once more congratulating himself on dispensing with Kate Burton's services for this interview. The journalist's cynicism jarred with him, but he suspected this disdain for her fellow women might have been a carefully calculated career move — acceptable camouflage in a notoriously chauvinistic profession.

'As a teenager, Maitland was one of those milk-white Blessed Virgin Mary types,' she went on. 'But definitely off limits, which was probably part of the fascination. March knew how the game worked — had his own groupies. If you believe the stories, Nick Gower had the hots for him in the early days when they were both making a name for themselves, but later on he threw Nick over and married Andrée—'

The DI was startled. 'Sorry, do you mean Nicholas Gower . . . as in the biblical scholar?'

'Yes, that's right. "Turin Shroud Man", we called him at the *Gazette*. Rumour had it that Gower and a few others were part of March's bisexual mafia.'

Suddenly a thought struck Markham. 'Was Edward Hamling involved?'

'I think he ran with that crowd, but he was more on the fringes. Back then it would have been the kiss of death to be too obvious.'

It was an unexpected piece of the mosaic.

Markham returned to the subject of Frederic March.

'The *Gazette* gave a lot of space to the Rosa Maitland business,' he said slowly. 'Are you saying there wasn't anything to it?'

The woman's mouth twisted. 'It was an infatuation,' she said bluntly. 'Apparently March called her his "porcelain princess" and a "china doll", pukey stuff like that.'

The motif of dolls kept recurring, Markham thought uneasily. Did Frederic March's fetish have something to do with Andrée Clark's peculiar hobby?

'March always hung around when Rosa was having lessons,' Calthorpe remembered, 'badgered her to have dinner with him and behaved like a regular "stage door Johnny". Maybe he even copped the odd feel.'

Once more, Markham felt relief that Kate Burton wasn't around to hear the nonchalant reference to sexual harassment. It struck an ugly note and made him wonder how the journalist had become inured to such behaviour. When she'd bought into the notion that it was somehow all in a day's work. Perhaps the truth lay in some suppressed trauma from her reporting days . . .

Calthorpe was unapologetic. 'But you know what they say, the past is another country and all that . . .'

*That tired old cliché*, Markham thought wearily, feeling profoundly depressed at his interviewee's perspective. The 'past' she was talking about happened a mere decade ago. Not before the Flood! On the other hand, recalling the Baranov investigation and its uncanny artistic environment — a world that seemed weirdly immune from standard social constraints — he could imagine how such a situation might have come about. Ordinary morality didn't seem to apply when it came to maestros and their muses.

'It wasn't just perving,' Calthorpe continued, aware of his disapproval. 'He was genuinely intrigued by Maitland as a dancer — her tremendous musicality. I remember him talking about how her dancing made it look like she was inhaling sunlight as well as air, as if she just couldn't get enough.'

'Very poetical.'

A harsh laugh. 'Well, that's how they carry on in those circles. There's an element of *droit de seigneur* with eminent men in the arts world. Easy for it to be misinterpreted . . . and Rosa was an impressionable teenager.' Slyly, she added, 'The publicity didn't exactly harm her career.'

'It didn't do much for March's, though,' Markham observed quietly.

'True . . . But he was old enough to take care of himself,' she retorted unsympathetically. 'Plus, he fanned the flames by threatening to sue.'

'Only his wife wouldn't support him.'

She frowned. 'Correct. That was the *coup de grace* for their marriage. Well, that along with the philandering and the MS.'

'Were they ever reconciled?'

'After a fashion . . . There were some appearances together and he visited her at Rosemount. Of course, with Gower being there and Hamling on the board, it was quite like old times.'

*And then she was murdered.*

Calthorpe was looking uncomfortable. 'Look, there's no great harm in Frederic March,' she said. 'He just fancied himself as some sort of impresario to whom the rules didn't apply . . . like Balanchine.' A puckish grin. 'He even imitated Balanchine's weird Wild West get-up — all string ties and gambler's waistcoats till he saw sense.' A harsh bark. 'At least he never went as far as having "rejuvenation" injections in a dodgy Swiss clinic.'

'Is that what Balanchine did?'

Calthorpe leaned forward, clearly enjoying having such a responsive listener. 'Oh yes . . . He got Creutzfeldt-Jakob disease because of all that stuff he swigged from horses and bulls.' A sardonic lift of the eyebrows. 'March might not have gone that far, but he fitted the rest of the template down to a T.'

'Remarkable of Andrée to forgive him.'

'As I said, she was no saint herself, Inspector. She could be jealous, greedy and downright wilful. Vindictive too. One time, she was so angry about not getting a particular role that she took it out on her partner, deliberately whacking him with her arms when she was doing a pirouette and digging her feet into the floor so that he had a hard time lifting her.' She shrugged. 'But she was an extraordinary artist . . . somehow unshakeable at the centre . . .'

The journalist seemed to become lost in her memories.

'Did you visit her at Rosemount?' Markham prompted.

'I saw her just a week ago. It's a beautiful nursing home . . . no dusty plastic flowers or dreadful smell of boiled cabbage. I remember the *Gazette* did a piece on some place out by Old Carton,' she shuddered, 'with Mrs Rochester-like wailing from behind closed doors and all these depressing rooms full of wheelchairs. Thank God Andrée never ended up anywhere like that.' Her face was troubled. 'Last time I visited, she was in bed with a cold. It *was* a bit odd . . . She kept pulling the sheets over her mouth and up to her face, as if hiding from something frightening. I mentioned it to that officious manager . . . Mary . . . Margaret or whatever her name is—'

Calthorpe was as bad as Noakes when it came to names. 'Maureen Frost.'

'That's right.' The bones in her face seemed to tighten. 'She gave me the brush-off, so I didn't make a fuss.' With some vehemence, she added, 'I wish now that I *had*.'

The DI remembered Chloe Finch's assertion that Andrée had been frightened of someone or something in the last weeks of her life.

'Were you aware of any unpleasant correspondence,' he asked. 'Any threats she might have received?'

'No, there was nothing like that.' A crooked smile. 'It was weird, though — weird even for Andrée, I mean. She quoted Shakespeare at me as I was leaving. *This above all: to thine own self be true, And it must follow, as the night the day, Thou canst not then be false to any man.'*

Calthorpe looked at him earnestly. 'Why d'you reckon she said that, Inspector? Was it a message? Did she mean that someone at Rosemount wasn't all they seemed . . . ? That they were putting on an act?'

'I don't know,' he said frowning. 'It could be . . .' He stopped, noticing the time. Noakes would be waiting for him at Waterstones. Bringing the conversation back on topic, he asked, 'Did you ever hear anything about this choreographer Richard Buckfast who I understand wanted Andrée to share her ideas with him?'

She laughed. 'Despite all its sophistication, ballet's quite prehistoric. There's no accepted written language, though some records are made through dance notation. A lot depends on people passing things down . . . a bit like folk legends.'

'Are you saying Andrée wasn't in the mood to share?'

'I don't know about that, but it wouldn't surprise me. From what I remember, Buckfast's an eager beaver, so he might have tried to wear her down.'

Markham drew a blank with Ray Franzoni. 'I remember hearing something about that,' Calthorpe said vaguely. 'But I didn't really know him and anyway the trustees closed it down pretty sharpish.'

Shortly afterwards, he took his leave.

'You'd have made a good dancer, Inspector,' she mused as they shook hands at the door of the flat. 'That black hair and the chiselled features . . . plus your height and the whole brooding aura. Yes, I can definitely see you as Albrecht or Siegfried.'

He suppressed a smile at the thought of George Noakes's likely reaction to this unusual tribute and answered simply, 'Thank you, Honor. Coming from a connoisseur like yourself, that's quite a compliment.' Regarding her thoughtfully, he said, 'It sounds to me as if the ballet was your favourite part of the Arts beat.'

'Yes, that's true . . . Whenever I felt oppressed by the chaos in the office, I liked to go and watch rehearsals in the studio. It was the best therapy I knew. Kind of helped me untangle my thoughts, and they never minded me lurking in the viewing gallery . . . It was all so other-worldly. Everyone laid bare, exposed in front of the mirrors — no cheating, no cover-ups.'

He thought about her words as he walked from Orrell Lane into the town centre.

*No cheating, no cover-ups.*

* * *

Noakes had come a long way from the days when he described ballet as 'pornography, pure and simple', the Baranov investigation having worked its magic on the former sergeant's unusually susceptible imagination. He listened eagerly to Markham's account of his visit to the Dance Academy and Honor Calthorpe, clearly intrigued by the glimpse of murkiness beyond the footlights and boggling at the revelation of Nicholas Gower's association with Frederic March.

On impulse, the DI said, 'Why don't you come along to the Arts Centre, Noakesy, tell me what you think of Andrée's ex and the other two.'

He grunted. 'Sidney won't like it.' The perennial refrain.

'What he doesn't know won't hurt him.'

Noakes glowed. 'I won't say no then, guv.' To Markham's amusement, the other spun gleefully round in his red leather moon chair. Then, somewhat abashed, he came to a halt. 'Sorry boss, I always fancy a twizzle when I sit in one of these.'

The open-plan café, surrounded by books, was located on the first floor of the large store. Markham liked the laid-back relaxed atmosphere and the friendly staff, as well as the feeling that this was somewhere he could be anonymous. Mid-morning, the place was quiet, so no risk of being overheard.

'How goes it at Rosemount?' the DI asked, sipping his cappuccino while Noakes made short work of a double chocolate chip muffin.

'S'like a morgue,' the other grunted. 'All hush-hush with folk looking sideways at each other an' Frosticles bollocking staff for gossiping . . . I mean, for chuff's sake, stands to reason they're wondering who had it in for Mrs C. That lass Chloe said everyone's twitchy an' the OAPs are dead upset. Old mister Turin Shroud's gone right off his grub apparently, an' he were only a skinnymalink to start with.' Noakes hoovered up the last crumbs. 'Sounds to me like the arty crowd's a better bet, guv, what with them being emotional an' *temperamental*. Not to mention Mrs C rubbing everyone up the wrong way.'

'I got the feeling they'd moved on with their lives, Noakes. All doing nicely, thank you very much and happy to let the past be the past.'

'Even Angelina Ballerina . . . y'know the teenager who said Mrs C's bloke had the hots for her?'

'Rosa Maitland,' Markham said austerely. 'I didn't get into that side of things with her, and she didn't volunteer anything about Frederic March . . . If Honor Calthorpe's right, it was just a harmless infatuation.'

'As in "There's no fool like an old fool"?'

'Quite.' Markham felt the ex-journalist was a canny student of human nature but didn't under-estimate the bitterness that must have been stirred up by Maitland's embarrassing revelations and the way they threw a hand grenade into Andrée Clark's marriage. 'I'm deferring judgment until I've had a closer look at him. It appears there's nothing much to go on in the police file, but then it wasn't a *bona fide* enquiry as such.' The top brass had made sure of that.

'What does Burton think?' Noakes asked through a mouthful of muffin. Before Markham could answer, he added with a wolfish grin, 'Bet she's got Shippers researching psycho Jerries.'

'God, Noakesy, I know you're free of the Thought Police these days, but don't let Kate hear you talking about Rosemount's residents like that.'

'Don' reckon I'm free of owt,' the other replied glumly. 'They've made me do so many safeguarding an' diversity tests, I could write the pigging book. Loads of bobbins questions about non-binary this, that an' the other . . . like it matters whether the oldies think they're Arthur or Martha.'

Markham suspected he wasn't looking at a top-scoring candidate but decided it was safest not to enquire too closely.

Suddenly Kate Burton was standing at their table.

'Where did you spring from?' Noakes demanded, looking suspiciously at the Waterstones carrier bag she was clutching.

'I was just having a look at the True Crime stuff, sarge.'

Like Doyle, she slipped easily into their former relations.

'Oh yeah?' Noakes was an aficionado of the genre, with a prolific knowledge of serial killers past and present.

'I got a book about the Mintiks case . . . *Murder at the Met*, where this violinist was killed during a performance by the Berlin Ballet at the Met in New York.'

Noakes riffled through his mental rolodex, clearly intrigued. 'Don' remember that one.'

'No spoilers, sarge, but the poor girl ended up down a ventilation shaft. They called it the *Phantom of the Opera* case . . . the police ended up hypnotising one of the dancers to help find her.' A shy smile. 'I'll lend it to you when I'm finished.'

'I guess the missus might like it,' he said gruffly. 'What with it being *cultural*.'

In other words, a vast improvement on tomes about Fred and Rose West or the Moors Murderers, Markham thought suppressing his amusement.

The DI got up. 'What'll you have, Kate? I'll get more drinks in.'

'No, these are on *me*,' Noakes insisted, gesturing them both to sit down. With endearingly transparent pride, he told them, 'I'm *corporate* now, see, so reckon I should stand around.'

Markham sank back down. 'Right-o, Noakesy. And then we'll see what we can make of Messrs March, Buckfast and Franzoni.'

* * *

Precious little, as it turned out, Markham concluded despondently forty minutes later in a rehearsal room of the main foyer in the Arts Centre, a modernist cement bunker that resembled a power station.

Frederic March was a tall whippet-thin man in his late sixties with prominent bony features and a receding hairline. Well past his prime, he nonetheless possessed an air of self-assurance which proved impervious to any insinuation that he might have harboured hatred towards his ex-wife for her failure to support him over the Rosa Maitland controversy. In fact, with his air of patrician reserve, he managed to convey the impression that he considered it distinctly ill-bred in them to press the matter. Noakes, having remained discreetly in the background during the questioning, burst out afterwards, 'What a slimeball trying to make us think he bailed out of the marriage cos Mrs C were doolally an' a nympho.'

'In fairness to the man, he talked about "wrongs on both sides", Noakes.'

'Yeah, but all that about "rampant human nature" an' her being obsessed with "climbing up the ballet totem pole no matter what it took".' Noakes's pudgy digits jabbed the air as though he wished it was March's face. 'Well, you could *tell* what he meant.'

Burton's expression was one of concentrated distaste. 'He seemed to think that as far as ballet was concerned, sexual misconduct came with the territory. There was something really *cold* about the way he spoke.'

Yes, Markham agreed, the man had been cold and self-contained, coming to life only momentarily when he spoke of his ex-wife's talent and his artistic collaboration with her. He had been careful not to push, being keenly aware that as yet there was no clear evidence of animus towards the dead woman other than sensationalist material in the tabloid press.

The conductor had beautiful expressive hands that he knew how to use to his advantage. Markham tried to imagine them clamped around Andrée Clark's throat and failed entirely.

Ray Franzoni seemed an equally improbable murderer, and again it was a case of "nothing to see here, move along".

Slight and bald, with neat white full beard, he walked with the off-duty dancer's weird flat-footed but springy gait, shoulders swaying with a hint of swagger and arms hanging loosely. According to his CV he was sixty-two, but there was something puckish and youthful about him, a transatlantic accent (a legacy of time spent Stateside) adding to the impression of hipness.

'Ancient history,' he said when Burton raised the subject of his allegations about the dead woman's teaching methods. 'We had different views on how to get the best out of the kids, that's all. Then various people blew it out of proportion . . . put two and two together and made five.' There was a hint of steel as he said this, which made Markham feel that whatever happened had somehow backfired badly on the ballet master and he was determined not to reopen that particular can of worms.

Richard Buckfast was even less promising. In his forties, with a lean frame, head of tight springy curls and somewhat androgynous features, he came across as having a one-track mind with little or no interest in anything beyond his art. He freely admitted having hoped that Andrée might share some 'juicy' ideas for an alternative version of *Swan Lake* — rumour said she had a totally fresh take on the unwieldy nineteenth-century production — but it was a case of 'no dice'. The insouciance seemed unfeigned, but of course the man was a choreographer and thus well versed in the art of illusion.

'I felt guilty, actually, because I'd made a ballet round her . . . a woman falling in love with Death. Then when she got MS, it was almost like I'd put a hex on her.'

Hearing this, Markham was struck by how eerily it paralleled the polio-themed ballet George Balanchine had created for his ballerina wife.

Now as they sat mulling over the interviews, Noakes growled. 'Buckfast's a tosser. All that clasping his hands an' bowing . . . Like we're in a Hindu temple or summat.'

'Very mannered,' Markham agreed, 'but maybe that's how they are . . . It's in the bloodstream.'

Noakes scowled. 'An' that BS about choreographers being like Pygmalion . . . having to use a hammer and chisel blah blah.'

Markham laughed, recalling what Honor Calthorpe had said about Andrée Clark comparing herself to Michelangelo. 'Actually, I found him quite interesting when he talked about how he became a choreographer — honest about his limitations as a dancer and how he almost *fell* into it . . . made up dances long before he thought of himself as being anything special.'

Burton agreed. 'Yes, the others came across as quite hard and cynical, but he was different,' she said. 'And he was keen to get across that Andrée didn't have a preference for pinhead students — you know, tall and long-legged with small heads. I liked how he said she compared a ballet company to the different sized pipes of an organ . . . all driven by the same wind and able to produce the same overall effect no matter what their shape and style.'

Noakes looked resigned on hearing this. *Trust Burton to fall hook line and sinker for a nancy boy like Buckfast.*

But Markham remembered the eerie organ music from his dream and felt a jolt. Strange how such patterns *would* recur.

The DI's mobile trilled shrilly, and they all jumped.

His face was very pale as he ended the call. 'That was Doyle,' he said. 'Maureen Frost is dead.'

## 5. STILL IN BLOOM

The morning of Wednesday 26 January saw the team, minus Noakes, assembled in Markham's office. It was a bright clear morning with crystalline blue skies and intimations of spring in the air, but the mood in CID was downbeat.

'Battered with a *spade*,' Doyle said in disbelief. 'In a *potting shed . . .*'

Carruthers too struggled to make sense of it. 'What was she doing in the grounds? I mean, isn't she meant to be the *administrator*?'

'The shed's in the herb garden,' Burton told them. 'Apparently Maureen liked to potter round outside now and again, but no one knows why she would have gone in there. There's a handyman who comes in on Thursdays, but he's the only one who ever uses it.'

'Her killer must have arranged the rendezvous,' Markham said with quiet certainty. 'And she didn't suspect a thing.'

He thought back to the horrifying sight that had greeted himself, Burton and Noakes when they arrived at Rosemount . . .

The dead woman had been slumped in an old rattan chair next to the gardener's battered footlocker, which was strewn with cans of Stella Artois and chewing gum wrappers.

At first glance, it looked for all the world as though she had been overcome by the moist muggy warmth of the hut and nodded off where she sat.

Her eyes, half filmed over, were empty and expressionless, but the back of her head showed that she had been savagely assaulted, blood and brain tissue thickly matted in dark purplish clumps. They hadn't needed the pathologist to tell them this was a frenzied attack.

It appeared no one at Rosemount had even noticed when Maureen Frost slipped outside, but Chloe Finch told them the administrator always took her coffee break at ten thirty come rain or shine. A search was only mounted by her colleagues coming up to one o'clock because by then the telephone in her office was 'ringing off the hook' with no one to answer it. It was Hafsah Peri who, mentioning that Maureen liked to wander around the raised beds in her rare moments off duty, led searchers to the shed. Rosemount's cook had promptly gone into hysterics and the scene was one of panic until the police arrived. The crime scene had been well and truly compromised by the time Markham, Noakes and Burton took over, but at least Dimples Davidson was able to pinpoint time of death at around eleven o'clock. Once again, the killer had exited Rosemount like a ghost once their victim had been dispatched.

It was the little packet of nasturtium seeds clutched in the corpse's right hand that had set the cook off. 'Mo loved spring,' she wailed. 'She must've been having a root around . . . wondering what to try out in her little garden.'

*Mo.*

Markham hadn't exactly figured the starchy administrator as someone who went by a diminutive, but it was a poignant reminder that this was a flesh and blood woman and not merely an executive robot . . .

Now Carruthers said, 'Did Noakes notice anything yesterday, seeing as he was handling security?'

Burton carefully avoided Markham's eye, but the DI had anticipated this.

'Noakes wasn't there when it happened because I'd asked him to accompany us to the Arts Centre,' he said smoothly. 'I wanted him to cast an eye over March, Buckfast and Franzoni.' God, that made the suspects sound like some kind of boy band. No doubt this nugget of information would in due course be passed up the line to Sidney, by which time he would need to have some platitudinous explanation ready. Something about wanting to see if Noakes recognised the threesome from visits to the home should do the trick and disarm the DCI.

As he sat there, outwardly imperturbable, Markham privately lamented the impossibility of cordoning off Rosemount or restricting access to the premises. Given the vulnerability of residents and the fact that this was a quasi-medical facility, the usual protocols had gone by the wayside. In any event, forensics from the garden shed would be of little use until they had a suspect firmly in the frame.

Carruthers narrowed his pale, glaucous eyes. 'The nurse, Hafsah, what about her being the one to find the body . . . is that significant?'

'Not really,' Burton said. 'Other people knew Maureen was green-fingered and the kitchen garden's nearest to the house, so it made sense to check there first.'

'It'd take some force, bashing her skull in like that,' Doyle mused. 'More likely to be a man with all that violence . . .'

'Dimples said not necessarily,' Markham countered. 'Uncontrollable rage could've produced a surge of unnatural strength. Mrs Frost would have been disabled after the first blow—'

'So the rest of it was overkill,' Doyle finished then blushed. 'Excuse the pun.'

'Yes,' Markham agreed. 'There seems to have been a need to disfigure the victim . . . almost wipe her out.'

Doyle shuddered convulsively. 'Which means it was *personal*? Unless there's some psycho on the loose.'

'There's a psycho on the loose alright,' the DI replied grimly. 'But they didn't plan on having Maureen Frost blab to the police.'

'You reckon that was it then, boss?' Carruthers asked. 'She saw something or knew something about what happened to Andrée Clark, and the killer figured she was going to come to us?' He thought for a moment, his eyes flicking over Markham's desk before returning to the DI. 'But she was the law-abiding type, wasn't she? If she knew anything, she'd have reported it straightaway.'

The DI considered this. 'Not if she was unsure,' he said. 'I imagine she had a strong sense of fairness and wouldn't bring her suspicions to us unless she was definite about it.'

'But we're talking about a vulnerable old woman who ended up strangled in her bed,' Doyle objected. 'Clark was an *invalid*, for God's sake. Wouldn't Maureen Frost have put the residents' safety first and left the soul-searching till afterwards?'

'There must have been some strong reason for her to keep schtum,' Burton said slowly.

'Like what?' Doyle demanded.

'Perhaps she was implicated in some way or felt she was somehow to blame for what happened?' Burton threw up her hands in a 'Search me!' gesture. 'Or she might have seen something, but the killer explained it away, so she didn't do anything about it . . . only they couldn't take the risk of her changing her mind later on.'

Carruthers steepled his long bony hands together. 'Or Frost could've had her own grudge against Andrée Clark and was glad someone had offed her. Problem being, the killer wasn't sure of Frost and instead wanted to make sure she never grassed them up. They could've been afraid she might try to blackmail them further down the line . . . use what she knew as some kind of lever . . .'

'At least it's not a patient this time,' Doyle blurted out. 'I mean, *another* OAP and the press would have a field day. Can you just imagine how Gavin Conors would spin it . . . ? *Granny Slayer Strikes Again!* or some garbage like that.'

Markham's lips set in a thin line at this allusion to the *Gazette*'s doyen of reptile journalism — the man Noakes, in particular, loved to hate, their feud spilling over into fisticuffs on one notorious occasion.

'I need to speak to the DCI,' he said evenly.

'We did him a briefing note,' Carruthers said eagerly.

'Only it needs updating,' Doyle added dourly.

'There'll have to be a press conference,' Burton said pulling a face. 'With all Rosemount's connections to the great and the good, the council will want us to put out some kind of bulletin.'

'Talking of the great and the good,' Carruthers remarked, 'presumably that's why Clark's funeral is lined up for Saturday.'

Markham was startled. '*Saturday*?' He wondered about the source of the new boy's intelligence before recollecting it would no doubt have come hot off the press courtesy of his uncle, 'Blithering' Bretherton. At any rate, he certainly wasn't going to give Sidney's spy the satisfaction of seeing that he was rattled.

'Saint Vitus Church at half past eleven followed by cremation at the North Municipal cemetery,' Carruthers confirmed with a smug air of having the inside track.

'Don't tell me,' Doyle said with heavy sarcasm, 'someone pulled strings to get it done that fast.' In unconscious imitation of his mentor Noakes, he added, 'You can bet poor old Frostie won't get the VIP treatment.'

'Ours is not to reason why,' Burton put in quietly, though privately she didn't like it any more than Doyle. 'With performers' schedules being planned out six months in advance, there was most likely pressure to put it on early.'

'More like Rosemount wanted to stress their pukka credentials and make a big splash by having a celebrity funeral,' Doyle said with a sour expression. 'They're probably looking for a spread in *Hello*! or *OK*! or one of the other glossies.' There was a certain vicious satisfaction in his voice as he added, 'Might regret turning it into such a big production now that there's been murder number two.'

Carruthers frowned. 'With Frost being found outside in a shed, they can talk about it being random. Like some sicko who just wandered in from the Newman,' he added in a burst of inspiration as he remembered Bromgrove's psychiatric facility.

No wonder the gold braid mob couldn't get enough of Carruthers, Doyle thought morosely. He was practically creaming himself at the thought of fitting up some poor bastard with mental health issues. He glanced at the DI who looked like he wanted to tell him to bog off and crawl up their backsides some more instead of cluttering up his office. Just as well Noakesy wasn't around cos he'd have come right out and said it. The young DS found that thought cheered him up immensely.

'What's the plan, sir?' Burton asked quietly, with a sinking feeling that Markham would want her alongside him for the interview with Sidney.

Her guess proved correct.

'We'll go and bring the DCI up to speed, Kate,' he said. 'In the meantime, there's everyone's movements to be gone through. Noakes took statements from the Rosemount lot yesterday and promised to e mail them over.'

Doyle noted with grim amusement how Carruthers stiffened on hearing this. He suspected the DI had noticed too. *Hard cheese.* Noakes was still one of them.

'Anyone with time unaccounted for has to be re-interviewed,' Markham instructed. 'Plus, we need to round up the arty mob and get alibis for yesterday morning.'

Doyle's eyes slid to Carruthers. God, he looked like a greyhound at the starting gate. Practically had his ears pinned back, he was so desperate to get out there. Wouldn't be surprised if he didn't fancy his chances with one of those bunheads at the dance academy. That type was *way* too scrawny for his own taste, he reflected critically, with their knobby hipbones and jawbones poking through the skin like fish spines. And if you wanted to go out for a meal, they'd never order anything decent, just ask for green salad without any dressing.

'Have you got that, Sergeant?' Burton's voice was sharp as she addressed Doyle, as if she could hear his thoughts.

'Totally, ma'am,' he replied, snapping back into the room. 'I can do Rosemount if Carruthers wants to take the dance crowd.'

Carruthers's eyes gleamed.

*You're welcome to it, mate*, Doyle thought. Plus, if he did the nursing home, it meant the chance of a natter with Noakesy, well away from Mister Hotshot Detective.

Markham approved the arrangement. 'At this stage I think we'll cover more ground if you divide the suspects between you, but I want you to be on the alert for anything that feels hinky . . . anything that doesn't seem quite right or sets the alarm bells ringing.'

'Roger that, boss,' Doyle said crisply.

Carruthers's eyes swivelled towards his colleague, but Doyle was the picture of sunny innocence.

'Come on, Kate,' Markham said. 'Time for our briefing.'

\* \* \*

Burton was really good at this, he thought admiringly twenty minutes later as his fellow DI made bright preliminary chat with Sidney about the latest achingly right-on initiative to be foisted on CID. He'd zoned out on hearing the words 'gender-fluid' and 'intersectionality', having no time for the kind of dreary virtue-signalling that was de rigueur these days. Noakes, of course, had never bothered to pretend he subscribed to any of it, wearing a look of mulish obstinacy that usually stopped the diversity apparatchiks in their tracks.

He knew that Burton, despite being as PC as they came, didn't enjoy the ritual backslapping and buttering up. 'It's all part of the machinery that makes life easy,' she had confided recently over breakfast in the canteen. 'These days I can do it on autopilot. Sometimes I just let my ears blur people's voices.' The braying, self-congratulatory, patronising kind. 'You know, the same way you can let your eyes blur the print on a page . . . Then the voices are just so much white noise.' Guiltily, she added, 'I'm not honest about it like Noakes, sir.'

'Thank God for that,' he told her. 'Mind you, at least his one-man "war on woke" kept the inclusion trainers in business.'

She had giggled at that. 'They never could chalk sarge up as one of their successes.'

Now his eyes wandered over the Hall of Fame, as the photomontage which took up the whole of one wall in Sidney's office was irreverently known. He couldn't see any pictures of Sir Edward Hamling, but there was one of Sidney's Brunhilde-like wife — statuesque, blond and bossy — posing with a group of ballet students at the Dance Academy. His lips curved in a smile as he remembered Noakes declaring during the Baranov investigation that the dancers' hair, arranged in wings over the ears, looked like bathing caps, merely confirming Sidney's impression of the sergeant's philistinism.

Sidney himself was looking decidedly chipper, his number one buzzcut (Prince William crossed with Bruce Willis) gleaming and the goatee long since consigned to history. There was no sign of his eczema either, causing Markham to reflect that previous flare-ups had perhaps been an allergic reaction to Noakes. The DCI had always been avuncular towards Burton (BAs in psychology helping the bonding process along) and no doubt rejoiced that she was no longer exposed to 'bad influences'. Wryly, Markham tried to imagine how Carruthers graded the team's performance in his off the record chats with Sidney. Presumably Kate aced it, whereas his own rating was no doubt nearer to C minus.

The word 'Rosemount' jolted him out of his reverie.

'A bad business,' Sidney said in the nasal honk that always grated on Markham. 'Are we to take it that these murders are linked?'

*FFS*. Did the DCI *seriously* imagine these were two unrelated attacks?

But he paused and willed himself to be fair. Instinct told him that the administrator had been killed either because of what she knew about the Clark murder or owing to some other connection with the dead ballerina. But they had nothing tangible, so Sidney's beloved option of the Bushy-Haired Stranger as the murderer was as safe a bet as any. No doubt the DCI was under pressure from the high command at both Rosemount and Bromgrove Ballet to damp down lurid speculation about murky goings-on that might have triggered a serial killer. After all, businesses went under every day for far less. Presumably sponsors and charitable donors would be swift to pull the plug at the merest hint that they could be embroiled in scandal, so Sidney had to play a canny game.

'Given the murders' proximity in terms of time and location, we're assuming that there's an interface, sir,' he said, managing to hide his frustration.

Spreadsheet lingo should do it. Sidney always went a bundle on clinical, bloodless terminology that safely transposed the dynamics of murder to coefficients on a graph.

Burton latched on to the actuarial metaphor as Markham had known she would. 'Obviously we'll be looking for points of convergence, sir.' She hesitated delicately before adding, 'So far there's nothing to suggest any ramifications in terms of reputational damage.' Which, roughly translated, meant that Markham's team would steer well clear of throwing mud at any of the Rosemount or Bromgrove Ballet bigwigs or exposing questionable corporate strategies. In other words, 'message received and understood'.

Sidney visibly relaxed as Burton launched into more doublespeak.

'We've asked Professor Finlayson to assist with the psychological profile,' she said earnestly, 'with a specific focus on oppositional defiant and antisocial personality traits, given that this looks very much like personal-cause homicide against an authority figure.'

'Some form of *hate crime*?' the DCI asked, intrigued.

'It's possible, sir. Mrs Clark was a prima ballerina and ballet coach for many years while Mrs Frost held a managerial role. In both cases, we could be looking at a breakdown in psychosexual defence mechanisms contingent on situational interdependence.'

Thank heaven for Burton and her love affair with the *Diagnostic and Statistical Manual of Mental Disorders*.

'Well Markham, let me congratulate you on this openness to criminal profiling. Very commendable,' Sidney said heartily. 'Nothing like science for promoting an *objective* perspective and ensuring you don't get carried away by that famous "instinct" of yours.' Ho ho.

'Absolutely, sir,' the DI replied impassively.

A conversation about suspects followed in which Markham deliberately downplayed the sensationalism, suggesting that he personally favoured pursuing a clinically rigorous analysis — as curated by Nathan Finlayson and the psychology boffins — over any potentially scurrilous lines of enquiry. An appeal to Sidney's 'man of science' credentials was always going to be safer than any discussion of eternal triangles, emotional crushes and professional jealousy.

They ended by agreeing to schedule a press conference for the following day, now that Sidney had reassured himself there was no question of the team straying into dangerous waters. Markham was pretty sure they could package the 'disturbed individual' spiel in such a way that Gavin Conors and Co would be titillated without being alerted to questionable shenanigans in high places.

Sidney could now afford to be gracious.

'How's that sergeant of yours getting along?' he asked jovially, privately reflecting that the absence of Markham's 'useful idiot' — with his deplorable wardrobe and uncouth ways — had greatly improved proceedings. Then a shadow crossed his face. 'I understand he's a security guard at Rosemount.'

*Security guard! Muriel Noakes would have a conniption to hear her captain of industry thus described!*

'That's right, sir.' Noakes wouldn't mind being busted a few rungs down the ladder if it meant keeping his involvement *sub rosa*.

'Useful to have one of our own in situ.' Sidney didn't look as though he derived any great comfort from this knowledge, but Markham gave him credit for putting a brave face on the reappearance of his nemesis.

'Indeed, sir, though of course Noakes is more than content to be a civilian these days.'

Sidney cheered up on hearing the magic word 'civilian'.

'Excellent, excellent.' The DCI's honk turned confidential. 'You're looking somewhat peaky, Inspector. Hardly surprising, seeing as you've scarcely had time to catch your breath after the Carton Hall investigation.' With an awkward attempt at paternalistic solicitude, 'Remember, my door is always open.'

*Peaky.*

*Damn and double damn*, Sidney must have heard about the split with Olivia. He writhed under the knowledge that the bush telegraph had been busy but, aware of Burton's silent sympathy, merely replied, 'Thank you, sir, that's good to know.'

After they had bowed themselves out of the presence and exchanged a few pleasantries with Sidney's new PA, a formidable lady who ruled her underlings with a rod of iron, the two detectives lingered in the corridor.

'I'll get on to the press office about tomorrow,' Burton said. 'Doyle and Carruthers are doing interviews, so you've got time for a breather.' Diffidently, she added, 'You do look all in, sir. The DCI was right about that at least.'

He smiled. 'Okay, Kate. I'll follow "doctor's orders" and head for home. But I have my phone, remember, so if anything comes in, I want to know.'

'Everything's in hand, guv. See you tomorrow at the press conference.' She grinned. 'Gavin Conors won't know what's hit him once I get started on ODD and APD.'

He could always count on Burton for the killer acronyms.

* * *

Markham felt better after a detour via Bromgrove Rise, enjoying the woods with their clumps of wild daffodils, violets and trilliums. Wandering idly, he thought of the nasturtium seeds that Maureen Frost would never see flower . . .

As with Andrée Clark, there were no immediate next-of-kin to be notified, the dead woman being a widow and only child whose parents were long dead. Sadly, he reflected that Rosemount had been her substitute family, which was why she was wedded to the job.

*Just like him.*

But he banished that thought as soon as it flashed into his mind, turning instead to the murders.

It seemed to be a case of two halves. The well-heeled nursing home on the one hand and Bromgrove's cultural elite on the other, with a dead ballerina somehow linking the two zones. Only for the life of him, he couldn't see *how*.

Markham took a last look at the Rise, his gaze straying to a bog pond at the boundary of the woods. It struck him that his own thoughts were revolving as aimlessly as the water's concentric ripples.

Spring had arrived, but he felt off-kilter. He just couldn't get to the heart of the case.

Sidney was right, he decided. He was bug-eyed from a restless night . . . best to get his head down for a bit and then take a fresh look at Noakes's stuff and Dimples's PM reports. Perhaps after a decent rest, some previously overlooked detail would jump out at him.

It was early evening when the flat's buzzer roused him.

His visitor turned out to be Olivia.

'You know you can always let yourself in, Liv,' he said with a hint of reproach. 'No need to be a stranger.'

'I thought it best,' she said before surprising him with a quick awkward hug.

Insisting that she stayed for supper, he installed her in the living room with a glass of Pinot Noir and Tchaikovsky on the stereo while he got to work in the kitchen on chili con carne, aided by restorative glugs of Chateau Neuf du Pape. Energised by her arrival, he interpreted this impromptu visit as a hopeful sign.

In the event, it was a relaxed evening free of tension. He could tell that the emotional repercussions from their breakup had also affected Olivia, her appearance as hollowed-out as his own and even the waterfall of red hair was lacklustre with none of its usual crackling electricity.

They talked easily about the case, which felt like a welcome relief. Somehow, Olivia had the gift of reflecting his best self, back to him, settings and suspects becoming more sharply defined as he basked in her attention.

'Rosemount's like a luxurious cocoon, Liv,' he said over coffee. 'All Aubusson rugs, massive fireplaces, overstuffed chairs, grandfather clocks and oil paintings—'

She laughed. 'In other words, George's natural milieu.'

He was willing to bet Noakes had already dropped by and visited his ex, but he merely replied casually, 'Oh yes, Quatorze the Fifteenth as he likes to call that kind of thing.' Then soberly, he told her about Andrée Clark's dolls and the sense of something deeply sinister at the heart of the nursing home.

'That's fascinating about the pointing doll,' she said when he had finished. 'Almost like the killer was using it to *accuse* Andrée of something.'

She was even more intrigued by his account of the artistic entanglements and rivalries connected with Bromgrove Ballet.

'Such an intense environment,' she observed. 'You think of the arts as being rarefied and spiritual, but they're just as earth-bound as the rest of us.' Lightly, she added, 'I suppose Kate has dug out her copy of Freud's *Abnormal Psychology* and got busy with all the Egos and Ids . . . Or has she moved on to Jung and *The Development of Personality*?' It was said gently and without the usual prickly resentment.

Responding in similar vein, he said, 'Well you know what she's like. And it's ideal for keeping Sidney at bay.' Then, adroitly, he turned the conversation to Olivia's own career, enjoying her wittily cynical account of the latest chalkface dramas at Hope Academy.

By the evening's end, Markham was more upbeat than he had been in days. Even though it felt like they were somehow protecting each other — tripping over their hearts in the process — he felt a renewed sense of their affinity which made him feel he could never be closer to anyone else. They were conspirators and soulmates.

He wanted her to stay the night but was too proud to ask. And she never suggested it.

He wanted to know if there was another man in her life but couldn't find the words.

As she was leaving, Olivia turned to him and said shyly, 'Thanks for a lovely evening, Gil. We should do it again soon.' So his restraint had its reward.

Lingering over his wine in the living room where Olivia's scent still hung in the air, some lines of poetry came unbidden into his mind.

*You hold the soul that speaks to me,*
*Although our conversation be*
*As wordless as the windy sky.*

It seemed like a sign, and he felt his despondency lift.

Although their personal tensions and friction were far from being resolved, the windblown rose hadn't lost all its petals, and everything was still to play for.

## 6. CUL-DE-SAC

Thursday 27 January was a rainy, sickish sort of day, but somehow Markham didn't mind. Uncomplicated physical exhaustion the previous night had swallowed him up in a dark and mercifully dreamless sea of sleep until he woke refreshed and rejuvenated at seven o'clock.

The press conference was scheduled for half eleven, so he planned to check in with Noakes at the nursing home and see if there was anything more to be gleaned from the staff and residents. Time spent with his old ally was bound to raise his spirits before the impending bout with Gavin Conors & Co.

When he got to Rosemount, he was ushered into what Noakes termed his 'broom cupboard' at the rear of the ground floor (though the utilitarian office was a sight better than Markham's own quarters in the station) by a vinegary looking bespectacled woman whose badge proclaimed her to be Mrs Cartwright the acting manager. With her old-fashioned chignon and sensible shoes, she reminded him of one of the fiercer administrators down at Bromgrove Central Library.

The DI murmured vague words of commiseration regarding Maureen Frost.

'Death is nature's own way of telling us to slow down and not take anything for granted,' Mrs Cartwright quoted gnomically. Once the door had closed safely behind her, Noakes pulled a rude face.

'I prefer the one about the Scotsman who whenever he felt sick sent for the undertaker immediately cos he "Didnae believe in dealing wi' middle-men".' Despite the questionable taste and execrable Glaswegian accent, Markham immediately felt cheered.

'Very droll, Noakes, but I'd lay off the jokes around our genteel friend out there.'

'Doyle had a good one for me yesterday,' the other continued unrepentantly. ''Bout the contortionist who had a coronary onstage and died in his own arms. *Geddit.*' Observing the DI's look of mild reproof, he sobered up. '*I ask you, guv,* what's all that cobblers about death being nature's way of sending us a message? She makes it sound like Frostie died all nice an' peaceful — conked out over tea an' cucumber sarnies or summat — when the poor cow were murdered, bashed round the head with a spade for chuff's sake!'

'We mustn't forget, everyone deals with tragedy differently, Noakesy . . . Remember the Ashley Dean case at Hope? It seemed to me then that most people see eternal life as consisting of reading excruciatingly bad doggerel verse.'

Noakes clearly recalled that case only too well. 'All them soppy schoolkids writing crap poetry . . . caterwauling . . . tying balloons an' soft toys to trees.' He shook his head. '*Gross.*'

'Indeed.' Markham smiled. 'Actually, I'm not sure Mrs Cartwright is correct when she talks about death being a reminder not to overdo things. You could argue that the absence of stress is called "Death". I reckon that's what George Bernard Shaw must have been thinking when he said, "Every day I perform two acts of heroic virtue. I get up and I go to bed."'

Even when Noakes struggled to follow the guvnor into the thickets of metaphysical speculation, he quite enjoyed being a philosophical sounding board.

'Thass prob'ly why doctors' surgeries are full of whingers an' layabouts moaning about their mental health,' he surmised. 'Need the stress of doing a proper day's work. That'd wake 'em up alright.' He warmed to his theme. 'Take Mrs Prune Face out there . . . swanning round spouting gobbledygook about nature when there's been two murders!'

'I don't remember seeing her before, Noakes. Is she a new member of staff?'

'They parachuted her in as "cover",' the other grunted balefully.

Markham was puzzled. 'Didn't Mrs Frost have a deputy for when she was sick or had to take time off?'

'Not *her*!' Noakes's voice held a grudging admiration. 'Apparently she never had time off. Did all the HR herself . . . it was only once in a blue moon she got one of the senior nurses to step in.' Head on one side, he added, 'I reckon that's how companies like Rosemount get rich, by squeezing their employees till the pips squeak.'

Markham considered this. '*Hmm* . . . It's not your standard retirement set-up . . . more a mixture of country house and private members' club. So I imagine there's a fair degree of latitude.'

'Yeah, 'specially with old Frostie being a fixture here since the year dot,' Noakes informed him. 'Lived two minutes away in a little bungalow just past the front gates.' He hesitated. 'I did a recce before forensics came an' cordoned everything off.'

Markham smiled. 'I wouldn't have expected anything less.'

Noakes beamed, then his face fell. 'Nothing doing in there though, boss. It were cleaner than a Butlin's chalet.'

'Any sign of someone having given it the once-over . . . anything out of place?'

'Not that I could see. There were a few files with household bills an' stuff like that. But nothing personal . . . no letters or diaries or anything juicy. Looks like she kind of ran her life from the office here.'

'And no sign of her mobile,' Markham ruminated, 'even though they said she always kept it on her, so we know the killer must've lifted it.'

Now Noakes's piggy eyes held real sadness. 'She's like some sort of ghost. Left no trace behind, almost like she were on the run. An' no real friends neither . . . not so much as a cat to keep her company.'

'What about the residents and staff here?'

Well, they weren't what you could call *friends*, not really . . . Mind you, they all seem proper upset.' Rosemount's new head of security sounded baffled as he said, 'I don' see how it could've been one of the old folk, guv . . . There were jus' Turin Shroud Boy an' the Merry Widow in the residents' lounge. The others all have mobility issues an' the nurses were working in pairs.'

'You said in your email there was no one on duty downstairs, Noakes . . . How come?'

'Well, once Chloe an' the other healthcare assistant saw them two settled an' comfy, they went back upstairs. Tuesday's when they sort the laundry with Periwinkle an' do a sort of spring clean, see. Half past ten regular as clockwork. You can set your watch by them on account of Frostie being dead particular about routines.'

The DI's face was grim.

'So the killer knew they were good to go,' he said, 'because routines here are sacrosanct . . . Mrs Frost taking her coffee break at ten thirty "come rain or shine" and the healthcare assistants busy sorting the laundry upstairs with Hafsah Peri.' He thought hard. 'How long does the house-keeping usually take?'

'Forty minutes or thereabouts. Hafsah's a right fusspot according to Chloe, likes everything perfect an' gives them grief if they don' get it right.'

'Your email said she wasn't with them continuously?'

'Yeah. One of the bedside lamps were on the blink, so she went to find another one in the basement — that's where they keep spare furniture an' stuff for repairs . . . According to her, she rootled around down there for a bit till she found what she wanted.'

'Okay. But what about the residents' lounge?' Markham asked, returning to the point that bothered him. 'Shouldn't there have been someone keeping an eye?' he asked, remembering Maureen Frost's description of Nicholas Gower and Linda Merryweather as being the 'less clinically vulnerable'.

'There's nowt wrong with Gower an' Merryweather 'cept for the fact that they're getting on,' Noakes said bluntly. 'They're fine on their feet . . . don' even need a zimmer. Same as Mrs C before the MS got bad.' He scratched his chin. 'There's a call bell thing in there, so they can get help . . . An' the cook brings drinks an' snacks round at half eleven. Plus, the mobile library woman visits just before lunch.' He sniffed. 'Coals to Newcastle with all the books they've got here, but I s'pose it's nice for 'em . . . different face, bit of a change an' all that. The hairdresser or manicure woman or whoever she is comes in after lunch. Then there's some arts group from the council who have a session in that room off the library.' He sighed gustily. ''S'like Piccadilly freaking Circus.'

'But you see, the place was quiet for that hour in the morning,' Markham pointed out. 'That was the killer's best chance, and they *knew* it.' The cubbyhole was too cramped for the kind of pacing that the DI always found an aid to cogitation. Restlessly, he drummed long fingers on Noakes's desk. 'Did visitors know about the home's timetable?' he asked.

'You mean like the housekeeping stuff an' Frost's coffee break an' all the rest of it?'

'Yes . . . You see, if it's all "regular as clockwork" here, then presumably people coming in from outside would know when it was safe to lure Mrs Frost out to that shed and be guaranteed no interruptions.'

'So you don' think it's an inside job then, guv?' Noakes was relieved.

'I'm not ruling anything out,' the DI replied. 'It could well be someone here who set up that rendezvous. Equally, they could have come from outside, assuming Rosemount's daily rhythms are common knowledge.'

'I guess most folk knew how things worked,' Noakes said slowly, his face troubled. 'With places like this, people kinda live by routine.'

Or die by it, Markham thought grimly.

'Look, boss, you don' reckon either of them *oldies* killed Frost?' Now Noakes sounded alarmed. 'Her skull were a right mess . . . Okay, they ain't *totally* past it, but she took a real pasting.'

'Dimples says it's not impossible if Mrs Frost was taken by surprise . . . He thinks there was a sharp blow to the back of the head from a hammer. Then, once she was unconscious and unable to fight back, they rained down more blows on her with the flat of the spade.' Or 'really let rip', as the pathologist had put it in his usual laconic fashion.

Markham nodded. 'Look, Noakesy, there's this blasted press conference to get through, but I'll come back with Burton once it's over. Then we can talk to Mr Gower, Mrs Merryweather and the staff. Maybe now the worst shock is over, they'll recall more about Tuesday.'

'There's Sir Edward Fishface too,' Noakes pointed out.

That brought Markham's eyebrows up sharply.

'*Sir Edward Hamling*? Was *he* here on Tuesday?'

'Well, Periwinkle said he popped his head out from the library when they started hunting for Frost.' Noakes gave another of his portentous sniffs. 'He's got the run of the place, what with being the big cheese, but he always holes up in there . . . Mrs Thing brings him tea an' biscuits . . . An' not jus' any old custard creams like I get,' he added venomously. 'Oh no, he always gets the *homemade* stuff.' Reason enough to dislike the director in Noakes's book.

'What time did "Mrs Thing" bring Sir Edward his refreshments on Tuesday?' the DI asked.

'She said half eleven . . . Then later on, when they were all looking for Frost, he came to help, not that he *were* much help by the sound of it,' Noakes said acidly. 'Jus' watched from the side-lines an' barked orders.' He looked wistful as he said, 'I don' suppose you need me for the press wing ding, guv.'

'Much as I would enjoy watching you and Gavin Conors renew auld lang syne, I don't think it's a good idea,' Markham replied drily. 'And it would give Sidney the idea that your role is *proactive* when I've gone to some pains to paint you as enjoying civvy street.'

'Bollocks to that,' Noakes gloomed.

Seeing that his old friend was genuinely downcast, Markham tried to rally him. 'Look, you've got a better office than me. Plus, there's decent refreshments on tap and,' his lips twitched, 'no doubt subsidised meals too.'

'Yeah, dinner's all in,' the other admitted. 'An' the grub's pretty good.' A smile split the battered features. 'The cook did "Home Made Apple Pie" for afters last week. I had a bit of a joke with her, said, "Whose home was it made in?" . . . an' she told me not to be so stupid cos "homemade" jus' meant it didn't come out of a tin.' A rumbling chuckle. 'I like winding her up. You should've seen her face when I said I'd never met a sane vegetarian an' asked if vegans are the ones with the pointy ears.'

Markham wished passionately that Olivia was there to hear this example of light badinage. He could almost hear her bell-like tones exclaiming '*Priceless*!'

'You know, you're scrubbing up so well these days that I thought you must have a clothing allowance into the bargain,' he teased.

Noakes looked highly gratified, smoothing the lapels of the loud tweed jacket which 'the missus' had decreed was eminently appropriate for his corporate-cum-country-side role. His regimental tie lent the ensemble a uniquely Noakesian touch that no doubt went down well with the likes of Nicholas Gower and Linda Merryweather, though Markham doubted that Hafsah Peri would appreciate it.

'I'll be back here before you know it, Noakesy,' the DI said encouragingly. 'Kate's got all her Freudian ducks in a row — absolutely raring to blind the journos with science.'

'Oh aye.' Noakes couldn't prevent a big grin from stealing over his face. 'I bet her an' Shippers have gone to town on it.'

'*Totally.*' The DI flashed an answering smile. 'Just think of it . . . All that subtle psychoanalytical theorising down the centuries . . . and in half a millennium, it boils down to us worrying about page three of the *Gazette*!'

He looked at his gloriously politically incorrect ally with affection. 'I know it's early days, but how's it *really* going here, Noakesy?' he asked gently.

The bristly chin lifted. 'Not so bad, boss.' Then anxiously, 'You ain't forgotten you're coming round to ours for your tea later?'

In fact, Markham had. But with radiant insincerity, he replied. 'How could I forget?' *Easily as it happened.* 'But please tell your lady wife not to go to any trouble.' *As if.* Waitrose was no doubt being plundered for organic delicacies even as he spoke.

'I told the missus. My guvnor could do with a decent Chicken Kev . . . *Geddit*, boss . . . *Chicken Kev*!'

Oh God. He could only imagine how that banter had been received at Chateau Noakes!

'Truth to tell,' Noakes continued more seriously, 'we wouldn't mind picking your brains about our Nat, guv.'

'*Oh?*'

Mention of the perma-tanned one invariably meant trouble.

'She does the odd freelance beauty treatment here, at the home . . . An' there'd been a bit of a to-do about pilfering . . .'

'*Pilfering?*'

'Cash going missing from residents' rooms, that kind of thing. Frost were gonna do an investigation an' all that . . .'

Only then she was murdered.

Bloody hell, Markham thought. This was all he needed. His wingman's daughter mixed up in a double homicide.

But his eyes locked on those of the man whom he knew to be 'true blue'.

'Natalie's got nothing to worry about,' he said firmly. 'But it's good to know about this, thanks Noakesy.' He rose with the elegant fluid grace that characterised all his movements. 'I doubt it's connected with the murders, but the more intel we have the better.' He shook hands, sensing that the other needed this affirmation that they were still brothers-in-arms. 'Go and warm up Mr Gower, Mrs Merryweather and Ms Peri for me. Kate can do her gentle-touch policing thing later on, but I need you to work your magic.'

Noakes straightened up like the old soldier he was. 'I'm on it, guv.'

* * *

It was still a tired wet day, miserable and drizzly, when Markham returned with Burton to Rosemount, the sky thickening from blue to grey, curdling over with clouds.

But the residents' lounge was warm and comfortable, agreeably scented by pots of early-flowering narcissi which adorned the recessed window boxes.

It was a gracious space on the right-hand side of the house, with pastel blue painted walls, deep seat armchairs, an abundance of appliqued poufs and an intimate writing-room leading off the main lounge. There were no stern-faced General Gordon style portraits, just two rather fine John Piper landscapes and a couple of Graham Sutherland engravings along with rolling vintage bookcases and handily placed coffee tables, plus some delightful eighteenth-century hunting prints in the little annexe. Through the windows, an enclosed courtyard with a patio draped in trailing clematis and star jasmine brought the outdoors inside in approved Country Life fashion. Looking around him, Markham could see how Muriel Noakes might fancy herself as a proxy chatelaine.

Noakes himself was suitably modest and retiring on this occasion, leaving the interviewing to Markham and Burton, though it was apparent that he had, as requested, done his best to 'warm up' Andrée Clark's neighbours on Bluebell Corridor since they both appeared relaxed under the questioning. Hafsah Peri's body language, however, was noticeably more constrained. Markham told himself not to draw any conclusions from the nurse's demeanour; in the circumstances, it was only natural for her to be concerned for the wellbeing of her charges.

It was certainly difficult to see either Nicholas Gower or Linda Merryweather as a cold-blooded killer. Gower in particular had an almost roguish charm that belied his formidable learning.

Oddly enough, to start with it felt almost as though the *detectives* were being comforted by the elderly resident and not the other way around.

'Maureen was a great one for spiritual edification,' the theological scholar told them with a mischievous air. 'Her latest initiative was ensuring all our Gideon bibles were replaced with the King James version.' A rueful grimace. 'She didn't appreciate my joke about the man in a Birmingham hotel who read, "If you have a problem with alcohol, ring . . ." followed by the local phone number. Sober but curious, he rang, only to find himself talking to the manager of the local off-licence.'

Burton shifted uncomfortably, as though unsure what to make of such off-beat humour. Noakes, however, looked delighted, beefy shoulders heaving up and down in delighted mirth.

'She was very religious then?' Markham's fellow DI hazarded awkwardly.

'I think it was more a type of nineteenth-century English patriotism,' Gower said wryly. '*Our Island Story* and all that.' The note of affection was clear as he added, 'Maureen might not have had a highly developed sense of humour, but she was a great one for inherited tribal customs.' Suddenly he looked every day of his age. 'One of a kind.'

Burton got back to business. 'You didn't notice anything unusual on Tuesday morning, sir?'

'Not until the hue and cry just before lunch when everyone was wondering where Maureen had got to,' he said. 'Up till then, I was just catching forty winks in here.' He shrugged. 'I lead pretty much a sedentary life of it these days.'

'Going back to the first . . . death . . .' Burton said. 'Can you think who might have wanted to harm Mrs Clark?'

'Oh, I'd say all of us at one time or another,' was the equable reply.

Burton shifted in her seat and Markham had the feeling the old man was enjoying her discomfort.

'As I'm sure you already know,' he said with ironic forbearance, 'I was a close friend of Andrée's husband. *De mortuis nil nisi bonum* and all that, but Freddie had a great deal to put up with. To paraphrase Noel Coward's verdict on Vivien Leigh and the dance she led Larry Olivier on, if Freddie had given Andrée a good clip round the lughole, he'd have been spared a whole heap of trouble.'

'Would you care to expand on that, sir?' Burton pressed, looking faintly scandalised.

'No, I don't think so,' came the polite but firm reply. 'It's not my place, and anyway I don't think the marriage has got anything to do with her death.'

Burton visibly bristled but kept her tone cool. 'How can you be so sure?'

Another shrug. 'I can't, Inspector. But Andrée attracted drama and controversy all her life, so it seems to me that the answer more likely lies in her professional relationships than on the personal side.'

Burton changed tack. 'Did you ever detect bad feeling between Mrs Clark and any of her visitors? Any of her former colleagues . . . people from the arts scene?'

He shook his head almost pityingly. 'No, nothing like that, Inspector. But then,' in a tone of gentle reproof, 'I'm caught up in my own academic interests — a monograph on Socrates . . . and no, I'm not referring to some world-cup sweeper from Brazil!'

Markham could see why Noakes enjoyed Gower's self-deprecating wit. But was there something almost too *glib* — too rehearsed — about it?

Burton got nowhere when she pressed him about Andrée's rumoured memoirs.

'That kind of autobiographical enterprise puts me in mind of a Zen proverb, when the Dalai Lama said that psychoanalysis is like stirring up a nest of hibernating snakes, removing the most poisonous ones, and leaving the rest to come out when the weather warms up.'

Markham found it a sinister image and wondered if Gower was really as detached from the entire sordid business of Kiss 'N Tell as he affected to be.

'Are you suggesting Mrs Clark's literary ambitions might have had unforeseen deadly consequences?' he asked, but the other merely gave a Cheshire Cat Smile. 'That's one way of looking at it, Inspector.'

Linda Merryweather was no more illuminating on the subject of Andrée Clark's circle.

'I wasn't one of her *intimates*,' she said cranking up her voice to the degree of poshness worthy of a former president of Bromgrove's Lady Taverners and making it sound as though contact with Andrée Clark's set was something she had by no means coveted.

'I believe the two of you didn't always see eye to eye over the residents' committee,' Burton prompted tactfully.

'*Trivia*,' the other said with a fat complacent laugh. 'I can barely remember anything about it.'

But Markham saw something shift at the back of those curranty eyes and felt sure he could detect a faint flush on the doughy cheeks.

Afterwards, when Mrs Merryweather had left them, Hafsah Peri unbent sufficiently to confide, 'I believe she wanted some insights from Madame on the ballet world . . . background help with a new book she was planning. She was going to write about a ballet company . . . dancers' relationships . . . their rivalries and love affairs.'

'And Mrs Clark wouldn't cooperate?' Burton asked.

With an air of hauteur that Markham imagined was borrowed from her beloved 'Madame', the nurse sniffed, 'By no means. She thought the idea was vulgar.'

'Presumably she didn't let Mrs Merryweather down gently,' Markham observed.

The woman looked embarrassed. 'She spoke her mind . . .' A pause. 'Possibly gave offence.'

Markham, observing her discomfiture, suspected there was no 'possibly' about it.

But the interviews left them no further forward. Like Nicholas Gower, Mrs Merryweather claimed to have been aware of nothing untoward on the morning of Maureen Frost's murder.

It transpired she had been working on the synopsis for her next book at the drop-lid oak bureau in the little writing-room. 'I'm dead to the world when plotting my next *oeuvre*,' she said, blithely oblivious to the unfortunate turn of phrase. 'Absolutely dead to the world.'

'She writes in longhand, you know,' the nurse told them afterwards with a certain amount of awe. 'Won't have anything to do with computers.'

Which must be a barrel of laughs for any potential publisher, Markham reflected while simulating the appropriate interest.

From his perspective, what mattered here was the fact that there was an opportunity for either Gower or Merryweather to sneak out without the other noticing.

Once they'd got rid of Hafsah Peri, Noakes voiced his objection to such a scenario. 'Okay, so they could've got out to the shed an' back without being spotted,' he conceded, 'but wouldn't they have got blood on themselves? You heard Periwinkle say they looked pretty much the same as always when she checked on them after sorting the laundry.'

'Yes, but remember, there's their cardigans and shawls and rugs . . . all the paraphernalia they seem to lug around,' Burton considered. 'Anything bloodstained could just have been stuffed in with the rest. And if it was housekeeping time, the staff would have been distracted — most probably just making cursory checks downstairs.'

Noakes grinned. 'You're right about all their clobber. It's always a real performance shifting Merryweather. Like she needs sherpas to go anywhere.'

'Plus, don't forget they went off to "freshen up" before lunch,' Burton pointed out. 'So there was time to get rid of any tell-tale bloodstains well before Maureen's body was discovered in the afternoon.' With a frown she added, 'Let's face it, the crime scene was such a dog's dinner with everyone and their mother traipsing all over the place, that even if anything turns up to connect residents with that shed, there'll be all the usual issues with secondary transfer.'

'I still think it's a bit of a stretch for an OAP, though,' Noakes objected. 'You could see Periwinkle didn't buy it.'

'Both Mr Gower and Mrs Merryweather are far from being totally helpless invalids,' Markham retorted. 'We don't want to take all that about catching forty winks and being dead to the world at face value.'

'And they *both* crossed swords with Andrée Clark,' Burton said. 'Gower felt she'd short-changed his, er, friend Frederic March.'

'Yeah, *Freddie.*' Noakes's fancy was clearly tickled by the unlikely triangle.

Burton ignored the interruption. 'While Mrs Merryweather was nursing a grudge on account of Andrée having slapped her down over the idea that they might collaborate on a romantic novel.'

'Mrs C didn't need to help out Mrs Fifty Shades of Grey with some Mills & Boon job,' Noakes said. 'Not seeing as she had a mucky book of her own in the pipeline.'

'We haven't got any evidence that it ever got off the ground,' Markham reminded him. 'No first drafts or proofs or anything like that. Sir Edward Hamling certainly didn't seem to think there was much substance to the story.'

'Yeah, but that's what he *would* say,' Noakes grunted, 'seeing the kind of X-rated stuff she had on him.' It rather sounded to Markham as though his wingman (somehow, he could not help still thinking of him as such) regretted the loss of a chance to 'read all about it' in some tabloid exposé. Perhaps the former sergeant and Gavin Conors had more in common than they realised.

Noakes turned to Markham. 'Where's Lord Snooty got to anyway?' he demanded suspiciously.

'Unavoidably detained,' Burton said tightly. 'He said he can come by the station later this evening,' she added, her voice faltering slightly in the face of Noakes's manifest scepticism. Clearly her former colleague was keen to watch Hamling squirm.

'Can I leave Hamling to you, Kate?' Markham asked lightly. 'Muriel is giving me my tea tonight, and I don't want to miss out on that.'

Noakes brimmed with a look of intense gratification, though he strove to appear nonchalant.

'Nice one, sir,' Burton said with just the right degree of casualness. 'I'll be lucky if Nathan remembers to do me flipping baked beans on toast.'

'You need to train Shippers up, luv,' Noakes told her with avuncular condescension. '"Behind every strong woman" an' all that.'

'I'll be sure to tell him that, sarge,' she replied faintly. Then, apologetically to Markham, 'There's an evening performance at the Academy on Sunday evening, sir. Some sort of testimonial—'

'I thought only footballers had those,' Noakes objected. 'Not the greasepaint mob.'

'It's taking off in the arts too, sarge,' Burton said. 'There was something the Royal Ballet organised for the Rudolf Nureyev Foundation a while back . . .'

'Oh aye. *Randolph Neveroff.*'

Burton looked pained but smiled and continued determinedly. 'There's no catching you out, sarge.'

'Will we be going to this shindig then?' Noakes demanded.

'Indeed we will, Noakesy,' Markham told him firmly. 'There's Mrs Clark's funeral to get through first, but I want to see more of her former colleagues. Rosemount's proved a dead end so far. We need to see what lies beyond the footlights.'

## 7. HOME COMFORTS

Muriel Noakes said nothing about Olivia Mullen over the tea table, but her tender solicitude towards her husband's handsome former boss aimed to convey that she was firmly on his side as a man 'used and abused'.

Simpering coyly as he handed over a bouquet of purple tulips, inwardly she rejoiced at having Gilbert Markham all to herself without any of that pseudo-intellectual grandstanding and clever-clever commentary that Olivia just didn't seem to realise was pure *showing off*.

Not that Olivia hadn't improved somewhat since the earliest days of Gilbert's ill-fated relationship. Muriel flattered herself that her own *sophisticated* example had helped to smooth out some of the rough edges — tone down the showiness and attention-seeking. But without a 'marriage of true minds', it was never going to be enough. Poor dear Gilbert had been taken in by sexual wiles and tricks, when what he needed was a deeper *spiritual* connection. Hopefully her own discreet refinement would act as balm to a wounded soul.

With softness and sympathy in mind, she had selected a floaty drop-waisted tea dress in floral hues teamed with rose pink peep-toe shoes, kept her makeup light but perfect and asked the hairdresser for a looser perm than usual. She was more than satisfied with her reflection in the mirror, ignoring Natalie's comments to the effect that it was 'OTT and made it look like she had a thing for Markham'.

Natalie herself was immune to the inspector's reserved charm and had never taken to his smart-aleck partner who she felt was always secretly laughing at them. It was too bad her dad had been taken in by Olivia Mullen's little-girl-in-the-big-wide-world act, but maybe now at least he wouldn't run round after her quite so much like some kind of pet poodle.

She'd made a bit of an effort herself, fitting in an extra session at *Tanfastic* and a makeup consultation at John Lewis. As luck would have it, she had a big fat zit on her forehead, but lashings of Clinique's *Even Better Glow* looked to have taken care of it. She'd had to remind herself not to overdo it in case she ended up looking like an Oompa-Loompa. Not classy.

'Chicken Kev' was off the menu, but Muriel dished up a very acceptable mushroom stroganoff followed by banoffee pie. Markham was touched to observe how she relished hearing about Rosemount's architectural splendours — from the stained-glass window that threw a confetti of blues, reds and greens over the hallway to the classic period cornices and crown moulding. Natalie ostentatiously cast her eyes up to heaven, but privately basked in reflected glory. A Jane Austen style pile was a step up from that grotty old police station, and now her dad wasn't at anyone's beck and call — well leastways not some jumped-up snot-nosed kid straight out of university on the fast track to promotion. And reporting to *Sir* Edward Hamling had a nice ring to it . . .

After two glasses of Shiraz, Natalie felt positively *benign* towards Markham.

To be honest, it wasn't surprising if her mum had a soft spot for the inspector. He looked a bit scrawny and tired these days (probably eating his heart out over that stuck-up schoolmarm), but he was definitely easy on the eye. And something about the way he spoke sent shivers up her spine. Dead cultured and come-to-bed at the same time. But he was always respectful and treated her like a lady. Which was more than could be said for Chris Carstairs and the rest of them in CID.

Actually, come to think of it, Markham's face was like one of those portraits her old art teacher at Hope used to chunner on about . . . some Rembrandt showing a posh bloke who was halfway decent looking . . . She remembered thinking it made a welcome change from the usual depressing paintings of peasants and farm workers who looked like they wanted to top themselves.

Evenings like this, her mum came out of herself, she thought, listening with increasing interest as Muriel shared snippets of gossip gleaned through the Friends of Bromgrove Royal Court, this being the elite group of patrons who sponsored the local theatre and its resident companies including Bromgrove Ballet.

'Andrée Clark was pretty *notorious* in her day, Gilbert,' Muriel said confidentially over coffee as Noakes watched proudly (when it came to culture, the missus could hold her own with the best of them, he always maintained). 'Apparently, during one of her screaming fits she had her back to the orchestra while she ranted at the other dancers onstage. Then she started pacing backwards, step by step, towards the edge of the stage. No one said a word. Even after she fell into the orchestra pit — *not one word* — and nobody went to help her because they were that fed up.' A brittle laugh. 'She wasn't injured, of course.' With an air of superior knowledge, 'Dancers learn early on how to fall. But it was the talk of theatreland . . . people dined out on that story for years afterwards.'

'Who was she ranting at, Muriel?' Markham asked casually. 'Anyone in particular?'

It was obvious Mrs Noakes was vexed at not having the full story at her fingertips. However, she rallied with admirable aplomb.

'They *said* the conductor husband was first in the firing line, but I heard she was shrieking at her partner for mistiming his lifts and carting her round like she was a sack of potatoes.'

This titbit elicited appreciative sniggers from Natalie and Noakes.

'She struggled with her weight from time to time.' Self-consciously, Muriel smoothed the filmy panels of her dress, grateful that her Spanx shapewear appeared to be doing its job. 'But when she moved into coaching, it didn't stop her criticising students who *gained*.' Clearly delighted at her own mastery of the technical lexicon, she continued, 'Can you believe it, she would accuse the poor dears of "beginning to look too healthy". And she told them that when they faced the audience their *rib cage* had to be *visible*.' A swift sideways glance at her own decidedly buxom offspring. 'I mean, for goodness' sake, nobody wants to watch *skeletons*, do they?' As she said this, it gave her some satisfaction to reflect that she had always suspected waiflike Olivia Mullen of having an eating disorder.

Markham murmured something anodyne and non-committal.

Satisfied that she and her handsome guest were in perfect harmony on this vital issue, Muriel resumed with renewed animation.

'Such unnecessary *body fascism*.'

*Blimey*, Natalie thought on hearing this. Mum had really been mugging up for DI Dreamboat. It was starting to sound like she'd swallowed a thesaurus.

But, like Noakes, she was quite impressed, even if it *was* a load of reheated feminist cobblers.

Seeing the lady of the house look at him expectantly, Markham realised it was time to do more than utter vague ums and ahs.

'A friend of mine on the *Gazette* would concur with you, Muriel,' he said with a charming smile. 'I was quite taken aback to learn the choreographer Balanchine took the ideal of the body beautiful to such extremes that he ended up contracting CJD.'

Natalie squirmed delightedly. 'What, *as in Mad Cow Disease*? That's *gross*!'

'The very same. I understand he took injections of parathyroid and adrenaline, known to have a convulsive effect on dogs. Later on, it was sheep placentas. Other famous people — Charlie Chaplin, Winston Churchill and Cole Porter — took these rejuvenating treatments as well.'

*Sheep placentas*!

Muriel felt it was incumbent on her to look deeply pained. *Winston Churchill*! She felt she would never be able to regard the orator of *We Shall Fight on the Beaches* in quite the same way again.

Markham forged on. As Liv might have said, it was time for him to give value for money — or at least for banoffee pie.

'Balanchine still appears to be Bromgrove Ballet's presiding deity, despite the dodgy pedagogy.'

Muriel was delighted to be 'in the know'.

'Didn't one of his wives catch polio and end up in a wheelchair?' she asked.

'That's right,' Markham confirmed gravely, grateful for Kate Burton's balletomane leanings. 'Wife number four, Tanaquil Le Clerq. There were all kinds of theories about it . . . People said she'd dipped her fingers into the canals of Venice when the company was on tour, and the waterways were contaminated with sewage. Another story had it that she was infected by the wife of the American cultural attaché who came down with the disease after hosting a reception for the company.'

Muriel pursed her lips. 'Didn't stop him moving on from her in the end.'

'Well, Balanchine was something of a serial monogamist,' Markham agreed. 'I gather he tended to fall in love with whichever young ballerina inspired him and then marry her. Apparently all the ballet mothers would gladly have thrown their teenaged daughters at him on the chance he might make her a star.'

Glancing round the table, Markham was amused by their rapt interest. Truly he had sung for his supper tonight.

'One of the baby ballerinas who turned Balanchine down wrote about it later,' he said. 'She figured there was a pattern — a time limit to his infatuations. They usually lasted seven years when his dancing girls were between the ages of fifteen and twenty-three. He married the first at fifteen, the next two at twenty-one and then Tanaquil Le Clerq at twenty-three. The ages of the wives stayed roughly the same while he grew older. His final major infatuation was with a dancer who was eighteen while he was fifty-nine. But he stayed with Tanquil for sixteen years, which was a matrimonial record for him. Guilt about her illness played its part in that. Then he fell in love with his final muse and divorced Tanaquil.'

'What happened with him and the last girl then?' Natalie asked wide-eyed.

'She rejected him for a much younger dancer. They ended up leaving the company, but he eventually allowed his muse back. Not the husband though.'

Muriel and Natalie looked satisfied at hearing about Balanchine's misfortune in love, as though — like the man himself — they considered it merely poetic justice.

'How weird that the same thing happened to Mrs Clark as the Tanny woman . . . struck down by an incurable illness and then her husband walked out on her,' Natalie said. 'Almost like a *curse*.'

Muriel appeared much struck by another parallel. 'It was the same with George Baranov, wasn't it?' she said slowly. 'His wife had MS and then he lost his head over some young girl who turned him down.'

'Yeah,' Natalie marvelled, 'almost like history repeating itself or reincarnation . . . P'raps Baranov was his clone or something.'

In the somewhat uneasy pause that followed this observation, Markham's keen dark gaze rested on her with the flattering intensity that Olivia once accused him of switching on and off at will. Certainly, it did funny things to Natalie's insides. Well, that and the Shiraz.

'I believe you've undertaken some health therapy at Rosemount,' Markham said, smoothly changing the subject from curses and clones. Instinctively, he knew better than to refer to 'beauty treatments', Muriel being decidedly sensitive to any blue-collar overtones.

'Yeah, that's right. I can do more *high-end* clients now that I'm freelance.'

'What did you make of Mrs Clark?' he enquired.

'She seemed nice enough when I did the Reiki.' A gossamer frown bisected her forehead's polyfilla surface. 'Though the dolls kind of freaked me out . . . She was always fiddling with them and messing with that creepy toy theatre.'

'But you'd have said she was of sound mind?' Markham pressed.

'Oh yeah, there were no flies on Mrs C. She could be quite funny sometimes. I remember she called her ex a Scrooge. Said he was the type to stop breathing if the air cost money.'

Noakes chortled happily at this, as much as to say, 'She's a chip off the old block.'

Carefully, Markham led up to the subject of money going missing at Rosemount. 'Not the kind of lady to be taken advantage of then?'

'Well, there was some loose cash went missing from her room. But it wasn't just her,' Natalie added. 'It happened to a couple of others as well.'

'When was this?' Markham asked.

'About a month before Christmas.' Further wrinkling of the well-grouted brow. 'It was strange really, the way Mrs Frost kind of put off doing anything about it. Then in the New Year, Mr Gower made a fuss about some antique cuff links going walkabout . . . that's when she told dad she supposed there'd have to be a formal investigation. Only he thought she was dragging her heels.'

Noakes nodded. 'It weren't nice for staff an'—' he groped for a term free of downmarket connotations — '*outside contractors.*'

'Yeah, everyone started looking sideways at each other,' his daughter agreed. 'Like we were *all* under suspicion.'

Markham sensed this was somehow important. 'And you thought it was out of character, the way Mrs Frost was behaving?'

Natalie was clearly pleased that CID's leading light requested her psychological insights, though the effects of the Shiraz (and, truth be told, a couple of voddie and tonics before she came out) made her answering smile distinctly lopsided. Luckily, Muriel's delight that they were in Markham's confidence meant she was oblivious to all else.

'She'd been snappish and mardy coming up to Christmas, but,' Natalie gave a martyred sigh, 'she was the kind who never liked tinsel and fuss.' A giggly hiccough. 'Didn't like fun or jokes or anything like that . . . got a right cob on when Chloe Finch told her the one about Bruno the Black-eyed Reindeer who's as fast as Rudolph but can't pull up as quickly.'

Seeing Muriel's expression cloud over, Markham interposed.

'I can top that, Natalie,' he laughed easily. 'What about the little lad in the grotto who marched up to Father Christmas, punched him on the nose and announced: "That's for last year"!'

Before Noakes could jump in with his all-time favourite about the dyslexic devil who stole toys from Satan's grotto, Markham continued smoothly, 'That's very interesting information about Mrs Frost's state of mind, Natalie. I suppose it's part of your professional skill set to notice such things.'

Muriel visibly relaxed as the prospect of her elegant supper descending into unseemly hilarity receded. It was gratifying that Gilbert Markham always spoke of Natalie's job in respectful terms. People were all too apt to assume that not going to university meant her daughter was an airhead, but now that she was specialising in *holistic medicine* there was every chance of her eventually becoming a partner in the Harmony Spa . . .

Her attention was jerked back to the present on hearing Noakes say jovially, 'At least you're not knee deep in bodies, guv.'

Markham grimaced expressively.

'*Not yet.*'

Seeing his hostess's look of consternation, he reverted to the subject of Rosemount.

'How do you find the nursing staff, Natalie . . . Hafsah Peri, for example?'

'I don't want to sound *raycist* or anything,' she began.

*Go on, force yourself*, Markham thought.

'She gives the impression she thinks she's better than everyone else, 'specially the healthcare assistants and people like that.'

'*Oh?*'

'Yeah. And she was kind of *possessive* about Mrs C . . . didn't like anyone else getting too close to her. I kind of wondered . . . Well, there was this one day when I went up there early and I saw Mrs C hand her something that looked like a cheque. Mrs C saw me looking and started talking about some charity or other for retired dancers . . . like she wanted me to think Hafsah was just passing it on to someone else. But there was something secretive about how they were. And Chloe told me once that she thought Hafsah dropped hints about family problems as a way of asking Mrs C for gifts. One time Mrs C gave her some doll from abroad which was worth a mint . . .'

'Did anyone bring this up with Mrs Frost?' Markham asked.

'*God no.*' Natalie tittered tipsily. 'Frostie and Hafsah were pretty tight, what with them both being there donkey's years . . . Plus, Mrs C was *dependent* on Hafsah, so she could make the old lady say anything she wanted.' In a burst of confidence, she continued, 'She's a sneaky type.'

Was Hafsah responsible for the thefts at Rosemount? Markham wondered. And if so, why had Maureen Frost taken so long to do something about it? Was there something afoot at the nursing home that had put the manager in Hafsah's power?

'Talking about sneaky,' Noakes said, with a grin, 'how's Roger the Dodger suiting you, guv?'

'Oh, I reckon you know the answer to that question, Noakes,' he said. An image of Carruthers's pale deadpan eyes rose up before him. 'Between friends,' with a graceful bow towards Muriel and Natalie, 'there's something very bloodless and anaemic about him.'

'He's a slimy git,' Noakes agreed. Or, as Olivia might have put it, Carruthers was one of 'the Brylcreem tendency'. 'Used to look at me like I were a real "cor blimey".' Perhaps in the current circumstances that should be *corps blimey*, Markham thought suppressing his amusement. 'Plus,' Noakes added balefully, 'he's always snitching to Sidney an' Nunky Bretherton.'

'That too,' Markham sighed. 'Kate and Doyle haven't taken to Carruthers but,' he flashed a conspiratorial grin at his old ally, 'they're good at running interference when necessary to keep him off my back. Right now, the psychological profile angle is keeping him out of mischief. Any day now I expect him to present me with a composite based on some half-baked Freudian theory or other . . . ideally something that won't frighten the horses at our next press conference.'

In her newly acquired role of professional expert, Natalie felt emboldened to enquire, 'You don't reckon it could be one of the old folks, do you?' The concern in her luridly made-up eyes reminded Markham of her essential kindness.

'I'm keeping an open mind, Natalie,' he said. 'Mrs Clark's personal and professional background was pretty complex.' Understatement of the century. 'I'm inclined to think the clue lies somewhere in her past.'

'Dancers can be dead bitchy,' she agreed. 'I remember the performing arts crowd at Hope . . . Always temper tantrums and tears.' She flicked her peroxide mane contemptuously. 'The boys were worst, calling the girls too bummy, too titty or too short in the neck.'

Seeing that Muriel looked as though something had gone done the wrong way, she added apologetically, 'Sorry, Mum, but they were just so *mean*.'

Markham suspected that teenaged Natalie Noakes had probably been no slouch in the spitefulness stakes, but merely nodded courteously.

'My eyes have been opened to the artistic temperament alright,' he said. 'I didn't detect any shortage of self-regard when I met Frederic March and Mrs Clark's former partner Toby Lavenham.' The Malignant Maestro and Mister Colgate Smile, as he had mentally designated them.

'That curly-haired choreographer, Buckwheat, were properly up hisself,' Noakes grunted. An' the midget Italian bloke with the name like a pizza topping—'

'Ray Franzoni,' Markham chuckled. 'And it's Buckfast not Buckwheat.'

'Whatever. A right pair of ponces if you ask me.'

'The women were definitely more appealing,' Markham found himself remembering Clara Kentish and Tania Sullivan with pleasure. 'Less concerned to act the big I Am.'

Now Natalie's eyes were avid with prurient interest.

'Wasn't there a row cos Mrs C's husband had the hots for some young dancer?' she asked. 'Like he was this big paedo.'

Despite wincing, it was apparent that Muriel was no less interested in the answer, well-bred ladylikeness and prurient fascination contending for the upper hand.

Nosiness won the day. 'Something about him being a little bit too . . . *tactile, over-friendly*?' she prompted.

'I'm not sure there was really all that much to it,' Markham replied, privately amused to see their faces fall. He felt he really ought to throw them a bone. 'There was some kind of infatuation by the sound of it, and then the rumour mill cranked into gear. Actually, when I talked to Rosa Maitland, I had the impression it was really Mrs Clark's coercive teaching methods that bothered her more than anything else.'

Natalie wasn't to be fobbed off so easily. 'What's she like, this Rosa woman?'

Markham knew better than to deliver an encomium to Maitland's beauty.

'Rather naïve and innocent,' he returned vaguely. 'Unformed somehow.'

Honour was satisfied by this faintly denigrating description, his hostess and her daughter assuming their best 'women of the world' air. For his part, Noakes looked relieved, as though a tricky social hazard had been safely negotiated.

Muriel suggested they adjourn to the drawing-room, ignoring how Natalie's Scouse brows shot upwards. No way did terms like 'lounge' or 'front room' pass her lips on gala days when Gilbert Markham was a visitor. There had been one or two close calls that threatened to mar the perfection of the occasion — Natalie holding her knife like a pencil, George turning his linen napkin over and over in bemusement, for all the world as though it was a towel for some post-football rubdown (she should be grateful he hadn't shamed her by asking what she'd done with the paper ones), or telling the one about the child who thought the vegetables were called 'Man Get Out', Natalie rolling her eyes at Richard Clayderman on the stereo (a favourite of the Royals according to *Woman and Home*) and the olives appetizers . . .

At least when she had served tea — Gilbert having expressed a preference for her special blend of Earl Grey — George and Natalie had remembered the drill (from Paul Burrell's *In the Royal Manner*): silver tongs for the sugar and only one lump so as not to appear greedy, then only half a swirl when stirring, with no noise when drinking . . . and never finish tea to the end, always leave a little in the cup like the queen. She had been afraid they would let her down by slurping or sticking their pinkies out for fun, but they had got that part right. George even managed not to pull a face at the sugar rationing . . .

Now they were in the final straight, and Gilbert had given every appearance of enjoying some home cooking and civilised chat. Her lips thinned as she recalled Olivia discoursing on the joys of 'vegging out' with Pot Noodles and an instalment of *Say Yes to the Dress*. The poor man had probably had it up to here with that kind of bohemian gipsy lifestyle.

No sooner were they settled in Muriel's chintzy sitting room (whose décor equalled Honor Calthorpe's flat for sheer fussiness), than Natalie announced she had to go.

'Need to be up bright and early for *clients* in the morning,' she said.

Markham rose and leaned in for a chaste peck on the cheek as befitted an old friend of many years standing. Somewhat panda-eyed but still valiantly batting her false eyelashes, the perma-tanned one disappeared into the hallway to order herself a taxi.

Markham inwardly calculated that another forty minutes or so should satisfy his social obligations. For all his hostess's gratingly arch manner and affectations, he sensed the vulnerability beneath and guessed there were hidden depths she kept well concealed. It had been touching to see how she flushed with pleasure at Noakes's muttered, 'That were champion, luv' at the end of the meal, suddenly looking almost girlish in spite of the lacquered blonde helmet (shades of Margaret Thatcher) and garden-party outfit. The dynamics of the marriage were a mystery to him, but of Noakes's devotion to his social-climbing wife there could be no doubt.

'Will you be joining us for the performance at the Dance Academy on Sunday evening, Muriel?' he asked courteously. 'I imagine as a Friend you can count on access all areas.'

'Mrs Councillor Anstruther-Stewart is taking me,' she said happily, while Noakes's expression telegraphed more clearly than words that the lady in question was one to avoid.

As Markham groped for further conversational gambits, the door burst open to disclose a wide-eyed Natalie.

'Kate Burton's out front,' she said in a rush. 'She says there's been a break-in at Rosemount.'

'Ah, I turned my mobile off the better to enjoy your company,' he said gracefully, with no sign of the chill that had settled over him at these words. Please God this incident wasn't the precursor to something worse.

## 8. HAPPY ENDING

Of course, Natalie Noakes had over-egged the pudding (or banoffee pie) and the reality turned out to be considerably less dramatic than her breathless announcement implied.

The 'intruder' turned out to be Ray Franzoni, challenged by a flustered Mrs Cartwright when she found him 'making free of the premises'.

According to Franzoni, he had come to Rosemount to do a 'recce' for some fundraiser due to take place at the nursing home later in the year. A telephone call to Sir Edward Hamling confirmed the truth of this claim, though it seemingly hadn't occurred to the ballet master that he should obtain clearance for the visit as opposed to simply wandering in.

Given that Hamling vouched for Franzoni who showed no discomfort or guilty consciousness, there was nothing to justify detention of Andrée Clark's former colleague. Not unreasonably, the coach was highly critical of the home's 'amateurish' security, which meant the police were on the back foot from the off.

'Sorry, guv,' Noakes mumbled after they had let Franzoni go, 'That's down to me. We need someone covering the front door twenty-four seven.' His scowl was ferocious. ''Specially if the likes of Pizza Boy ignore the notice telling 'em to bring the bell at reception.

'Mister Franzoni was in the hall at the bottom of the stairs when Mrs Cartwright caught him,' Hafsah Peri told them. 'I think he wanted to look in Madame's room.'

'Why would he do that?' Markham enquired but the woman merely pressed her lips tight together as though she not trusting herself to say more.

Afterwards, as they conferred in the staff room, Kate Burton told him, 'There's nothing doing upstairs, guv. Mrs Clark's room's been processed by forensics. It's clean as a whistle.'

'And yet Ms Peri seemed to think Franzoni was up to no good . . . on the prowl,' the DI mused.

'It might've suited her to turn the spotlight on him,' Burton suggested. 'If Natalie's right about there being some kind of funny business going on here . . . an extortion racket perhaps . . . then she'd be keen to have us look elsewhere.'

'An' Cartwright didn't say he were going upstairs,' Noakes concurred. 'She were jus' wittering on about it being trespass.'

'What else do we know about Franzoni, Kate?' Markham asked.

'Volatile, bisexual, in and out of therapy, but that's nothing unusual with his crowd. Very intense, with a reputation for being a bully . . . screaming at dancers that they all "looked like shit and danced like shit".' She frowned. 'Which is a bit rich, seeing that he accused Andrée of the same thing.' The DI's eyes narrowed, 'There was a piece about him in the *Gazette* from way back. It said there was this lad who told him he wanted to be a soloist and rattled off all the ballets he wanted to dance . . . apparently, Franzoni smirked and said, "Why don't you make a list of the things you want to do. And you can add to the list, 'Leave the company'!"'

'Hmm, he sounds a real charmer,' Markham observed on hearing this.

'Oh yes,' Burton continued. 'According to the *Gazette* article, one of the other coaches said that lessons with

Franzoni were good for the kids' careers because they learned how *not* to treat people. There were other stories about him too. Stuff about pestering some young lad who was a soloist, bombarding him with messages and texts . . . But it never went anywhere. Word has it that Hamling looks out for him.'

Noakes was in bullish mood. 'As in they've got summat going between them?' he demanded.

She shrugged. 'Nobody's come right out and said it, but reading between the lines . . .'

Noakes looked disgusted. '*What a chuffing shower!*' he exclaimed. 'Makes me glad our Nat never kept on with the ballet lessons.'

An image of Natalie Noakes in her perma-tanned glory bourréeing her heart out, like Miss Piggy in the Muppet Show's *Swine Lake*, popped into Markham's mind eliciting a bark of laughter that he hastily turned into a cough.

Burton remained commendably po-faced, though the DI suspected she had a similar apparition before her eyes. 'That's the arts for you, sarge,' she said at last. 'And you know, maybe in many ways they've got a more evolved attitude when it comes to sexual morality.'

Seeing that Noakes didn't look as if he cared for Burton's brave new world, Markham said crisply, 'Well at any rate, as things stand, we've no grounds to bring Franzoni in.'

'It was interesting though . . .' Burton murmured as though talking to herself.

Noakes stared at her. 'What was?'

'While you were talking to Mrs Cartwright, I had a word with Chloe Finch. She remembered something from when the Dance Academy crowd came in to see Mrs Clark over the New Year. She's almost certain she heard Andrée say, "I'm not scared of you at all".'

'Was she talking to Franzoni?' Markham asked.

'Chloe said she couldn't be sure, just that it stuck in her mind because it seemed an odd thing to say.

Indeed it was, heightening Markham's sense of unease. As they parted from Noakes, the words echoed over and over in his mind like a sinister refrain.

*I'm not scared of you at all.*

\* \* \*

After the frustrating events of Thursday and an equally unproductive Friday, Markham was almost glad of the expedition to Saint Vitus Church for Andrée Clark's funeral on Saturday morning.

Situated literally around the corner from Rosemount, at the bottom of the winding front drive, it was a modest little building of grey flint with dressings in white limestone and a tiled roof. Built in the mid-nineteenth century on the site of a medieval church which was developed and then demolished in succeeding centuries, it boasted a crenelated tower from which — to Noakes's evident approval — a Union Jack flag fluttered defiantly in the breeze.

Passing through the gabled porch where they collected orders of service from a rickety little table, they were immediately assailed by the damp and musty smell peculiar to such places. Markham liked it but noticed Doyle wrinkling his nose in fastidious disapproval. Carruthers also appeared distinctly underwhelmed as the group moved into the dim interior, slipping into a box pew at the back led by Markham and Noakes with the other three close behind.

Architecturally, the church was fairly nondescript, with a three-bay nave, north aisle and chancel accessed through a tall arch, with Italian style pulpit to the side. Whitewashed walls, grey flagstone flooring and hexagonal granite pillars gave an impression of cool austerity, only relieved by some garish stained-glass windows and ornate plaques honouring local bigwigs. On the wall opposite their pew, a stone tablet listed the dead from two world wars, while next to it a Romanesque funerary frieze of some classical matron roaming moodily beneath cypresses commemorated the family of a local JP.

His gaze wandering through the shadowy gloom to an iron wrought votive stand next to the pulpit, Markham reflected that the inner workings of his mind resembled the little tea lights flickering and wavering, like so many lanterns in the dark.

The church was slowly filling up, but the DI barely noticed, his attention suddenly caught by a heavily gilt-framed reproduction next to their bench. A brass plaque beneath the painting was simply engraved *Lavinia Fontana: Noli Me Tangere*, alluding to the encounter between Christ and Mary Magdalene when she mistook him for a gardener after the resurrection.

It was particularly suited to a rural church, he thought, charmed by the depiction of the Saviour as a barefoot labourer in simple tunic and wide-brimmed hat, while his voluptuous penitent resembled a well-fed country girl. Warm russets and ochres imparted the glow of an Indian summer to softly tinted skies, with even the empty tomb in the background transformed into an idyllic arbour hollowed out of a tree trunk and twined round with hawthorn flowers. Were it not for the angel perched inside and the Magdalene's halo, one might almost have mistaken the scene for a celebration of Harvest Home.

One detail, however, made Markham catch his breath.

Christ was leaning on a long-handled spade.

Noakes had followed his guvnor's gaze.

'A spade,' he whispered, 'a chuffing *spade*.'

It was an eerie coincidence in light of the weapon that had been used to bludgeon Maureen Frost.

The Saviour's hand hovered tenderly over his disciple's head — *Don't touch me, for I have not yet ascended to heaven* — but it was that long shovel which somehow compelled the two detectives' attention.

Markham smiled reassuringly at the man he still thought of as his number two. 'It's a beautiful picture,' he said simply.

Noakes affected equal nonchalance. 'The lass looks a bit gormless,' he commented before adding kindly, 'Mind you, bound to be gobsmacked seeing as she thought he'd gone for good an' it were all a great big mess. *Finito*. End of the road.'

Christ's features were in shadow, partly concealed by the brim of his hat. And there was nothing celestial about his casual posture. But Markham fancied that an enigmatic smile lurked about the figure's mouth and found himself hoping that this boded well for Andrée Clark and Maureen Frost wherever they now found themselves. Involuntarily, he remembered his dream of black-robed figures processing into a surreal watery grave and gave a convulsive shiver. Noticing that Carruthers was observing him covertly, he composed himself and turned his attention to the mourners.

Clara Kentish, Tania Sullivan and Rosa Maitland came in together: *The Three Graces*, white-faced and sheathed in black. Maitland's profile held the purity of a Botticelli angel, its delicate lines emphasised by the simple low ponytail which contrasted with the more formal chignons of the older women. Kentish looked as if a gust of wind could blow her away, huddled anorectically in the depths of a black shawl coat. Sullivan, in a long poncho, was wearing a surprisingly heavy amount of makeup which would not have looked out of place in *Carmen* or some equally flamboyant production.

Frederic March, even more cadaverous than when Markham had last seen him, turned up with Toby Lavenham, the latter carrying a sheaf of lilies that he no doubt fancied made him look like Albrecht in *Giselle*. Unsurprisingly, there was no sign of Ray Franzoni, but Richard Buckfast arrived a few minutes after the others. Appearing ill at ease, he had dark circles under his eyes, his lips looked dry and cracked, and the springy curls seemed as though they had been plastered to his head. There was no trace of the faun-like boyishness that had previously struck Markham.

At the front, Sr Edward Hamling towered over the rest of the Rosemount contingent, a handsome almost brooding presence impeccably attired in superbly cut pinstripes. Though it was cold and blustery outside, he disdained an overcoat and appeared unaffected by the chill of the church.

Hafsah Peri and Chloe Finch stood either side of Nicholas Gower and Linda Merryweather, the tableau giving an unfortunate impression that the two residents were somehow in custody. Today Merryweather was more Russian babushka than stentorian-voiced toastmistress, almost swallowed up by a voluminous flapping raincoat and scarf. Gower, parchment pale, had the same will-'o-the-wisp insubstantiality as Clara Kentish, and Markham remembered what Noakes had reported about the academic being off his food.

He noticed that Hafsah Peri was wearing a beautifully cut cashmere trench coat and wondered yet again whether it was possible that the nurse was supplementing her income via some form of extortion . . .

There were others unknown to him, but the artistic mourners were easily distinguished by their eye-catching attire (some of it funky, such as an ensemble of black velvet hot pants and jacket topped off with veiled fascinator) and elegant carriage.

As Andrée Clark's coffin was carried in to the accompaniment of Gluck's *Dance of the Blessed Spirits* from the little organ loft above them, Markham recalled Honor Calthorpe's description of her as a miracle of lightness flitting about the stage. There was no sign of the former journalist in the congregation, which did not surprise him. It would doubtless have evoked too many bitter-sweet memories. Nor was Gavin Conors in attendance, but the presence of a pimply anoraked youth who kept darting furtive glances at the detectives from across the aisle suggested that the lead reporter had sent one of his henchmen.

A huge, framed head shot of Andrée from *Swan Lake* was placed on top of the coffin after it had been carefully deposited on the trestle in front of the altar. The same picture adorned the front of the orders of service, and underneath it was a quotation:

*When you have a garden full of pretty flowers, you don't demand of them, "What do you mean? What is your significance?" Dancers are just flowers, and flowers grow without*

*any literal meaning, they are just beautiful. We're like flow-*
*ers. A flower doesn't tell you a story. It's in itself a beautiful*
*thing. —George Balanchine*

Suddenly Markham recalled Clara Kentish telling him that the great choreographer had said 'that Ballet was a woman and man the gardener,' and his eyes wandered superstitiously to the *Noli Me Tangere* painting with its mysterious shimmering landscape.

As the organ struck up the ubiquitous *Jerusalem*, he contemplated the young Andrée Clark's lushly exotic features, mentally comparing it with the post-mortem photographs of a shrivelled, almost simian little woman on the mortuary slab, patches of straggly hair sticking like seaweed to her tiny head. It was a heartrending juxtaposition.

The service, taken by a surprisingly youthful vicar, was more or less in line with the Book of Common Prayer. Markham was amused that his homily incorporated more Balanchine, though this time with a clear nod to the Deity: 'God creates, man assembles.'

There was no eulogy as such, though Clara Kentish stepped forward to read Andrée's favourite poem *Thanatopsis*. Somehow the lines about resting on a heavenly couch and lying down with patriarchs seemed almost comically inapposite to one whose business was perpetual motion.

Still, Kentish read well, her gentle but clear delivery carrying to the back of the church. Far less simpatico was Frederic March's rendition of some mumbled lines which ended with a quotation from Aeschylus's *The Persians*: 'Death is long and without music.' There was something curiously spiteful in what sounded like a gloating malediction, for surely, Markham thought, music was all in all to a dancer.

'Pretentious tosser,' Noakes grumbled under his breath, earning himself a stern look of reproof from Burton.

She was even more scandalised when during the vicar's final exhortation that they should beseech the Almighty with sighs, she heard the former DS mutter 'six and three-quarters'.

But Noakes's pièce de resistance came with the final hymn, *Hail Redeemer, King Divine*, when he seemed positively to be engaged in a fight to the death with the wheezy little organ, his colossal bass virtually obliterating the accompaniment. Roger Carruthers certainly looked as though nothing could ever compensate him for the sheer mortification of such a spectacle, while Burton and Doyle braved the incredulous stares and gamely sang along.

As they followed the congregation into the pocket-sized handkerchief graveyard, Markham murmured, 'Great *esprit de corps* back there, team.' And with a mischievous glance at Carruthers, he added piously, 'Of course as Scripture says, "He who sings prays twice".' Though it might fairly be said that where Noakes was concerned, the old proverb should run, 'Those around he who sings badly pray three times'.

Burton felt profoundly grateful that DCI Sidney had missed Noakes's performance. Markham too was relieved that Sidney and Superintendent Bretherton were off addressing the Specialist Firearms Command. Though no doubt, he reflected grimly, Carruthers would be sure to give them chapter and verse later.

According to specific instructions in her will, Andrée Clark's cremation was to be strictly private.

'Like Princess Margaret,' Noakes had commented approvingly, being well briefed on such matters by his royalty-obsessed wife. 'A proper send-off in church an' then the depressing bit out of the way without anyone peering an' gawping.'

Now he said, 'Thank chuff we don' have to go to the crem, all plastic an' artificial . . . with canned music an' that creepy strobe lighting like you're in a disco.' He shuddered.

'The grounds are quite nice, though,' Burton put in, recalling previous visits for the funerals of murder victims. She had liked the woods and little memorial areas with their good old-fashioned cottage-garden flowers.

Noakes's mind was running on temporal matters.

'Did Mrs C leave much dosh, guv?' he asked Markham out of the side of his mouth, furtively checking that none of the congregation was within earshot.

'I made discreet enquiries,' the DI replied. *And twisted some arms.* 'There were sizeable bequests to Rosemount and Bromgrove Ballet, with some small gifts to carers and friends, but I would say nothing worth murdering for.'

Burton nodded her agreement. 'We're looking for a grudge-killer,' she said quietly.

Doyle glanced around the cemetery uneasily. 'Kind of figures when you think of how they messed with that doll . . . made it look like the thing was *pointing* at her.'

Markham suddenly remembered Olivia's words. *Almost like the killer was using it to* accuse *Andrée of something . . .*

Noakes shuffled restlessly. The other mourners had moved well away, as though the detectives were surrounded by a *cordon sanitaire* and ordinary folk risked contamination should they breach it.

It had turned increasingly chilly while they were inside the church, with grey-green storm light darkening the little cemetery and no hint of the warm 'lambish' winds and tentative green shoots that Markham had savoured such a short time before on Bromgrove Rise. No sign of pale wildflowers, just straggling bushes that looked as if their leaves were afflicted with jaundice.

It was a setting that was somehow appropriate for the obsequies of a murder victim, he thought.

'How come the padre didn't say owt about Frostie?' Noakes demanded suddenly as they began to drift towards the lychgate. 'I mean, prayers for our departed brothers an' sisters seemed a bit bobbins.'

'I believe there's to be a memorial for Mrs Frost in due course,' Markham replied. 'Mrs Clark had decreed a simple, brief service without any "twiddles"—'

'Didn't stop her ex an' that skinny dancer going off-piste with the godawful poetry,' Noakes shot back.

'Well, I imagine allowances were made . . . in light of the tragic circumstances surrounding her death.'

Noakes looked as though he still thought it was a poor show but moved on to more pressing concerns.

'There's a buffet back at Rosemount,' he said. 'It'll be a decent spread cos of the Black Baron an' his posh chums.'

Markham's lips twitched. 'Don't let anyone hear you call Sir Edward Hamling that,' he warned. 'Well, seeing as you're head of security, I suggest you lead on,' he added encouragingly.

Noakes brightened on hearing this. He'd been to more than his fair share of grisly wakes with the guvnor over the years and always had to be careful in case it looked like he was guzzling on duty. But these days it was different. *Now* he didn't have to worry about the likes of Carruthers or some other greaser whingeing to the top brass about him 'letting the side down'. Yup, *today* he could tuck in without feeling guilty.

It was a shame Muriel was off with her women's group. He'd have liked her to see Mrs C's send-off. On the other hand, it hadn't been the celebrity funeral he expected. Just that spotty nerk from the *Gazette* there to cover it and not much of a crowd at all. Most likely it was something to do with her having been *murdered*, he thought darkly. Your typical tuppenny-ha'penny toff would be afraid something might rub off on them, he concluded scornfully. A curse or bad luck, something like that.

Doyle's voice jolted him back to the present. 'What's that?' the youngster asked, pointing at an intricate carving in the lychgate's timber pediment.

'It's the tree of knowledge,' Noakes said, taking sly pleasure in Carruthers's evident surprise. 'The one that got Adam an' Eve into trouble in the Bible cos they weren't supposed to eat from it.'

'*Right*.' Doyle squinted upwards. 'Yeah, now I can see the snake . . . and there's little figures at the base.' He moved nearer. 'Like dolls.'

*Dolls.* A disconcerting parallel, Markham reflected. As for the tree of knowledge, it was like something out of the Brothers Grimm . . . somehow a mocking reminder that so far in this investigation hard information was decidedly thin on the ground.

The DI took one last look back at St Vitus's depleted shrubberies and thought of the hearse making its lonely way to Bromgrove North Municipal Cemetery.

He had to hold fast to his (battered) belief that Andrée Clark's bare new self — free of earthly blots — had slipped shining into a better life. But in the meantime, there was a killer waiting to be lured out of the shadows.

* * *

The funeral buffet was laid out in the nursing home's library which was decidedly grand with its dark woodwork, ornate fireplace, deep Wilton rugs, art deco lamps, floor to ceiling mahogany bookcases and heavy dark-wooded reading tables. Some rather fine oil paintings depicted various local landmarks, Markham recognising with pleasure Bromgrove Rise and Carton Hall amongst them.

It was all old plush, with an abundance of curios and leather bindings and a general air of quiet sumptuousness. After the chilly church, the detectives were grateful for the log fire and buffet which was indeed generous, with platters of homemade sandwiches, mini quiches, stuffed canapés, cheeses, cake, pastries and trifle along with tea, coffee, soft drinks and wine for those who wanted it (the theatricals predictably did, Burton noted disapprovingly, beadily speculating as to the 'designated drivers').

Noakes certainly didn't hold back, Markham noted with amusement, though at least on this occasion he didn't pile savouries and pudding onto his plate in pyramidal abandon, being apparently mindful of the corporate proprieties. Carruthers hovered in the background, remembering his uncle's words: 'The man's an appalling gannet,'

Superintendent Bretherton had advised, 'barely house-trained.' But Noakes was aware that the new boy's eye was upon him — Sir Edward Hamling's likewise — and behaved with unusual circumspection (for him). There was little inter-mingling between the various factions, with mourners wandering in and out, though a hum of subdued chat denoted that the event might be said to have 'gone off well'.

Courteously, Markham circulated amongst the guests, breaking off now and again ostensibly to examine the library's treasures but in reality to prevent mourners from feeling that they were under observation. The rest of the team followed his lead and dutifully mingled, Doyle and Carruthers making a beeline for Ms Velvet Hotpants and the more attractive visitors. It might well be, as Noakes was wont to observe, that female dancers in the rehearsal studio looked 'like they'd got a muffin tied to their head', but in a social context they were decidedly easy on the eye and duly appreciated as such by the two younger detectives.

Markham wondered how long to give it, feeling sure there was nothing to be gained by lingering over the funeral baked meats and keen to get back to the station where he could calculate their next move. Eventually, he made his way over to the vicar and Sir Edward Hamling, well-practised when it came to acting as social wadding.

But before he could embark on the usual desultory chat, there was a minor commotion across the room and Burton made her way anxiously towards him.

'Mr Gower's gone missing, sir,' she said without pre-amble. 'He seemed quite upset when people got back and didn't feel up to coming in here. Chloe Finch says she walked down to the lake with him, he was well wrapped up and had one of those contraptions for sitting down on outdoors . . . combined walking stick and folding chair . . .'

Carruthers had joined them. 'You mean a shooting stick,' he amended.

'That's the one,' she confirmed without rancour, aware that her colleagues would have resented the clever clogs correction. She was getting used to the new recruit, however, and sensed the underlying insecurity which prompted his one-upmanship.

All morning, Markham had experienced an insidious sense of threat. As though he was continually menaced by something on the periphery of his vision. But now he felt evil breathing down his neck.

'Presumably Chloe didn't stay with Mr Gower?' he asked.

'He wanted to be alone,' Burton replied. 'Told her to get off and help Mrs Cartwright and the others.'

Noakes and Doyle had now joined them.

'There's a fricking *killer* on the loose.' A combination of too much cake and rising concern made Noakes's corned beef complexion almost purplish. 'What was she *thinking* of?'

'She was a bit emotional herself after the funeral,' Burton explained. 'Didn't think it through ... wanted to give him some privacy.'

'Would she normally just *dump* one of them outside like that?' Doyle asked.

Sir Edward Hamling's authoritative baritone interrupted them.

'As I think I've told you before, detectives, Rosemount isn't a *prison*. Nick Gower isn't gaga or disabled. He enjoys spending time in the grounds when he feels up to it.' His expression was glacial as he contemplated Doyle. 'Staff are devoted to the residents, but obviously they respect their autonomy. No doubt Ms Finch exercised her professional judgment.'

This was Burton's cue.

'Yes, she told Mr Gower she'd be back in three quarters of an hour to check he was alright,' the DI told them. 'He was wearing an alarm pendant in case he needed to call anyone. Like I say, she only meant for him to get a breath of fresh air after the funeral ... But when she went to help him back to the house for a cup of tea, he wasn't there ... just the shooting stick lying on its side.' Burton rumpled her bob distractedly. 'Chloe's adamant there were no signs of him being suicidal or anything like that. He just said he wanted to blow the cobwebs away before joining the "Plum cake fest" in the library.' That acerbic reference to the funeral buffet was certainly typical of Gower, Markham thought. 'I've radioed it in, there's uniforms headed out there right now,' Burton said urgently.

'Let's get down there and join them,' Markham instructed. Hamling hastened forward but he held up a restraining hand. 'This is best left to the police,' he said firmly. 'And your security manager, obviously.' Not that Noakes had any intention of being left out of things, but best to pre-empt any tale-bearing about the former DS being treated as ex officio CID.

Burton's mobile trilled.

Her face as she listened confirmed what Markham deep in his heart already knew.

Death had come once more to Rosemount.

* * *

The body, frail and brittle as driftwood, had been found not far from the abandoned shooting stick, face downwards in a tangled bank of sedge on the left-hand side of the lake.

'I would say his face was pushed face down into the water and then held there,' Dimples Davidson told them. 'It would have taken less than a minute to drown him.'

Doyle looked down at the dead man whose face was peaceful, the eyes closed and the suspicion of a half-smile at the corners of the mouth. But for the sodden garments and strands of sparse grey hair plastered to his scalp, one might have thought the man had died peacefully in his bed. Poignantly, the personal alarm was still round his neck.

'Any chance he could've gone for a bit of a wander and fallen in, doc?' the young DS asked, visibly upset.

'There's bruising on his arms and neck,' Dimples replied, 'which suggests that force was applied.' His keen eyes raked the scene. 'I would say the killer frogmarched him this way because the grass or rushes or whatever they are grow thick and tall here. It would provide an effective screen in case anyone was watching from the house.'

'With the wake in full swing, it was a safe bet that no one noticed what was happening outdoors,' Burton observed grimly. 'And anyway, the library's round the side, looks out onto the woods and up to Weston Ridge . . . There's no view of the lake from there.'

'The killer must've been spying on Gower,' Noakes said glumly. 'An' then when they heard the lass was going to take him out here . . . *bingo*, they were in there like a rat up a drain.'

Suddenly Markham had a flashback to the conversation with Honor Calthorpe when she described the *petits rats* of ballet's early days. It conjured up images of weasels and stoats and other sly predators . . . scheming, planning, and contriving how best to snare their prey.

'What was he doing outside anyway?' the pathologist asked. 'Surely it's a bit cold for birdwatching.'

'I was counting on safety in numbers, Doug,' Markham replied sadly. 'Keeping them all together. Mr Gower suddenly fancied some fresh air before joining the bunfight back there, and the nurse thought there was no harm in it — just forty minutes or so to recharge his batteries and then back inside.'

Dimples heard the note of self-reproach in the DI's voice. 'Don't be too hard on yourself,' he said gruffly. 'You could hardly have started counting heads or taking a register . . . not with it being a *funeral*.' He looked down again at the corpse. 'He didn't die hard, that's one small mercy.'

With a signal to the two paramedics who waited respectfully behind him, he said. 'We're going to move him now, Markham. The ambulance is parked down the drive out of sight of the house.'

The detectives withdrew to the strip of lawn which bordered the lake, heads bowed as the sheeted stretcher was carried up the red sandstone path and round the side of Rosemount towards the driveway. Looking at the small island in the middle of the lake, Carruthers said unexpectedly,

'Maybe subconsciously he knew the killer was coming for him and he wanted it to end out here. Somewhere beautiful.'

It was indeed beautiful now that the afternoon sun was filtering through the cloud, illuming the grounds in a pale radiance, making them seem as if rinsed clean.

'Almost like an Easter scene,' Burton murmured softly.

'Only there ain't any rabbits, or any lambs doing that weirdy thing . . . y'know, when they spring in the air, all fours at once,' Noakes observed more prosaically.

Markham could tell they were in shock. Time to take charge.

'Let's leave the SOCOs to do their stuff while we take statements.' Briskly, he added, 'Mr Gower died in the time between Chloe Finch leaving him at the lake and coming out to look for him. Anyone who can't give a good account of themselves for the relevant period is automatically suspect, so this gives us a real chance to narrow the field.'

Burton had spoken of Easter, he thought as they trudged back to the house. The ultimate Happy Ending for a devout believer like Nicholas Gower.

But *he* was concerned with the narrative which went before. Not the story that turned out well in the end, but the story of what human malice had perpetrated against three defenceless victims. Another plotline altogether.

## 9. INTRIGUE

Markham called a team meeting in CID on Sunday morning to review all the alibis for Nicholas Gower's murder.

The January weather continued to seesaw between benign and foul, a stiff breeze hurling white blossoms from a sad little wild cherry tree at the corner of the station carpark and making a mock snowstorm. As he contemplated browning petals stuck to the pane of a neighbouring Fiesta, they seemed to Markham almost like messages left by a malign nature.

They seemed to say, *Your investigation is going nowhere fast.*

Normally he would have been cheered by seeing early daffodils in the large ceramic planters with which Bromgrove Council sought to make the station more 'user friendly', the flowers opening out hopefully like little constellations. But today he felt no Wordsworthian lift of his spirits at the golden trumpets and their concert of yellows, unable to forget Nicholas Gower's pitiful corpse stretched out amongst the lakeside weeds at Rosemount . . . that wet, plastered forehead . . .

He had liked the man and knew that Noakes felt the same.

'Sure, I called him a Holy Joe, but he were down to earth . . . didn't ram the religious stuff down your throat,' was his friend's verdict. 'One of the nurses said he didn't bat an eyelid when she told him everything about the afterlife was bullshit. He just smiled and said, "Well dear, why not think about it as what's left behind from the way you've lived." She thought that was great.'

Markham knew Noakes would dearly have loved to join the session in CID, but his old ally knew better than to ask. Sidney was definitely mellower these days and, where his bête noire was concerned, it was undoubtedly a case of absence making the heart grow fonder. But there was no point pushing their luck. Moreover, Markham felt a secret sympathy for the DCI who he increasingly suspected was fundamentally a decent man in hock to all manner of hierarchical pressures and intrigue. While *he* had the luxury of being able to ignore the cabals and politics — one reason why he didn't care about further promotion — Sidney was caught on that endless treadmill silently pleading 'Stop the World: I want to Get Off'.

Olivia, he knew, had no time for such compassion towards the man she called Judas Iscariot. 'He's a horror, Gil, and you know it.'

But now it increasingly seemed to him that Sidney's real face was somehow concealed by this oversized corporate mask he was forced to wear. If you looked into his eyes, you could see the real man in there somewhere, screaming . . .

Anyway, there was no point making Sidney's life more difficult by smuggling Noakes into the department and leaving the DCI to deal with the H-bomb when it was detonated — as would surely be the case if Roger Carruthers had anything to do with it.

Markham felt strongly antipathetic towards Carruthers. In his inmost soul, he knew he was being unfair and that the loss of Noakes had a great deal to do with his lack of enthusiasm for the new recruit. But there was something so cold and watchful about the man, and it was obvious Doyle couldn't stand him. Burton of course, in her thoroughly decent, conscientious way was endeavouring to draw him into the magic circle. Carruthers's cerebral streak clearly appealed to her at a level, though Markham had a shrewd idea his vaunted enthusiasm for psychology and criminal profiling was to some extent put on.

Noakes had pronounced him a 'con artist', but it was Markham's responsibility to make the team gel and he determined to give the newcomer a fair chance. As yet, he couldn't find a key to the man's character but there *had* to be a way in. If he was being totally honest, perhaps Carruthers's chilly reserve was too close to home. The cat that walked by himself. He knew that his own nickname with the lower ranks was 'Lord Snooty', while unclubbable habits hadn't endeared him to the higher echelons. So it behoved him of all people to make allowances and avoid being judgmental.

He wondered what Olivia would make of Carruthers and smiled inwardly. Obviously, she would have detested him simply for not being George Noakes. He could almost hear her denouncing the new boy's cellophane personality!

*Olivia.*

*She* would have known how to jolt him out of his doldrums.

He wondered whether she would show up for the Dance Academy show that evening. Ever since the Baranov case, she had been fascinated by the ballet, calling it as fleeting as fireworks or soap bubbles but somehow utterly transformative.

*Oh no.* He spotted the blinds twitching in Bretherton's eyrie (why wasn't the man off playing golf?). No doubt the superintendent would find a way covertly to raise the topic of 'Markham's introspective streak' with HR, on the basis that he appeared to be communing with the daffodils in a very unpolicemanlike fashion. Better get inside before anyone else decided he was having a nervous breakdown in the car park!

\* \* \*

The team trickled into Markham's office shortly afterwards, Burton clutching a bag from the Bagel Deli round the corner.

'Don't worry,' she said as Doyle eyed her toasted offerings warily, 'they're not humous or anything like that. I got pastrami bacon and cheese for you guys.'

Carruthers had turned up with drinks from Costa, an encouraging sign that he was trying to build bridges (though Markham couldn't repress the uncharitable thought that this particular DS was bound to claim back on expenses). He'd even made sure to remember that Burton favoured a vanilla soy latte, earning himself a decidedly gracious smile from that quarter.

Doyle's contribution was some walnut buns, while Markham had brought pistachio pastries from his favourite bakery.

They were certainly maintaining the time-honoured Noakesian tradition of combining brainwork with gastronomy, Markham thought affectionately as he watched his colleagues happily munching away.

'An army marches on its stomach,' as Noakes always said, and the DI had found such occasions — however unorthodox — certainly helped with team bonding.

At last, they were ready to begin.

'Right, *alibis*,' the DI said looking at them expectantly. 'The wake started at around half past twelve or thereabouts, with people drifting in and out of the buffet. Mr Gower's murder took place in the time between when Chloe Finch left him by the lake at half past one and when she came back for him at quarter past two. So, we need to pinpoint where everyone was for those forty-five minutes.'

Burton, predictably up to the mark, whipped out her notebook and specs in a trice, carefully scrutinising the list of suspects' movements.

'As you say, it was all quite, er, *fluid* at the wake, sir. And with folk feeling shaky after the church service, we can't be absolutely positive . . .' She cleared her throat. 'But to summarise: According to the ballet crowd, they pushed off just after half past one because they had classes and rehearsals scheduled later, so they wanted to get back into town. Toby

142

Lavenham and Clara Kentish drove themselves, while Tania Sullivan dropped Rosa Maitland at home because she wasn't needed till five. Frederic March left about five minutes after the dancers. The choreographer guy, Richard Buckfast, did some sort of disappearing act, but Mrs Cartwright found him in the downstairs writing-room later on after everyone else had left. She had the impression he was a bit the worse for wear. According to Buckfast, he'd fallen asleep in there. Let's see . . . No sign of Ray Franzoni. Hafsah Peri was busy in the basement sorting out a *Medisave* delivery.' The DI paused and turned to Markham. 'Obviously there were other people at the buffet too, sir. We've taken details for them, but I'm presuming we can pretty much discount any outsiders for now.'

Markham nodded. 'Correct, Kate. There's no doubt in my mind that Mrs Clark and Maureen Frost were killed by someone with an intimate knowledge of Rosemount's routines, which means we can narrow it down to the people you've listed.'

'You've forgotten Sir Edward Hamling,' Doyle reminded Burton.

'I was coming to him.' Burton checked her scrip. 'He was in and out of the buffet. Linda Merryweather had come over faint after the service, so he stayed in the residents' lounge with her for a bit . . . Didn't realise Mr Gower was out in the grounds . . . thought he might've gone upstairs to be on his own. Hamling ended up going into the rose garden to clear his head and then went back to the library.'

The DI took off her specs and folded the piece of paper carefully. Her expression was frustrated as she said, 'I'm not sure we can rule *any* of them out.'

Carruthers frowned. 'What about the dancers?' he asked. 'If they left Rosemount at half one, then they were away from the grounds when Gower was killed. That means they're in the clear, right?'

Burton grimaced. '*Wrong*,' she said decisively. 'Suppose the killer overheard Chloe arranging to leave Mr Gower down by the lake. They could easily have headed off with the others then parked out of sight in one of the lanes by the meadow and cut across to the lake,' she replied. 'If anyone saw them pulling up, well they could say they were just stretching their legs . . . having a ramble. *Think about it*,' she insisted as he went to protest. 'Lavenham or Kentish were by themselves, so either of them could've doubled back without anyone being any the wiser. The same goes for Frederic March.'

'Sullivan and Maitland were together, though,' Doyle pointed out. 'Which means they're each other's alibi.'

'Sullivan could've dropped Maitland back at home and then nipped back to Rosemount,' Burton countered. 'It's only about ten minutes each way and not much traffic at the weekend.'

'Did anyone see Sullivan arrive at the Academy?' Doyle asked.

'She wasn't expected there till three to give a character class. The janitor didn't notice anything unusual when she clocked in.'

Carruthers pondered this scenario. 'What about Maitland? Could *she* have turned round and gone back to Rosemount? Did the neighbours notice anything?'

'Maitland turned up for a rehearsal at quarter to five,' Burton informed them. 'We drew a blank with the neighbours, but she *does* have a nippy little Mazda . . . quite the demon driver by all accounts.'

'*Hell*, you're right.' Doyle sounded disgusted. 'Potentially they're *all* in the frame . . . including the old bat with her funny turn and Hamling taking that stroll after he did his Good Samaritan number. Not to mention Rip Van Winkle in the writing-room . . . *he* could have been in and out without anyone seeing a thing.' Doyle sounded more like his erstwhile mentor than ever, thought Markham as he heard this outburst, though George Noakes would doubtless have expressed himself even more colourfully.

'Less of the "old bat", Sergeant,' he said mildly. 'One day we'll *all* be in the same boat, only hopefully living out our twilight years free of homicide.'

'Sorry, sir,' Doyle said meekly enough while reflecting that it was the most excitement Merryweather and the rest of them had experienced in *years*.

'Did anyone see Hafsah Peri doing the stocktake or whatever she was supposed to be doing in the basement?' Carruthers interjected. 'I mean, *she's* got to be in the mix too.'

Burton grimaced. 'Apparently nobody liked that job, so they were more than happy to let her crack on . . . To answer your question, nobody saw hide nor hair of her till the hue and cry over Mr Gower.'

'Didn't Noakes say Peri was down in the basement when Maureen Frost was killed?' Carruthers enquired beadily. 'Seems like she's got a love affair with the place.'

'Hmm.' Burton considered this. 'It's in character,' she told him. 'Chloe Finch said Hafsah positively *thrives* on doing the stuff everybody else hates.'

'Anal retentive,' Doyle said, nodding sagely.

'What about Mrs Cartwright?' Carruthers enquired hopefully.

'Flitting about the place but didn't notice anything amiss . . .and she's not a serious contender,' Burton replied.

'No,' Markham said heavily, 'she isn't.'

'Looks like we've got sweet FA then,' Doyle concluded.

Burton shot her colleague a repressive look, tucking a stray lock into place behind her ear.

'I'll get uniform to check those routes between Rosemount and town, sir,' she said. 'See how the timings stack up.'

Carruthers was deeply sceptical. 'You really think one of the arty lot peeled off and scooted back to drown Gower?'

'I think it's *possible*,' she said, barely concealing the irritation in her voice.

'Apart from Maitland, they're oldsters,' he said bluntly. 'Surely they wouldn't have been able to carry it off.'

'Dancers, even ex dancers, are *athletes*,' Burton replied. 'Lithe, steel-muscled, incredibly trim and capable.'

'Not once they've *retired*, surely?' This was Doyle.

'They've got muscle memory,' she assured him. 'It means they stay fit well into middle and old age . . . Think about performers like Margot Fonteyn and Rudolf Nureyev.'

'Oh yeah,' Doyle grinned. 'I remember Noakes talking about that guy . . . only he called him Randolph Neveroff.'

Markham was pleased to see Carruthers give a tiny smile at this, even if he did hastily supress it.

Doyle was coming round to the idea. 'If you're right about them being super-fit and they were pumped up to do it, ma'am, then I guess they *could've* tipped Gower off his shooting stick thingy and shoved his head under the water . . .'

'Dimples says it wouldn't have taken much strength,' Markham advised them. 'Especially if Gower didn't struggle.'

'D'you reckon that's right, guv?' Doyle asked. 'That he never fought back?'

'There were no defensive injuries,' Markham replied gently. 'He might not have had the chance.'

For all Doyle's earlier flippancy about the 'old bat' — what Markham realised was a defence mechanism — the DS was clearly upset. 'It was an *execution*,' he muttered.

'Over very quickly, Sergeant,' the DI said, trying to find some semblance of reassurance. 'As with Mrs Frost, he had to be silenced because he represented an immediate threat.'

'Did you notice anything when you interviewed Gower, sir?' Carruthers asked. 'Like he was holding something back?'

The DI turned to Burton. 'Mr Gower seemed totally calm and collected to me,' he said. 'What was *your* take, Kate?'

'I'd agree, boss . . . He shied away from getting into any showbiz intrigue, but I'd say he found that kind of gossip unpleasant. A very private man.'

Markham nodded thoughtfully. 'He was with the other mourners in the churchyard after Mrs Clark's funeral, but I didn't notice that he lingered with anyone in particular.'

'He walked back to the home ahead of us,' Doyle informed them. 'Sir Edward Hamling lent an arm.' The youngster grinned. 'Gave Chloe Finch and Hafsah Peri short shrift into the bargain . . . more or less told them to bog off when they started fussing over the old guy. You could see they didn't like it.'

'Well, Hamling and Gower go way back, don't they?' Carruthers surmised. 'Didn't that journalist woman mention Gower falling for Frederic Marc and Hamling might've wanted a piece of the action too by the sound of it . . . a bisexual mafia or something like that.'

The new recruit certainly had a retentive memory for salacious intel, Markham reflected wryly. No doubt his nose for intrigue would serve him well in CID.

Now Burton recalled, 'Mr Gower talked about "Freddie" having to put up with a lot from Andrée. It seemed like there was still some affection there.'

'What about Gower and the Black Baron?' Carruthers asked, unconsciously adopting Noakes's nickname for Sir Edward Hamling — a hopeful indication, perhaps, that the man wasn't totally lacking a sense of humour.

'We don't know if Mr Gower and Sir Edward were *involved* once upon a time or anything like that,' Burton said carefully. 'But they seemed to be on good terms . . . no sign of any tension.' She screwed up her eyes, remembering. 'When they got up to the house, people milled around a bit, chit chat and small talk . . . then Hafsah began complaining about it being too cold to hang around outside so everyone headed to the library—'

'Except Gower,' Doyle finished glumly. 'If he hadn't gone walkabout, he wouldn't have ended up getting murdered.'

'Oh, I think the killer would have found another way,' Markham said with quiet certainty.

'But Gower might've come to *us* first,' the young DS insisted.

'I'm not sure he would necessarily have done anything in haste,' Markham replied.

'Not even if he thought they'd killed two people?' Doyle sounded incredulous.

'Perhaps he hadn't figured out it was them,' Carruthers suggested. 'Could be he just said something that spooked the killer . . . made 'em think he was somehow on to them.'

'Or he might have had an idea who it was but didn't know for sure,' Burton added. 'He'd be like Mrs Frost . . . wanting to be fair and decent.'

Doyle's aghast expression suggested that he thought decency in such circumstances was decidedly overrated.

'What about Franzoni?' he asked at length.

'Home alone,' Burton said. 'Holed up in his flat watching TV. No one to vouch for him, I'm afraid.'

'Frederic March?' the young DS without much hope.

Burton sighed. 'Same goes for him. Once back home, he spent the rest of the day going over scores . . . didn't notice the time till he felt hungry round about seven.'

'He's a Jerry too,' Carruthers mused. Then, catching sight of Markham's wintry expression, 'Sorry, sir, I meant to say *getting on* . . . wouldn't be up to racing cross country and finishing off Gower.'

'He's not *that* old,' Burton protested. 'Composers these days have to have incredible stamina. Like Daniel Baremboim . . . coming up to eighty and audiences can't get enough of him.'

'Isn't he the one who cheated on that cellist?' Carruthers asked.

Trust him to be au fait with all of *that*, Markham thought impatiently.

'Yes, that's him,' Burton confirmed. 'Thing is, Baremboim's a total dynamo. When Rudolf Nureyev planned to move into conducting, he gave an interview about it . . . said people thought there was nothing to it — just waving a baton around — but Nureyev wouldn't know what had hit him when it came to drilling a hundred musicians. Made a big thing about conductors having to be at peak fitness and at the top of their game.'

Doyle didn't want to hear any more about musical maestros or Randolph Neveroff. 'The DCI is going to *love* this,' he groaned theatrically. 'Half a dozen suspects and technically they could *all* have done it.'

So much for the alibis, thought Markham. He was starting to get a thumping headache as the different scenarios went round and round in his head . . .

'Look,' he said after a long pause. 'Let's call it a day for now and regroup at the Academy later.'

Doyle was startled. 'Aren't they going to cancel the performance, boss?' he asked. 'Out of respect for Mr Gower and all that?'

'Bromgrove Ballet have cleared things with Rosemount, and it's been decided to go ahead,' Markham told them. 'The evening's a tribute to Andrée Clark as well as a fund-raiser for the home. Everyone seems to have agreed that Nicholas Gower wouldn't have wanted to see it cancelled.'

'I spoke to Sir Edward Hamling earlier, sir,' Burton said. 'Apparently, Mr Gower was a great follower of ballet. Said it was very poignant because it was so fleeting . . . He used to compare it to an ice sculpture or sand painting that you knew would dissolve into nothing.'

It could have been the epitaph for Gower himself.

'Very poetic,' Markham said expressionlessly. 'Right, I'll see you over there at half seven.'

'Is Noakesy coming?' Doyle ventured.

'Wild horses and all that,' the DI replied drily, suppressing a smile as the youngster visibly perked up. At least if Doyle had to miss an evening's football on the box, his fellow armchair pundit would be around to ease the pain.

After Markham's colleagues had left, he sat for a long while, fingers steepled in thought, the cast of suspects revolving in his mind as though on some infernal carousel.

Finally, he rose, impatiently sweeping case papers from the desk into his briefcase.

Time for a break from all his theorising. Perhaps an escape into high culture would bring something to the surface.

He could only hope so . . .

\* \* \*

In the event, nothing broke upon Markham's mind that evening. No great illumination or thunderbolt.

But the whole experience was agreeably civilised, and he received a flatteringly warm reception from Academy staff on arrival at the school.

His quick eyes took in an addition to the foyer's collage. 'You've acquired some new pictures,' he exclaimed, pointing to photographs of a slim dark man with handsome sideburns standing next to a circus elephant with finger raised.

Tania Sullivan chuckled. 'That's George Balanchine working on his elephant polka,' she told him.

Then Clara Kentish came over, looking flushed and happy. 'You must see the one of Balanchine teaching his cat Mourka to do leaps and jetés,' she laughed, pointing to a startling portrait of the same man, older and greyer now, with a white-and-ginger-coloured cat leaping in the foreground. 'Everyone got in on the act after that.'

Noakes hove into view and leaned in to have a look.

'Blimey,' he said admiringly, 'they must've put summat special in his *Whiskas*.'

Kentish giggled. 'People said it was the only time they had seen Balanchine nervous before a performance . . . his tic went into overdrive.'

Markham was intrigued. 'Tic?'

'He had a kind of twitch, a sort of nervous sniff. It caught on . . . became almost fashionable in the end.'

Noakes didn't appear too impressed. '*Creepy*,' was his verdict.

Rosemount's security manager was resplendent in a dark double-breasted suit which gave him the look of Yorkshire's answer to Nikita Khrushchev but did an excellent job of minimising his paunch. Muriel being safely installed in the auditorium with Mrs Councillor Anstruther-Stewart, he and Markham were able to relax and inspect the display at their leisure, genuinely fascinated by how dancers' shapes had evolved over the years.

'That one's got no neck, like a monkey,' Noakes said, 'an' them lot are quite chubby,' he added, pointing at a photograph from the 1930s that showed plumpish self-conscious young women in one-piece bathing suits. 'That lass in the front looks more like a prop forward than a ballerina.'

'*Shhh*,' Kate Burton hissed, appearing alongside them and glancing nervously around the lobby. Markham's fellow DI had made an effort with her appearance, wearing a clinging green jersey dress and black suede boots, with dangling art deco earrings that added a dramatic accent to the outfit. Markham was amused to see how Doyle and Carruthers did a double take on seeing their colleague out of her usual trouser suit. Like him, they were dressed in blazers and skinny chinos, Doyle trying not to boggle at Noakes's Soviet-era ensemble. '*Suits you, sir!*' he winked at his mentor who pretended not to hear.

As Doyle and Carruthers wandered off to scope out any stray ballerinas, the other three lingered over the display.

'The teachers are a bit hands-on,' Noakes grunted, eyeing a photograph of a ballet master adjusting dancers' positions as Toby Lavenham sauntered over, immaculate in a handsome suit, with a carnation in his buttonhole, beautiful hair and polished shoes, making everyone except Markham feel suddenly underdressed and short of the mark.

'In the early days, coaches followed the Russian way,' he said easily, overhearing Noakes's comment. 'It was all about whacking, pushing, tugging . . . lots of physical contact . . . Nobody thought anything of it.'

Markham recalled Clara Kentish and Honor Calthorpe making the same point.

'Oh, aye,' Noakes grunted and continued along the line of pictures, examining a section devoted to 'distinguished *danseurs nobles*'. It was comical to see how Burton watched her erstwhile colleague anxiously, clearly dreading that he might utter some appalling gaffe to the effect that ballet was a sissy occupation for men and male students were at risk of catching an incurable case of homosexuality.

But Noakes, as ever, surprised her.

'Check out the bulging muscles on them two,' he observed admiringly, moving in for a closer look.

'Ah yes, Jacques d'Amboise and Edward Villella . . . They were both sports jocks,' Lavenham said affably, 'and Villella was a championship boxer.'

It was clear that Noakes liked the sound of this.

Markham desperately wished Olivia was there to see this most unlikely bonding of the ballet master and Bromgrove CID's former resident philistine.

And suddenly, as if he'd conjured her, there she was in the foyer, looking impossibly elegant in a tunic dress and leggings that would have got the thumbs-down from Muriel Noakes but looked just right on his willowy ex, accessorised with a colourful pashmina and jewellery that he didn't recall having seen her wear before. With the vibrant red hair in a half-up, half-down hairstyle, she looked as glamorous as any doe-eyed ballerina.

Mathew Sullivan, Olivia's colleague from Hope Academy, had accompanied her, which was a surprise. Markham found himself unsettled by Sullivan's obvious air of enchantment even though the school's deputy head had come out as gay during the Ashley Dean murder investigation. But Markham still couldn't derive any comfort from the notion that he was simply there as Olivia's walker.

Sullivan and Noakes having become friends through their mutual devotion to five-a-side football, the former DS wandered over to the lanky bespectacled teacher whose boy-ishness and subversive wit set him apart from Hope's decid-edly stodgy senior management. Markham wondered if it had occurred to his wingman that this might be the start of something between Sullivan and Olivia.

After a brief hesitation, the DI forced himself to join them followed, after a moment's hesitation, by Burton. Somehow he drew comfort from her quietly sympathetic presence as he tried not to notice how Noakes's massive head swivelled back and forth in the manner of one refereeing a ping pong match.

'Hello, Liv, Matt. I believe we're in for a treat,' he said. 'Plotless and modern in the first half with some moon-drenched romanticism to follow.'

Was it his imagination or did Olivia's escort momentarily appear uncomfortably self-conscious?

But Sullivan then merely replied, with the trademark laconic humour that Markham knew greatly appealed to his ex, 'Evening, Gil. Wonder if they'll ever put together all the first acts that the folk who always come in late never see and make a new ballet from them.'

Noakes guffawed appreciatively.

'How d'you like the picture show?' he asked, waving a meaty paw at the collage.

Sullivan smiled. 'We had a quick dekko earlier, Noakesy. Evolution of the ballet from Petipa . . . Very impressive.'

'Petipa to *Petipaw* if you include the moggy.'

It broke the ice, and Olivia laid an affectionate hand on Noakes's arm. 'I can see you moving into the arts at some point, George.' She laughed. 'Be honest, you've caught the ballet bug.'

Their old friend was immensely gratified and looked as if he only wished Muriel could have been at hand to hear the implied tribute. However, 'Them bunheads make Katarina Johnson-Thompson look a right couch potato,' was all he said.

Olivia's eyes were starry, Markham thought admiringly. However, he noticed that she managed completely to ignore Kate Burton who waited quietly at his elbow.

'I'm sure they'll transport us to fairyland,' Olivia said, 'but I bet backstage is nowhere near as glamorous — creaking scenery, cracking gilt plaster and bundles of sweat-stained costumes.'

'Hope you enjoy it, Liv,' he said lamely, cursing himself for not being able to come up with something more original.

A brittle smile, and she had gone, shepherded by Sullivan towards the stalls.

Lavenham had watched this little bit of byplay with interest.

'Ballet's not as ethereal as people like to think,' the ballet master said wryly, his gaze following Olivia's graceful form. 'More like a spider web of intrigue — machinations, plots and counterplots.'

'Pretty much like CID then,' Doyle muttered as he and Carruthers re-joined the group. And once again, Markham was pleased to see Carruthers's answering gleam. All in all, he was beginning to have hopes that the newcomer's arrival was not necessarily the unmitigated disaster that he had feared.

'Eyes and ears open please,' he instructed his colleagues as the five-minute bell announced that the performance was about to begin. 'I'll check backstage during the interval, and I want you to mingle out front . . . see who cosies up to whom, any unusual behaviour, that kind of thing. We can compare notes tomorrow.'

\* \* \*

Despite the twin spectres of the investigation and his ex, Markham found himself soothed and tranquilised by Bromgrove Ballet's stellar performance.

He thought of Sidney's likely reaction to his raptures. 'Markham's *mystical* side, legacy of Oxbridge, blah blah.'

Safe in the darkness of the auditorium, he suddenly found himself grinning at the notion of the DCI and Bretherton putting his psyche under the microscope. Like lepidopterists dissecting a prize specimen.

God knows what they would have made of his reaction to Rosa Maitland, fleet, fragile and incredibly lovely in a display which almost lifted her performance into the realms of poetry.

It was during the intermission when, checking backstage, he overheard a strange incident — a flustered exchange between Clara Kentish and Maitland.

'Somebody *shoved* me at the beginning of my solo,' he thought he heard Rosa Maitland tell her teacher. 'Pushed me onto the stage.'

'Did you see who it was?' Kentish demanded urgently.

'No, when I turned around, they were gone. But it was really *aggressive* . . . I nearly fell.'

The exchange left Markham feeling uneasy, but there were others to think about.

*Toby Lavenham.* The ballet master following in Balanchine's shoes . . . the personality of a Don Juan combined with a pinch or two of Pygmalion and more than a trace of Svengali . . .

And cadaverous Frederic March, there in the audience, intent on Bromgrove Ballet's dancers, the youngsters still with a little tender puppy fat on them, not pared down to the bone the way Balanchine and those creepy Russian ballet masters liked their dancers.

Reconnoitring the bar, he saw Richard Buckfast and Ray Franzoni huddled together, heads touching as though oblivious to all except artistic considerations. How far would Buckfast go to lay hands on Andrée Clark's designs for new ballets? he wondered. Assuming the former ballerina had in fact come up with something worth stealing . . .

Sir Edward Hamling was holding court on the outskirts of the crush, cutting an imposing figure in his habitual pin-stripes — superbly tailored as always. He showed no sign of distress in the wake of Nicholas Gower's murder, but the DI knew better than to draw any conclusions from the lack of visible emotion. Mingling at such events was all in a day's work for Hamling, and Markham suspected the philanthropist rarely if ever let his mask drop. Much like himself if it came to it.

'Everything's so *beautiful*, Matt.' Inevitably, the DI picked out Olivia's bell-like tones from the swelling throng. 'All that heightened emotion — exhilaration, adoration, jealousies, longings, fears — made visible.'

The DI wondered how Sullivan would feel if he were to unleash his own jealousy in the shape of a sharp uppercut . . .

*Get a grip, Markham*, he told himself. Mentally promising himself an 'exorcism' at Doggie Dickerson's boxing gym as soon as possible, he managed to maintain an expression of sphinx-like inscrutability.

Suddenly a snatch of conversation caught his attention.

'He has his hands in everything that one . . . an *octopus* . . . a crooked octopus.'

*Who were they talking about?* Markham asked himself.

Mentally, he admonished himself for being beguiled by the strange, civilised happiness that ballet bestowed, in keeping with the aristocratic austerity which so closely corresponded to his own conception of art.

*Follow the money*. Wasn't that the watchword these days?

Tomorrow he would shine the spotlight on Rosemount's financial structure and see if there was anything more to Hafsah Peri's influence on Andrée Clark than vague rumours. Come to think of it, he hadn't seen anything of the nurse or Rosemount's staff tonight despite this being by way of a testimonial to their patient.

Noakes loomed up in front of him.

'We should meet up some time tomorrow, Noakesy,' he said. *Well away from the station obviously.*

To hell with Sidney, Bretherton, Carruthers and the rest. He *needed* Noakes back at base.

'Nothing doing here then, guv?' Noakes asked sympathetically, thinking privately that *Men In Tights* hadn't proved as bad as anticipated. Certainly the missus looked well pleased from where he was sitting.

'We need to refocus, Noakesy,' Markham told him. 'I'm going to have another crack at Hafsah Peri.'

The piggy eyes gleamed. 'Sounds good to me, guv.'

'Right, off you go. I believe Mr Balanchine's *Firebird* pas de deux beckons.'

## 10. A VEIL IS LIFTED

'Sir Edward wants an end to this scurrilous media speculation, Markham.'

It was Monday morning and DCI Sidney had, unusually
for him, descended from the upper regions to Markham's
office, brandishing a copy of the *Gazette*.

'With respect, sir, the *Gazette*'s hardly all that influential
. . . small fry really. The arts pages always peddle mildly racy
gossip, but nobody takes it too seriously.'

'I assure you, Sir Edward is taking it *very* seriously,
Inspector.'

*Oh no.* The last thing he needed right now was Sidney
flapping and fussing about some tediously up-himself
grandee.

The DI adopted his most emollient tone.

'What seems to be the trouble, sir?'

The DCI dropped heavily into a chair across from
Markham, wincing at the contrast with his own ergonom-
ically designed furniture.

'Unsubstantiated rumours about staff at Rosemount
taking gifts from patients.' A portentous frown as Sidney
thumbed through the paper. 'Specifically, their "entertain-
ment columnist",' he made that worthy sound like a carrier

of the plague, 'implies that Andrée Clark's nurses may have had thousands from her . . . to say nothing of other benefits.'

'Do they single anyone out by name, sir?'

'No,' the DCI honked, 'but that hardly matters, does it?' He thumped Markham's desk for emphasis. 'The thing is, this stuff about her being "cut off from the world in her lonely room" and "totally dependent on a small group of people",' he air quoted irritably, 'is all mixed in with speculation about the woman's mental competence and the fact of three people having been murdered at Rosemount.'

Markham noted idly that Sidney's eczema was back.

'And it's not just Sir Edward,' the DCI added beadily. 'I need hardly tell you how concerned the chief constable is . . . Not at all helpful for Bromgrove's *image* right now.'

Especially with those civic awards nominations coming up, Markham thought cynically.

'And just to top it off, this *hack*,' Sidney literally spat the word, 'has included snippets about dollhouse dealers and toy collectors so that the whole setup sounds distinctly iffy . . . as though the poor woman was caught up with fences and crooks and all kinds of peculiar characters.'

'May I sir?' he asked, reaching out for the paper.

Markham swiftly scanned the offending article as his boss sat like a thundercloud.

'*Well?*' Sidney barked impatiently.

'Typical hot air and puffery, sir.' Plus, it was badly written, a far more serious crime in Markham's book. 'A hint here and a nudge there, but it doesn't add up to anything.' What the current prime minister would doubtless call an 'inverted pyramid of piffle', he reflected wryly.

The DI endeavoured to arrange his features in the nearest he could get to a soothing expression. 'Actually,' he affected a yawn, 'it sounds to me as if it was a slow news day and,' he pointed out cannily, 'you'll see how careful they are not to allege anything concrete against Rosemount? Most of it's a rehash of stories about Mrs Clark's days as a ballerina

. . . backstage anecdotes, that kind of thing . . . mildly spiteful but nothing really damning.'

He might have got away with it. At the very least, Sidney's blood pressure looked as though it was returning to normal.

Markham pressed home his advantage. 'Seriously, sir, it's mainly tired old stuff with a bit of salacious spin. I'd say they were hard put to get much of a story out of it.' He paused. 'As for the issue of staff taking advantage, Mrs Clark was known to be generous towards one particular nurse, but I don't believe there was any professional impropriety.' He hesitated before ploughing on. *In for a penny.* 'There *was* a spate of petty thefts a while back.' Mentally, he apologised to Nicholas Gower for lumping his antique cufflinks in with the missing cash. 'But regrettably this *does* tend to happen from time to time in such places.'

He had been startled when Olivia told him about thefts from the staff room at Hope Academy; even more taken aback by her nonchalant assumption that the thief was undoubtedly one of her own colleagues.

Sidney was puzzled. 'Didn't the manager do something about it?' His face darkened, the eczema empurpling as the realisation hit him. '*Don't tell me*, it was that woman you found battered to death in the gardener's shed . . . Maureen Field?'

'Frost, sir. *Maureen Frost.*' He cast around for an explanation, deciding to stick to the truth and keep it simple.

'George Noakes's daughter Natalie goes into Rosemount from time to time,' he said suavely. 'Homeopathic medicine and holistic therapies.' Muriel would like that. 'It was *her* understanding that Mrs Frost planned to conduct an internal investigation but was obliged to hold off . . . on account of there being a changeover of facilities staff—' i.e., from the decrepit specimen hanging on for dear life to one George Noakes — 'and the Christmas holidays coming up . . . always their busiest time of year.'

Privately, Maureen Frost's reticence — so much out of character — troubled Markham, but as yet he couldn't see how it fitted into the scheme of things.

Sidney looked less than delighted at the involvement of another Noakes.

*What, will the line stretch out to the crack of doom?*

But the DCI seemed resigned to the inevitable. 'Remarkable how your former sergeant,' with testy emphasis on *your*, 'has managed to get himself mixed up in a murder enquiry so soon after his . . . *retirement.*'

'Ah well, sir,' he replied, mildly. 'You know how it is.'

Sidney looked as though he didn't, but the anodyne platitude seemed to normalise things.

'So you don't think there's anything significant in all of this?' the DCI waved a hand at the newspaper. 'Anything *germane* to the investigation?'

Markham hated corporate jargon but knew enough to parrot it back.

'I'll be asking our criminal profiler to advise on the extortion aspect, sir . . . whether it's central or tangential.' *Nathan Finlayson, come on down!* 'And of course, I'll consult with Sir Edward.'

Sidney wasn't entirely appeased, scratching his chin with irritable vigour.

'And all this about Mrs Clark collecting dolls and toy theatres, what the *Gazette* calls her obsession with, er, *little people* . . .' Sidney's voice trailed off helplessly.

Markham suppressed a grin. Clearly, as Doyle might have said, the whole concept of miniatures 'freaked him out'.

'There's a real vogue for tabletop models these days, sir,' he said. 'Including theatres with scenes and characters painted on the walls. Given Mrs Clark's artistic sensibility, it was only natural she should become absorbed by it as a hobby.'

Sidney looked as though he wondered why Andrée Clark couldn't have turned her hand to flower arranging or something equally suitable. No doubt Mrs Sidney would have been happy to show her the way.

'We're all taken by customs and culture, sir,' the DI said mischievously. 'All of us are a little peculiar, you might say . . .

With Mrs Clark, it was the Mariinsky Theatre and the glory days of Russian Imperial ballet.'

Sidney's chin jutted out. In *his* case, it was collecting stamps and trainspotting. *Infinitely* more respectable than this bizarre fiddling around with dolls and costumes.

But obviously, he had to pay homage to diversity.

'*Artistic*, yes of course.' The DCI paused to let this acknowledgement register. 'But are we sure Mrs Clark's, er, *contacts*, the people she went to for this stuff, have no connection to these murders?'

'Kate Burton has checked them out, sir. They're in the clear.' He sought to reassure Sidney. 'It was actually a fairly lowbrow hobby,' he said. 'A bit like playing with Barbie dolls, only in this case they were vintage and antique. Auction days were the equivalent of a day at the racetrack . . . an adrenaline rush if you like.'

Clearly Sidney *didn't* like, but he nodded nonetheless.

'I was sorry to miss the performance yesterday evening, Markham.'

*Liar, liar, pants on fire*, the DI thought.

'Mrs Sidney was in raptures . . . said they surpassed themselves.'

*Bully for her.*

'It was a most enjoyable evening, sir,' he replied, his tone colourless. 'A fitting tribute to Mrs Clark, and indeed to Mr Gower who was a devotee of dance.'

'Sir Edward is concerned about possible *aspersions* being cast on Bromgrove Ballet,' Sidney replied.

'As things stand, we haven't found anything to suggest a connection between these murders and the ballet company, sir.'

The DCI looked profoundly relieved, but Markham experienced a wave of frustration. Increasingly, he felt that the clue lay in the strange egotistical world of the performing arts, if only he could unlock it.

*Welcome to the big time!*

Aware of his boss's expectant look, he improvised. 'I'm going to interview Mrs Clark's nurse Hafsah Peri later today.'

Sidney visibly brightened.

*God help us*, Markham thought, he'll be ecstatic if we can pin this on some 'nobody' as opposed to a ballet notable or the likes of Frederic March. An obscure health professional with a grudge was unlikely to attract the kind of banner headlines that would ensue should the killer turn out to be a member of Bromgrove's cultural elite.

After Sidney had finally departed, with the usual disconcerting admixture of condescension and what appeared to be genuine concern for his 'peaky' subordinate, Markham arranged with Kate Burton that they would interview Hafsah Peri at the end of the nurse's afternoon shift.

'See if you can schedule a meeting with Sir Edward Hamling afterwards, please Kate,' he instructed.

Her eyebrows rose at this. 'Are you having doubts about him, boss?' she asked.

'I overheard someone at the Academy talk about a "crooked octopus" who had his hands in everything,' the DI told her. 'I'd be interested to know if they were referring to some kind of financial skulduggery or whether this was just the usual throwaway gripe about management.'

'I've had Carruthers and Doyle toothcomb the accounts for Rosemount and Bromgrove Ballet, sir,' she said, a frown puckering her forehead. 'There wasn't any sign of unethical practices, but I'll ask DI Johnstone in Fraud to take a look . . . and do some digging on Hamling.'

'Cheers, Kate.' Deadpan he added, 'DCI Sidney still thinks I'm looking under the weather.'

His punctiliously correct colleague groped for an appropriately polite response. 'Well, this is certainly one of those cases that takes it out of you,' she said neutrally, albeit there was a lurking concern in the big brown eyes that reminded him of Noakes's description of her as his faithful Doberman.

He flashed her a grin. 'Well, obviously this calls for a restorative session in the gym to bring me up to peak fitness.'

'You mean Doggie Dickerson.' She grinned back, the solemn features suddenly transfigured so that she looked positively pretty, with the gamine impishness of a teenager. He was always fascinated by such metamorphoses, and a vague unhappy sense of loss came over him like a cloud at the thought of her evident contentment with life.

Perhaps Olivia's jealousy was not so misplaced after all . . .

'Yes, there's nothing for it but a workout at Doggie's,' he said, doing his best to sound cheerful. 'Who knows, he might even have some words of wisdom to impart, what with being in the Body Beautiful business and all that.' *Nobody thought!*

\* \* \*

Doggie Dickerson (best not to enquire too closely as to how he acquired the moniker) was by popular consensus a 'dreadful old villain' who ran a boxing club in Marsh Lane. Rejoicing in the title of Bromgrove Police Boxing Club, in reality the 'club' was a down-at-heel, dingy setup where CID detectives and local criminals pounded away side by side, an unofficial truce operating within its sweaty precincts whereby anonymity was the order of the day (until they got outside again).

Noakes was very partial to Doggie, the two being fond of reminiscing about National Service and exchanging politically incorrect limericks or what Olivia termed 'barrack-room ballads'.

The proprietor himself looked scarily like an extra from *Sharpe*, with his eyepatch, tombstone yellow gnashers (unnerving when bared in a snaggle-toothed grin) and a horsehair wig which was always skew-whiff and gave him the appearance of a pantomime Judge Jeffreys. Markham greatly enjoyed Doggie's parade-ground exhortations to regulars — '*Stand by your beds!*', '*Barrack shun!*' and '*Give it some spit 'n' polish!*' — but there was no doubt he was an 'acquired taste'. One for which the council and police authority had scant appreciation, having tried every trick in the book to get the place closed down.

Doggie's battles with Environmental Health were legendary, but he somehow outwitted every clipboard-toting official and managed to keep his mildewed and distinctly grotty little kingdom open in spite of all.

Markham infinitely preferred Doggie's premises to the Harmony Spa or Bodyworks or any of the other salubrious but thoroughly antiseptic and characterless health facilities that had proliferated in Bromgrove. There was something truly authentic about the whisky-scented, rheumy-eyed, frock-coated proprietor and his smelly locker rooms that suited him down to the ground. The fact that Sidney and CID's head honchoes took a dim view of the outfit was one more thing in its favour as far as he was concerned. He knew he could always count on running into one of his colleagues for a cathartic bout, since it was an open secret that most of them vastly preferred the club's unique atmosphere and gritty clientele to anything on offer elsewhere.

Doggie, being a great one for fads and crazes, had gone through a New Age phase involving close study of astrology, cabbalism and other occult practices. However, this had ended when his girlfriend, Marlene from the bingo hall, had dumped him. ('She had to give up bingo when she started getting blotto,' Doggie confided sadly.) There had been one memorable occasion when he had persuaded Markham and a few select patrons to join him in his office for a session with the Ouija board, only for the putative séance to dissolve in hilarity when Noakes pronounced solemnly, 'There's a horse here that wants to say "Hello".' Doggie was huffy with Markham's wingman for quite some time in the wake of that particular fiasco.

Today, however, Doggie's Gandalf garb was a distant memory, the proprietor looking far sprucer than was his wont, the dressing gown-cum-overcoat being replaced by a suit that was *almost* respectable, though the overall effect in conjunction with the eyepatch and wig was still that of Long John Silver on shore leave.

Doggie was delighted to welcome his 'fav'rite 'spector', proudly showing him the newly renovated VIP locker room (for 'premium members').

'You've done a good job on the regrouting, Dogs,' Markham congratulated him after opening pleasantries and the proprietor's polite enquiries after Noakes. 'And those shower curtains look new. Have you come into money . . . ? Or are the Health and Safety lot on your back again?'

'Evelyn said it was time to smarten fings up, Mr Markham.'

*Evelyn? God, it was hard to keep up with the old villain's romantic adventures.*

'Nice one. Where did you meet the lady?' Presumably not at Bingo.

'A mate of mine set us up . . . kind of like a blind date.'

'Right,' Markham said faintly. 'Well, it appears there's been a bit of a wardrobe makeover since I last saw you, too.'

A bashful leer. 'She likes everything nice an' smart, Mr Markham. Dead fussy about that.'

It would be a long-term project with Doggie, Markham thought, but full marks to his latest squeeze for attempting an overhaul.

As he wondered how to broach the subject of this one's marital status, Doggie helped him out. 'Evie's divorced. Her daughter Violet teaches Tap and Zoom part-time at that dance school.'

*Zoom!*

'I think you mean *Zumba*,' he suggested swallowing his mirth.

'That's it,' Doggie said easily, unabashed. 'Tap is for the kiddies an' the other's for adults . . . Y'know,' with a grotesque wiggle, 'sexy moves . . . like in *Dirty Dancing*.'

Markham did his best to banish mental images of Doggie shaking his booty on the dance floor.

But one thing had caught his attention.

'Do you mean the Dance Academy?' he asked.

'Yeah.' A knowing smile. 'The place where that woman from the retirement home used to teach after she finished being a ballerina.' Doggie tapped the side of his nose, 'Don' worry, Mr Markham, I know you come in here for a break an' not to be pestered. Thass why I didn't want to ask about any discoveries.'

'You're alright, Dogs. To be honest, discoveries are somewhat thin on the ground right now.' He paused. 'How does Violet like working there?'

'Well, she says the management are snotty types, Mr Markham. They look down on part-timers who teach modern 'stead of the posh stuff on tippy toes.'

'They're behind the times when you think of the dancers on *Strictly*.'

'Yeah, well, Vi has all her qualifications . . . She says you wouldn't believe some of the ballet mums.'

'How so?'

'Dead pushy . . . always trying to sneak into classes or bend people's ears. One of 'em follows her kid everywhere . . . even to the bog . . . went an' got the sprog's portrait painted in a ballet costume — y'know, a tutu thingy, like she'd already reached the top an' had her name in footlights or something.' Doggie became increasingly loquacious with this most respectful of listeners. 'Vi said they can be dead spiteful too. She gave one student a good luck crystal before a show an' the poor little cow burst into tears . . . turned out this witch whose kid hadn't been picked only went and told her she'd been crap in rehearsals.' He scowled. 'Some of the kids are just as bad . . . sounds like they'd kill their granny to get ahead.'

'What about the boys?'

'There's not so many of them an' you don't see mums with the lads as much. Shame really cos Vi says some of 'em are brilliant the way they jump around like springboks.'

Markham smiled at the striking image.

'Sometimes Vi takes a peek at the ballet lessons. The ballerina teachers don't mind. They're really nice an' even the old ones can move like you wouldn't believe. She says it's like they've got grasshopper muscles.'

Markham felt himself beginning to relax. The inimitable Doggie Dickerson always did him good. Apart from finding Doggie's company oddly soothing, he always felt that he learned something.

'What about the male staff?' he asked. 'Are they as nice as the women?'

'In love with themselves,' came the withering reply. 'An' there's some designer bloke who's a real Handy Andy. Like a freaking octopus according to Vi.'

*Octopus.*

Markham wondered if this was the same person he had heard described as a 'crooked octopus' the previous night.

'When Violet said "designer", was she talking about a painter or stagehand?'

Doggie squinted sagaciously. *'Nah* . . . She said it's some curly-haired guy who works out the dance movements.'

*The choreographer Richard Buckfast.*

'There's this other bloke who looks like a film star, but Vi says he's got a mean streak. Heard him shouting at some kid saying she walked like a bull terrier, though he's ever so smarmy when there's parents around.'

*Toby Lavenham, Andrée Clark's former partner.*

'Vi says the ballet kids are the most competitive an' some of 'em are downright screwy. There's this dancer everyone says is the next big thing an' they all want to be like her.'

'Rosa Maitland?'

'Yeah, that's the one. A nice kid but doesn't seem like she's all there. Sort of frightened looking. Vi saw her in the auditorium one time, said it was weird—'

'What was?'

'How she was kind of showing herself off an' looking away at the same time.'

Markham recalled the pouter-pigeon profile and air of inaccessibility.

'Mind you,' Doggie pursed his lips, 'she were in this itsy-bitsy, white costume that made it look like she had nothing on . . . Vi thought she looked embarrassed.'

A cheery voice interrupted the conversation.

''Lo, Dogs, Gil.'

The two men turned to see Markham's colleague, DI Chris Carstairs, approaching.

'Haven't seen you for a while, Mr Carstairs,' Doggie greeted the DI cordially. 'But you've timed it well, what with Mr Markham coming in for a workout.'

'They're keeping my nose to the grindstone in Vice, Doggie,' Carstairs replied. 'Guess my sixth sense told me Gil might be looking for a sparring partner.'

'Well, Mr Markham was just ahead of you on points last time,' Doggie pointed out affably, 'so stands to reason you'll be looking for a win.'

His fellow DI thumped the proprietor's arm affection-ately, sending up a cloud of dust and a distinct odour of mothballs; together with the aroma of Johnnie Walker, it made Markham feel quite lightheaded.

'Might have known you'd be keeping a tally,' Carstairs laughed. Then winking at Markham, 'Come on, let's be hav-ing you . . . Just pretend I'm Sidney, that should put you in the mood.'

Having done the honours of his establishment, Doggie headed for the door.

'Hey, Dogs. Before you go,' Carstairs called, 'I saved this one up for you . . . When did a boxer after winning a world title urinate in the centre of the ring? *Crufts* — 1979.'

Doggie did a fair impression of splitting his sides, while Markham decided his colleague deserved a pummelling on the strength of this witticism alone . . .

An hour later, back at the station aglow from walloping Carstairs, Markham felt a surge of renewed energy that not even the sight of his drab office could dispel.

Kate Burton was an attentive audience as he relayed the titbits he had gleaned from Doggie.

'It's a strange environment, the ballet world,' he concluded, leaning with his back against the office window. 'But then we knew that from the Baranov case.'

She was fascinated by details of the 'pushy mums'.

'I remember that type from ballet classes when I was a kid,' she said ruefully. 'I had two left feet, though, so I wasn't a threat.' Unexpectedly, she added, 'Nathan wants us to try Salsa, so maybe I'll be better at that.'

Something twisted in Markham's gut, but he merely replied lightly, 'I'll be wanting the two of you to give me a demonstration.'

Her face flushed rosily. 'Don't tell Noakes, will you, sir? Only you *know* what he's like.'

The DI chuckled. 'Yes, I imagine you can do without any ribbing of the "Shippers Does Salsa" variety.'

She smiled gratefully. 'He rang earlier, boss. Hafsah Peri's coming in at two and Sir Edward Hamling,' her tone took on a certain edge, 'believes he can "fit us in" around three.'

'Excellent, Kate, thanks. You should grab yourself some lunch before we interview them. As Noakesy always says, an army marches on its stomach.' Through his window, the early afternoon sun felt warm on his back. 'You know, I can't help thinking I *missed* something back there with Doggie.'

Kate looked startled.

'A *clue*?'

'Something that might help us, if only I had the wit to work out what it was.' Moving across to his desk, he said, 'What are Doyle and Carruthers up to?'

'Recovering from another trawl of Rosemount's finances.' She grimaced expressively. 'Carruthers thought about becoming an actuary before he decided on the police, so you'd think it would be right up his street.'

'Dimples once defined actuaries for me as "Those who can't stand the excitement of accountancy".'

This sent Burton on her way with a smile.

* * *

There was a breakthrough of sorts before the end of the day, but Markham wasn't sure what to make of it.

Hafsah Peri surprised himself and Burton by turning up with her solicitor Mr Quinn, a weary middle-aged man with a bald pate, handlebar moustache and nicotine-stained fingers. After the preliminary exchange to establish that she was attending in a voluntary capacity et cetera et cetera, they got down to business.

Yes, she had received sums of money and cheques from Mrs Clark from time to time but then, she believed, so had others (while declining to name names). 'Madame' only had to hear about there being some sort of need and she would want to help. 'She had great sympathy for any problems people had,' the nurse told them. 'She had such a kind heart.'

The solicitor added stiffly, 'Mrs Clark was certainly not being pestered for gifts. She regarded Ms Peri as loyal and devoted and would seize on any opportunity to be generous.'

'What about ethics of the nursing profession?' Burton enquired.

It appeared that this had 'never come to mind'. Nor, it was claimed, did she know anything about thefts from patients' rooms.

The development came with Hafsah's admission that Maureen Frost had challenged her about accepting gifts after seeing her pocket a twenty-pound note. The administrator also brought up the thefts, though she didn't accuse Hafsah outright.

'Mrs Frost was a conscientious and principled manager, so why did she not take any action over the gifts? Why did she not institute disciplinary proceedings, for example?' Markham asked. However loyal and devoted Hafsah Peri might be, something about her mixture of servility and defiance made him instinctively uncomfortable. She could well have been an excellent nurse while adroit at trotting out sob stories for Andrée Clark and subjecting her to emotional pressure.

Suddenly, as the glittering watchful eyes like anthracite coals observed him from under lowered lids, it came to him.

'Were you blackmailing Mrs Frost?' he asked.

'Mrs Frost and my client reached an *understanding*,' Quinn told them. 'It was felt there was no need for *unpleasantness* in the circumstances.'

Markham addressed the nurse, ignoring the solicitor. 'So, you had something on Maureen Frost?' he said simply. Then, with steel in his voice. '*What was it?*'

The woman seemed hypnotised by the tall dark inspector whose eyes now bored into her.

'She went with women.'

There it was, finally. But he wanted to be clear.

'Are you saying that Mrs Frost was homosexual?'

'Yes, I saw them once at her bungalow . . . kissing.' Her voice became a hiss. 'It was *immoral*.'

'No, Ms Peri.' Markham never raised his voice, but something about it raised the hairs on the back of Burton's neck. 'What's immoral is not only your homophobia but the way you manipulated what you knew about Mrs Frost's personal life for your own ends — to save yourself from a disciplinary hearing and, most likely, dismissal.' With icy disdain, the DI continued, 'Was the woman you saw with Mrs Frost known to you?'

There was something like shame in her voice as she muttered, 'No, I never saw her before.' Again, the defiant bravado. 'But it wasn't *right*. They could've sacked Maureen.'

It was Burton's turn for anger. 'Her sexuality wasn't grounds for dismissal. She was a very private woman who would have hated people knowing.' A flush travelled up the DI's neck. 'Not because she'd done *anything* wrong, Ms Peri, but because it had nothing to do with how she did her job and wasn't anyone else's business.'

Afterwards, she exploded to Markham. 'What an ignorant bigot!'

'But not, I think, our murderer.'

Burton calmed down as quickly as she had flared up.

'No,' she conceded reluctantly. 'Hafsah had Andrée and Maureen right where she wanted them, so there was no need to kill either of them.' Her voice dripped acid as she added, 'No need for any *unpleasantness*, as Mr Quinn would say.'

'But do you reckon she was Rosemount's thief, Kate?'

'Oh yes. And I wouldn't be surprised if she was siphoning off supplies — there was all that poking around in the basement, remember? But we've got no way of proving it.' Burton turned hopeful eyes on Markham. 'At least we can see she gets the boot from the nursing home, sir. And maybe do her for obstruction of justice while we're about it.'

'I'll think of something, never fear,' he promised grimly.

'What about this mystery woman Hafsah spotted at Maureen's bungalow, sir? Could *she* be the one we're looking for?'

They regarded each other tensely for a long moment.

Suddenly his intercom buzzed with the announcement that Sir Edward Hamling was downstairs in reception.

'If he was creating noise about that lightweight garbage in the *Gazette*, what's he going to say about *this*?' Burton groaned. 'Just imagine it . . . *Lesbian scandal uncovered at death-struck care home.*'

Markham's lips quirked. 'Careful, Kate. You're outgunning Gavin Conors.'

She grinned back.

'Come on, better get this over with,' he told her. 'At least we've got hold of another piece of the puzzle.'

A veil had been lifted. Behind it was their killer.

## 11. SMOULDERING EMBERS

The 'Black Baron' lived up to his nickname, turning a louring countenance on Markham and Burton as they entered the more salubrious of the station's interview rooms.

'I want to know why your officers have been making a nuisance of themselves with Rosemount's HR and Accounts department,' Hamling demanded as soon as he saw them.

Markham laughed easily as though the objection was too absurd for words.

'As I'm sure you realise, Sir Edward, we have an extensive remit when it comes to issues such as *fraud.*' He paused to let the word sink in. 'Obviously, we prefer to do things the nice, easy way, with everyone at your end co-operating and assisting our enquiries.'

He let the possibility of a far more unpleasant, embarrassing alternative hang in the air.

Hamling regarded him narrowly, the two men being roughly the same height so he couldn't look down his nose at the tall dark DI who, for all his pinstriped elegance and graceful manner, had the appearance of someone who would have no compunction about resorting to strong-arm tactics.

'Look, Inspector. There's no mystery here,' Hamling said. 'At least not so far as *I'm* concerned. Ballet and the arts have always depended on people like me . . . philanthropists hovering on the fringes.' His mouth twisted. 'No doubt Joe Public would say we've got more money than sense.'

There was a sadness about the other's tone that brought Markham up short. Somehow, he thought, *Hamling isn't the one we're chasing.*

*But does* he *know who it is?*

'I understand, sir,' the DI said with a gentleness that surprised Kate Burton. 'There's a long, honourable tradition of patrons like yourself keeping the arts afloat . . . I suppose we might call you the heirs to Diaghilev and Lincoln Kirstein. If it weren't for Kirstein, neo-classical ballet and Balanchine would never have stood a chance.'

Hamling looked at Markham with marked respect.

'I see you understand, Inspector.'

The DI felt the old, familiar pang as he reflected that his interest in the performing arts owed everything to Olivia and her fascination with the Baranov case.

But he let none of this show, aware of Burton's eyes still riveted on him.

'Give me something, Sir Edward,' he said quietly.

'You should speak to Linda Merryweather,' was the unexpected reply. 'I think there's something she wants to get off her chest.'

Burton was startled. 'A *confession*?'

'No, I don't think so . . . more like information that could help you.'

'Has she confided in you?' Markham asked.

Hamling shook his head. 'No, but there's something preying on her mind.'

Markham looked at him long and hard for a moment before turning to Burton. 'Let's go straight to Rosemount and speak to Mrs Merryweather.' The DI dismissed Hamling with a graceful nod. 'Thank you for your assistance, Sir Edward. We may need to speak again.'

The other regarded him levelly. 'Good luck, Inspector.'

As if he knew this was endgame.

\* \* \*

Markham and Burton, accompanied by Noakes, found Linda Merryweather in her comfortable quarters on Rosemount's Bluebell Corridor.

Markham had an impression of solid warmth — carved oak cabinets, landscapes in gold-leaf frames, russet velvet armchairs and a sofa punctuated by forest-green throw pillows — but his and Burton's attention was wholly focused on the plump writer of romantic fiction who seemed undecided as to whether she was pleased or disconcerted by their visit.

'You may as well know, Andrée turned me down flat when I suggested we might collaborate on a novel about the ballet world.' Then with some compunction, Linda Merryweather added. 'I think she wanted to make her own splash with a tell-all memoir and didn't want me stealing her thunder. Also, she was becoming more dependent on her day nurse who I suspect turned her against me for reasons of her own.' She pulled a face. 'Bit of a snake in the grass that one.'

She shot a significant look at Markham, and he understood that this shrewd elderly lady had long been wary of Hafsah Peri.

'Even though she wasn't interested in a writing partnership, Andrée liked to reminisce and gossip about Bromgrove Ballet.' A disapproving sniff. 'To some extent it was power play — lifting the lid to let me know there was a store of juicy nuggets that she was saving up for her own book. But I think now maybe she was trying to tell me something . . .'

'That she was frightened?' Burton prompted.

'I think so, yes.'

'Who was she frightened of?' Markham asked. The answer suddenly came to him with the speed of an arrow as he recalled Tania Sullivan's casual reference to dancers 'battling it out' over lead roles. 'Was it Clara Kentish?'

'I'm not even sure I *did* think that it *could* be her to start with.' Mrs Merryweather looked embarrassed by her own incoherence, but the DI nodded encouragement and she seemed to take heart from that. 'It was only the day of Andrée's funeral that things started to click into place.' Agitatedly, she picked up the hideous carpet bag, rummaged in it for a hankie, blew her nose stertorously and then resumed. 'I noticed Nicholas — Mr Gower — standing with Clara after the church service when everyone was getting ready to walk up to the wake. He said something to her, and she flinched as if he'd struck her . . . almost recoiled. Her expression was really strange, and her eyes seemed to turn black. It was over in seconds . . . then she turned away from him, and people started walking back up the drive.' She bit her lip. 'Nobody else noticed anything. I even wondered afterwards if I'd imagined it. But something about the look in her eyes spooked me.'

Noakes patted the plump arm reassuringly. 'Did Mr Gower seem bothered, luv? Did *he* clock the weirdy behaviour?'

'No, it looked like he was making casual chit chat . . . I think he was wiped out after the service in church and pretty much just going through the motions. I don't think he noticed her reaction. But I was leaning against the lychgate just getting my breath and saw how her face changed.'

'I bet not much gets past *you*,' Noakes said admiringly. 'Being a novelist . . . student of human nature an' all that.'

The reputedly crass and uncouth former member of CID had touched the right chord, as he so often did in his dealings with those who were vulnerable and frightened.

'Well, it's true I'm a pretty sharp observer,' she said with pardonable pride, her fear momentarily forgotten.

'Is that why you came over a bit shaky when you got back to the house?' Noakes continued. 'Cos it upset you?'

'I instinctively felt something was badly wrong,' she said. And now her bottom lip was trembling. 'I wanted some time by myself to process it . . . Sir Edward kindly stayed with me to start with, but really I just wanted to be on my own. And then suddenly it was pandemonium and people shouting that Nicholas was dead. The whole thing felt like a waking nightmare.'

Fearing that that they were losing her, Markham interposed swiftly. 'You're doing really well, Mrs Merryweather. You talked about things "clicking into place". What *things*?'

He sensed Burton and Noakes holding their breath.

'I remembered one time when Andrée was chatting with me and Nicholas about dancers from the company,' she began slowly, 'and I said something about how easy-going and, well, *normal* Clara and Tania Sullivan seemed to be . . . I was expecting them to be real prima donnas, you see. Well, Andrée turned round and said that with Clara it was all a façade and she was really quite dangerous.'

'You're sure she said *dangerous*?' Burton asked urgently.

'Oh yes. Andrée could be terribly melodramatic, but there was something very serious about the way she said it.'

'Did she explain what she meant by that?' Burton pressed.

'She said that Clara was insanely competitive — couldn't get over the fact that Andrée had become a star while *she* never got promoted past the rank of soloist.' The novelist frowned. 'She said that in the early days Clara pretended to be interested in helping her but later she found out Clara had been talking about her behind her back, laughing at her, putting her down.'

'But Clara visited her here, along with the others?' Noakes pointed out. 'So looks like they made it up.'

Mrs Merryweather shook her head slowly.

'On the surface maybe. But Andrée never seemed comfortable round her . . . her body language was a dead giveaway. At the time, I thought perhaps it was a guilty conscience. Andrée ran over quite a few people on her way to the top, so it crossed my mind that Clara might have been one of the victims she left in her wake.'

'But now you think it was more than that?' Markham was anxious not to put words into the woman's mouth, but he wanted to be certain.

'Looking back, yes I do. I can see now that I had niggles but ignored them. There were stray bits of conversation when people said that Andrée was the reason why dancers missed out on opportunities, that she stopped them getting a piece of the action, demoralised them . . . Toby Lavenham said that Clara suffered the worst. She laughed it off, said it was nonsense and she was very happy with how her career had turned out. But she didn't *look* happy, and I had the feeling she was quite bitter underneath it all.' Her voice dropped to a whisper. 'Seeing Clara outside the church — the strange way she looked at Nicholas — suddenly brought everything to the surface.'

Markham could almost hear Sidney in his ear honking a warning to the effect that hindsight was a wonderful thing.

Burton was clearly thinking along similar lines. He could tell his fellow DI wanted more, wanted something *concrete*.

'Did you ever witness any altercation between Andrée and Clara?' she asked. 'Anything to suggest that Andrée was afraid of her?'

'When the dance crowd visited just after New Year, I'm almost sure I heard Andrée say something like, "I don't scare easy" . . . Or maybe it was "I'm done with being scared" . . . I definitely heard the word "scared".'

Burton and Noakes looked at each other, thinking of the words Chloe Finch claimed to have overheard: 'I'm not scared of you at all.'

*But it wasn't enough to go on*, thought Markham. *Nowhere near enough.*

However, Mrs Merryweather's next words made the atmosphere electric.

'Of course, Clara's sexual orientation might've been why she missed out on promotion. It'd be like Andrée to get under her skin about it,' the elderly writer mused.

'Who told you she was gay?' Noakes demanded excitedly.

'Nicholas let it drop one day when we were discussing LGBT rights and how society had moved on from the days when he and Clara had to keep their private life under wraps.' She looked surprised at their evident interest. 'They were never standard bearers for the gay movement  or anything like that. I suppose they were what you might call "closeted". Nicholas said that back then the ballet world was full of men who wore long, flowing scarves and billowing sweaters . . .

they camped around waving cigarette holders and called each other drag names.' Her lips thinned. 'Always disappearing to what they called the "cha-cha room". He said ballet was dominated by gay men. It was *their* milieu, but the same wasn't true for women. He figured it was why Clara never made it to principal . . . the powers that be just weren't comfortable when they found out about it even though she'd been terribly discreet.'

Markham wondered if it had in fact been Andrée Clark who made sure to drop a hint about her rival in the right ear.

'According to Nicholas, Clara reinvented herself after that,' the woman continued. 'Projected this kind of sexless aura so that people assumed she just wasn't interested . . . you know, wedded to her art, no interests outside it. Over time nobody remembered it had ever been different.'

*But Nicholas Gower remembered*, thought Markham. *And his knowledge could have proved fatal.*

'How did Clara get on with Mrs Frost?' Burton asked. She kept her tone casual, but Markham knew she was thinking that a connection between Kentish and the second victim made the dancer a viable suspect. A glance at Noakes confirmed that he realised the significance of the DI's question.

'Oh, I think she liked her,' the elderly lady said pleasantly, with no indication that she'd picked up on Burton's ulterior motive. 'Maureen was quite the ballet fan in her youth. I remember her talking about visits to the Coliseum in London to see the English National Ballet, though I think it was called Festival Ballet back then.' She looked pleased at the opportunity to reminisce. 'Maureen didn't often open up, but I remember one Christmas after I moved here, she told us about a visit to Spain when she was on some student exchange . . . They were taken to see these ancient caves — you know, the ones with wall paintings — and the guide told them about some large flat stones that had been found covered with patterns of scuffmarks. He said they were left by prehistoric people who strapped animal hooves to their feet and stomped out rhythms, patterns and dances . . . Later,

179

when they were watching some amazing flamenco dancers in one of Barcelona's gypsy cave restaurants, she felt like there was this kind of umbilical cord stretching from 60,000 B.C. to the floor under her feet, reverberating with millenniums of rhythms. She never forgot it.'

Noakes looked somewhat taken aback at this reference to primeval voodoo, but Burton was clearly intrigued by the glimpse into Maureen Frost's hitherto unreadable character. Markham too found it a poignant anecdote.

Seeing Mrs Merryweather lost in thought, Burton and Noakes preserved a respectful silence after this little tribute to the departed.

Meanwhile, thoughts flashed through Markham's mind at warp speed.

Thanks to Hafsah Peri, they now knew that Maureen Frost was gay. If she and Clara Kentish had ever overlapped — maybe even been romantically involved — and then she saw or heard something which pointed to Clara being the killer, it would have placed her in a quandary.

Markham found it hard to imagine that Maureen would have protected the killer of a helpless invalid, still less connived at murder. On the other hand, it was possible, given their shared history, that she had rumbled Clara but been unable to turn her in.

Other scenarios presented themselves to him in rapid succession.

Perhaps the manager *hadn't* been certain Clara was Andrée Clark's killer. If that was the case, then Clara might have somehow managed to reassure the manager and allay her suspicions, thus buying herself some time. But then for some reason she decided that Maureen Frost too had to die, perhaps because Frost had changed her tune and begun to express doubts or because the manager initially believed whatever story Kentish had fed her but wanted her to tell the police . . . or — most unpalatable of all — perhaps she simply decided that the other woman was a threat that had to be eliminated.

Their elderly interviewee appeared tired, but Markham had one more question for her before he could let her rest.

'Do you recall ever hearing Mrs Clark talk about receiving unpleasant correspondence?' he enquired.

Immediately Mrs Merryweather became reanimated.

'I asked her about that once. She talked about tiresome fans but said other dancers were the worst . . . anonymous notes left at the stage door before a first night . . . "Your arabesques *stink*", malicious stuff like that. It was strange. She told me you need to be wary of certain people . . . think about their hidden motives and not let them get too close . . . not let them into your life. I remember she looked furtive and nervous when she said that.'

'Did she mention anyone by name?' Burton asked.

'No, but I remember after the New Year visit from the Bromgrove Ballet lot, she seemed jittery and out of sorts . . . told Maureen she was too tired for any more callers.'

'Did any of 'em ever visit Mrs C upstairs?' Noakes asked.

'I know the odd person went up to her room, but I'm not sure about Clara . . . the nurses will be able to tell you that.'

'You've been a tremendous help, Mrs Merryweather,' Markham said warmly, noticing that she had picked up the carpet bag and was pulling at some stray threads. 'Obviously it's important that you keep everything we've discussed to yourself for now.'

The writer's face puckered like a child's.

'I'm not going doolally am I, Inspector? Imagining things about people?' She looked between the three of them, tremulous now. 'Clara's so elegant and graceful. I remember a photoshoot in the *Gazette* about the Dance Academy . . . there was a picture of her in this flowing skirt with a scarf tucked at her waist and ballet shoes . . . that beautiful long neck and the wonderful carriage. She looked so gentle with all these boys and girls listening to her for dear life. Maybe she would have liked a child of her own, but she never had one . . . It just doesn't seem *possible* that she could be a killer.'

Noakes stepped in. 'Yeah,' he said gently. 'She must've been brilliant in *Swan Lake* an' all them floaty ballets . . . the ones with princes an' things.'

It served to distract her, and she looked brighter now.

'Yes, Clara definitely belonged to the romantic era. She loved the story about Rudolf Nureyev asking Balanchine if he could come and dance with his ballet company. Balanchine said Nureyev would find his ballets too abstract . . . told him to go away and dance his princes then come back when he was tired of them. But Nureyev never got tired of his princes and the princes never tired got tired of *him*.'

'And Andrée? Was she a romantic dancer?' Burton asked curiously.

'She did all the great romantic roles, of course. But she was overtly erotic whereas Clara was restrained and ethereal. I remember Clara saying that the stage should eliminate sex, otherwise there's a risk of ballet regressing to the early days when people saw it as a form of titillation . . . you know, rich men ogling dancers, eyeing them as if they were show ponies. She said it was a terrible thing when young dancers became coarsened and lost the purity of their art.' Suddenly, Mrs Merryweather shuddered. 'She told us about a dancer called Emma Livry back in the nineteenth century . . . The poor girl was fluffing her skirts out backstage to make them look full and round for her entrance. Somehow, by fluffing her costume she managed to fan the flames of a gaslight and went up in flames . . . turned into a human torch with forty percent burns . . . she died eight months later from blood poisoning caused by her wounds.'

'*Jesus*.'

'That's a prayer I trust, Noakes,' Markham said austerely.

'*Too right.* Blimey Mrs M, that's pretty gruesome for over the teacups.'

'Oh, Clara made quite a study of it. Apparently, there was a holocaust of young ballerinas because of the gaslighting . . . it allowed the house lights to be dimmed and created a sort of ghostly illusion.'

Her face clouded over.

'What is it, Mrs Merryweather?' he asked gently.

'It was the way she talked about Emma Livry.' She frowned. 'You see, Emma wouldn't wear skirts that were treated in chemicals to make them fire resistant. She said it made them ugly and they didn't suit her. The way Clara talked, it was almost as though she thought that Emma was punished for being vain. There was something *ruthless* about the way she gloated over the details . . . Emma lying face down on a stretcher for months having lemon juice poured into her wounds and not daring to move in case she ruptured the tissue forming across her back.' They winced at that. 'Clara said Emma's mother was a prostitute who tried to keep her daughter from being devoured by predatory men only to see her devoured by flames on stage. She showed us this picture from an exhibition at the Paris Opera Museum, "Blazing Ballet Girls", a tiny coffin-like box with what was left of Emma's costume . . . She said the stays of Emma's corset had become encrusted in her flesh and her mother passed out watching the doctors try to remove them.'

'*Chuffing Nora.*' Noakes normally florid complexion had visibly paled.

Despite the grisliness of the subject, Mrs Merryweather was clearly pleased to have such an attentive audience.

'All terribly morbid. Well, at least Nicholas and I thought so, but Clara seemed fascinated by the whole story . . . right down to the epitaph inscribed on Emma's tombstone: *Earth, tread lightly on me who so lightly weighed on you.*'

After Mrs Merryweather had left them, Noakes said, 'One thing's for sure. That Clara's got a screw loose somewhere. I mean, banging on like that about bleeding ballet suttee to two old folk. Must've properly freaked 'em out.'

'Oh, I reckon they were well able for it, Noakesy. But you're right about there being something unbalanced about that intensity . . . something that disturbed Mrs Merryweather and raised a red flag about Clara.'

Burton said, 'Interesting about Clara wanting to *eliminate sex* onstage . . . Sounds like she made it a rule to live by.'

'D'you reckon that's why she wigged out down at the church when she an' Gower were chatting?' Noakes demanded. 'He said summat about them two being part of the gay scene back in the day an' it gave her a shock cos she thought all that were dead an' buried. 'Scuse the pun.' He frowned. 'Does that mean Gower had twigged the connection between her an' Frost . . . an' he were kind of *warning* her?'

'Clara could always have bluffed it out,' Burton observed. 'The fact that she and Maureen maybe had something going didn't necessarily make her a killer . . . didn't mean she'd committed the murders.'

'But it could've been a reason why Maureen might've decided to protect her . . . only, things went wrong, and she became a threat,' Markham said quietly. 'Nicholas Gower was a shrewd and highly observant individual. He could well have sussed out the tie between Clara and Maureen with all its implications; maybe, like Hafsah, he saw something.'

He thought about the interview they had just concluded. 'Or perhaps, like Mrs Merryweather, he had become uneasy about Clara . . . Perhaps things were plucking at his memory and touching a hidden chord in his mind . . . maybe those snatches of gossip about Andrée damaging Clara's career . . . maybe Andrée's wariness around Clara or what she said about her being dangerous—'

'Mebbe his old mate "Freddie" March had filled him in on stuff too,' Noakes interrupted.

'True,' the DI acknowledged. 'It's quite possible Frederic March regaled Mr Gower with all kinds of gossip about the dancers' rivalry, and after Andrée's murder this contributed to his latent misgivings about Clara.'

'Why didn't he tell someone?' Noakes demanded.

'He was tired and worn out,' the DI said simply. 'And I think he would have wanted to be sure that his suspicions were well-founded. As you may recall, according to Sir Edward he was a great devotee of dance. Clara Kentish was one of the ballet greats . . . okay not in the first rank of talent, but quite a star nonetheless.'

'You make it sound like he turned a blind eye to murder cos he were this chuffing ballet fan,' Noakes protested.

'No, it's not that,' Markham replied. 'I think his suspicions were all nebulous, half-formed in his mind. He knew nothing for certain.'

'He must've known when she bleeding came for him down by the lake,' Noakes persisted.

There was an uncomfortable silence as they imagined the truth of those unthinkable misgivings suddenly rising up before Nicholas Gower in one devastating conviction.

'So what exactly *did* Gower say down at the church when Kentish backed away from him?' Burton asked. 'Whatever it was, presumably *that's* when she decided to kill him.'

'Who knows, Kate?' Markham suddenly sounded very weary.

'Mebbe he came right out with it,' Noakes suggested. 'Told her he knew she'd killed Mrs C and Frostie.' He was on a roll now. 'With him being this big ballet fan, he could've said he were giving her a head-start so she could turn herself in or make a run for it.'

Burton's eyebrows shot upwards.

'You really think he'd do that straight after Mrs Clark's funeral?' she challenged.

'If he were all tired and worn out like the guvnor says, then he might've,' Noakes said stubbornly. 'Or with the emotion of the church an' everything, mebbe he weren't thinking straight.'

'I'm not sure Mr Gower would have been as direct as that, Noakesy,' Markham said thoughtfully. 'However, I *can* imagine the stress of the occasion and his private fears might have led him to talk in a way that betrayed the direction of his thoughts . . . Perhaps he sympathised with Clara for what Andrée had put her through over the years and the missed opportunities, perhaps he brought up the fact of her being gay . . . Whatever he said, there was a self-consciousness or an uneasiness that came across, so she saw that deep down he was beginning to suspect her.'

'Would Mr Gower have realised that he'd been too obvious and given himself away?' Burton wondered.

'I doubt it,' Markham replied. 'He was probably quite overcome after the funeral — don't forget he and Mrs Clark were neighbours at Rosemount — and his suspicions of Clara were only just rearing their heads. Having watched Clara read a poem in memory of her colleague, he might have thought like Mrs Merryweather that he'd got it all wrong.'

'It's a shame them two didn't compare notes,' Noakes growled.

'They're old school, Noakesy. Wouldn't have wanted to breathe a word against Clara Kentish unless they were sure.'

'More's the pity.'

'Calumny and detraction count as sins,' Burton told her disgruntled ex-colleague.

'Oh well, that's alright then,' Noakes said with withering sarcasm.

'Cut it out you two.' Markham's voice was sharp.

'Sorry, boss,' came contrite mumbles.

Noakes was never meek and mild for long. 'So, what's the deal?' he demanded. 'Are we going after Kentish or what?'

'Yes, she's our prime suspect now,' Markham said decisively. 'I know we're short on hard evidence, but it's enough to try and provoke her into showing her hand.'

Noakes was like a terrier. 'How are we gonna do that?'

'We regroup at the station and come up with a strategy. Then first thing tomorrow morning we sell our prime suspect and plan to Sidney.'

Markham noticed that his former wingman was looking wistful.

'You can come along for the ride, Noakesy. As our "civilian consultant". You may not have been *in situ* at Rosemount for very long, but you can vouch for Mrs Merryweather . . . Sidney'll need convincing of her credentials.'

His friend was visibly delighted.

'Any chance you could make a special effort on the wardrobe front?' Markham suggested delicately. 'That outfit you wore to Mrs Clark's funeral was bang on the money.' The other looking highly gratified, Markham continued, 'No need for the same tomorrow obviously,' otherwise Sidney was likely to mistake Noakes for a KGB operative left over from the Cold War, 'but a *business suit* should go down well.' As opposed to today's mismatched flannels, pullover and jacket. Muriel would surely be able to disinter something appropriate now that the prospect of a consultancy role had been dangled.

Burton looked dubious, but Noakes beamed.

'I'll take it up a level, boss,' he promised.

'Right, we can hitch a lift back to base with Kate and after that it's all hands on deck. We've had a lucky break.' If that's what you could call the latest developments, he thought wryly. 'And now we need to make the most of it.'

As they left Rosemount, having fended off Mrs Cartwright who was clearly bursting with ill-concealed curiosity, Markham's thoughts were focused on just one thing.

What had triggered Andrée Clark's murder?

Jealousy that had festered for many years only to erupt when some hidden nerve was touched?

Or did Clara Kentish see herself as on some kind of twisted ideological mission to punish a dancer who exemplified all that she deplored in ballet culture?

Or was a 'crooked love' part of the puzzle?

He couldn't get that image of the burning ballerina out of his head.

A butterfly that flew too close to the flame.

## 12. LIGHT IN THE DARK

Tuesday 1 February saw the team and Noakes assembled in Markham's office. The weather had turned once again, a stiff wind and rain rattling the ill-fitting sash window, but the atmosphere was one of anticipation and supressed excitement. Even Carruthers was visibly champing at the bit with no sign of his previous ennui and ill-concealed boredom.

True to his word, Noakes had risen to the sartorial challenge and sported a fairly decent suit, of ancient vintage admittedly but nothing that the DCI could cavil at. Even the regimental tie looked less like a noose and more like regular workwear, from which Markham deduced that Muriel or Natalie had taken the renegade in hand. Most remarkable of all, his ex-wingman had assumed responsibility for the refreshments (even the prospect of apprehending a killer failed to shake Noakes's priorities, first of which was appropriate provisioning). Distributing paper bags and coffee trays from Costa, he said solemnly to Kate Burton, 'Yours is a granola square an' soy wotsit, luv.' At least he didn't talk about 'that birdseed crap', a sign of the momentousness of the occasion. He had even remembered Americanos for Doyle and Carruthers, having come a long way from the days when he demanded of bemused Costa staff what was the American component in said beverages.

Burton had briefed her colleagues comprehensively the previous afternoon and, once breakfast had been distributed, Doyle was clearly impatient to know the game plan.

'Are we really certain it's Clara Kentish, sir?' he asked through a mouthful of bacon roll. 'I mean, d'you reckon the old lady has all her marbles?'

'I would say *Linda Merryweather* is perfectly *compos mentis*, yes Doyle,' Markham said drily, giving his younger colleague a look of mild disapproval. 'She struck me as remarkably clear and lucid given the circumstances.'

He sipped his black coffee fastidiously before continuing.

'If Mrs Merryweather is right, then Nicholas Gower mentioned something to Clara just after Andrée Clark's funeral service . . . Whatever he said came as a shock.'

The DI nodded to Kate who briskly summarised. 'It might be that Mr Gower challenged her directly . . . said something to the effect that he knew she was the murderer. But it's more likely to have been inadvertent — he dropped a reference to her sexuality and private life, or he commiserated with her about the way Andrée had behaved over the years . . . Either way, he gave the impression of knowing more than he actually did, or made Clara think that something had put him on his guard.'

'He could've brought up what Andrée said to him about Clara being dangerous or said he'd noticed Andrée wasn't comfortable round her . . . seemed afraid of her,' Carruthers interrupted eagerly. Somehow, flushed with enthusiasm, the newcomer seemed less amoeba-like than usual and, to his surprise, Markham found himself warming to the young DS.

'I was coming to that,' Burton pointed out crisply, less appreciative of the DS's interruption. 'The point is that something he said — or something about his manner — rattled Clara so badly that she decided it wasn't safe to let him live.'

'If she thought he was wondering whether or not to dob her in, that would have meant curtains for the poor sod.' Doyle drew an eloquent finger across his throat.

Burton looked pained at 'dob her in'.

'The thing is, Clara was smart enough to bluff it out,' Carruthers said, echoing Burton's previous observation to Markham and Noakes. 'She could have thrown sand in the old bloke's eyes . . . maybe even turned things round . . . got him thinking about the dodgy nurse.' A cool customer himself, Carruthers clearly felt the killer could have salvaged the situation.

'Don' forget, she's off-balance cos of Frostie,' Noakes said sagely, having made short work of his breakfast muffin. 'That were *personal*, see, what with them having been an item.'

'They might not have been romantically involved,' Burton pointed out.

'Yeah okay, but even if they were part of the same scene,' Noakes observed with an ineffable "man of the world" air, 'it meant they had *history* . . . the murder would've been like a *crime passionel.*'

Burton winced at his dire pronunciation of this term of art but conceded the point. 'Yes,' she agreed, 'like you say, that kind of emotional investment would mean Clara was wound up pretty tight afterwards . . . it probably wouldn't take much to trigger her.'

'D'you think it was personal with Mrs C too?' Doyle asked.

'Don' get much more personal than strangling the poor cow,' Noakes pointed out lugubriously.

But Doyle looked thoughtful. 'No, I meant I was wondering if Andrée messed with her head . . . kept her dangling . . . that kind of thing.'

Noakes stared. 'What, as in gave Kentish the idea she'd be up for a bit of the other?'

'*God*, sarge, you always sound like one of those seaside postcards,' Doyle shot back in exasperation. 'There's nothing so unusual about it. Nobody bats an eye these days.'

'I'm not your "sarge" anymore,' the other muttered with a sidelong glance at Carruthers.

'Don't worry, I get it,' Carruthers said unexpectedly. 'I know that's how everyone still thinks of you.'

He was rewarded for this obviously unrehearsed and genuine observation by an approving smile from Markham. Despite the newcomer's apparent sang-froid, he felt a glow of pleasure at this sign of acceptance. It was rare to see the boss smile, Carruthers thought to himself. Took years off the bloke so he looked almost human.

Doyle grinned, for once dropping his guard with Carruthers.

'Yeah, I guess it's Noakesy's honorary title,' he said, '*emeritus* or something . . . like they use for the Pope . . . the one who retired.'

Seeing that Noakes didn't appear to relish any papistical connotations, Doyle continued swiftly, 'Okay, so maybe Andrée screwed Kentish up somehow. What else have we got? So far, it's a bit thin if we want to convince the DCI.'

Burton cleared her throat.

Noakes and Doyle exchanged glances of the *Now we're in for it* variety.

Blushing slightly, she said, 'I'm not going to bore you rigid with a whole load of stuff about the ballet. But like Sir Edward said, it's a brutal world. A female dancer's working life is short. Only the likes of Margot Fonteyn go into their forties and fifties. With the rest, they end up on the scrapheap in their thirties.'

Despite himself, Doyle was curious.

'Why can't they keep going for longer?' he asked. 'I mean, haven't they got any number of nutritionists and physios and fitness people to help them?' Avoiding Noakes's eye, he added somewhat defensively, 'There was a programme on BBC 4. Paula made me watch it.' Paula being the ex-girlfriend who had forced him to choose between her and a career in CID.

'Back then they weren't as enlightened about the health side of things,' Burton explained. 'Plus, ballet was sexist and ageist, which was another reason why ballerinas had such a short shelf life. *Think about it.*' Now her tone was intense. 'Retirement's like death for dancers. But Andrée had the celebrity marriage and notoriety to fall back on whereas Clara really had nothing.'

'There was her job at the Dance Academy,' Carruthers pointed out.

'Yes, but she's only been on the permanent staff for the last two years,' Burton told them. 'Before that, it was a case of taking the odd class here and there by way of filling in when other people were off sick . . . I found out that she'd tried to set up her own ballet school but couldn't attract enough students, so it bombed.'

Now her colleagues were interested, a picture of Clara Kentish starting to form in their minds.

'I gather her life was hand to mouth and pretty precarious for a long time,' Burton went on. 'And it must have been scary . . . letting go of the one thing she'd spent her whole life training for and feeling she was more or less redundant, fit for nothing and invisible — out in the cold once she hung up her ballet shoes.'

Noakes was coming over to the idea. 'An' meanwhile, good ole Andrée were having a ball . . . TV shows an' gossip columns an' lots of attention.'

'Exactly,' Burton said, pleased by this endorsement. 'Even her marriage hitting the rocks and the furore about Frederic March harassing young dancers didn't really do her any harm. It was the same with people making allegations about her teaching methods. *All PR was good PR.*'

Markham nodded. 'If anything, it made her even more bankable,' he said. 'A valuable commodity.'

His fellow DI said eagerly, 'That's right, sir. All the affairs and rumours and sexual shenanigans just made Andrée more glamorous . . . and she *milked it* for all she was worth.'

'It must have been gall and wormwood to Clara Kentish as she watched from the sidelines,' Markham observed with compassion in his voice.

'She'd always been outshone by Andrée,' Burton went on. 'Andrée was the flashier dancer who knew how to be sexy and could pull out the pyrotechnics at the drop of a hat. Apparently, Clara was more lyrical and expressive . . . very keen on storytelling and connecting with audiences emotionally rather than trying to dazzle with acrobatic tricks.' Out came Burton's notebook and on went the glasses. 'I looked at some recordings of Andrée's TV appearances . . . There's this one where she sticks it to Clara.'

'She actually mentions her by name?' Markham asked eagerly.

'Yes, sir.' Burton consulted her notes. 'She talks about Clara drawing a curtain over the mirror in one of her classrooms to — and I quote — "get the dancers to find meaning within themselves and not in a reflected image". She laughs about this being navel-gazing and the kind of thing dancers fall back on when they're technically "dead as a doornail".' She grinned. 'Andrée had quite a way with words. Really waspish and withering.'

'Being ridiculed on TV . . . That had to have stung,' Carruthers said. 'Did she say anything else about Clara?'

'She talks about various contemporaries including Clara,' Burton replied. 'She's careful not to be *too* bitchy, but there's one place where she discusses partnering and gives Clara as an example of how *not* to go about it . . . Says Clara's pickiness demoralised male dancers, because she was such a perfectionist and drove them mad by endlessly analysing the motivation of particular movements.'

'But Andrée criticises other people too, right?' Doyle said. 'So it's not like she's just having a go at Clara.'

'I reckon Clara was more vulnerable and thin-skinned than some of the others,' Burton replied. 'Plus, some of the details Andrée shared were unkind . . . Like, she mentioned in one of her interviews how Clara was so nervous that she was always chewing wool—'

'*Wool?*' Noakes and Doyle said in unison.

Markham had the feeling Burton was rather enjoying the effect of this revelation on her colleagues.

'Yes, and not just any old wool,' she told them with a grimace. 'It had to be the crinkly stuff . . . overcoats and her teddy bear were quite useful from that point of view apparently.' Burton thumbed through her notebook again. 'Apparently there was also quite a lot of sniggering in dance circles about her superstitious streak. There was some choreographer who smoked like a chimney and sat in her dressing-room on one particular first night trailing ash everywhere. Clara scored a success in that ballet, so she kept pestering the poor guy to come and give her more ash every time she did a first night . . . And she wouldn't ever sign her name on a programme for fans on the day of a performance because she was convinced it would make her fall over.'

'*Jeez*,' Noakes grunted, 'she sounds a right barrel of laughs.'

'Well, she *does* come out of it all as being terribly precious,' Burton conceded. 'But there's something snide and underhand about the way Andrée took cheap pot shots at her . . . I mean, she could just have trotted out those anecdotes without saying who she was talking about, but she made a point of identifying Clara by name.'

'Assuming Clara's ego was fragile . . . her self-esteem and sense of identity had somehow been fractured and then Andrée mocked her publicly . . . well, there's another trigger,' Markham observed.

'If she thought Mrs C planned to put funnies about her in them memoirs to have a good laugh at her an' make money out of it, mebbe that's why she finally snapped,' Noakes theorised.

'So, it was all a slow burn kind of thing,' Carruthers remarked. 'Resentment and dislike building up over the years and then *Pow*! she lost it.'

Burton nodded vigorously. 'Yes, I think it must have happened like that. She was obviously highly strung and probably really suffered from being pigeonholed as the talented soloist who never quite made it, or at least didn't scale the heights like Andrée. And it sounds like she was a total novice at ballet politics, whereas Andrée knew how to play the game . . . There's this article in *Dancing Times* which implies that Andrée ousted Clara — talked choreographers out of creating ballets on her and persuaded management to make her second rather than first-night cast . . . bagged the juiciest roles for herself, that kind of thing. There was a strong suggestion that Clara was actually the more interesting dancer but couldn't get the breaks because of how Andrée hogged the limelight.'

'If Clara was more talented, maybe that's why Andrée was so keen to undermine her,' Carruthers speculated.

'More than likely,' Burton agreed. 'But professionally, she managed to out-manoeuvre Clara all down the line.'

'Was there anything in that ballet magazine about Clara's private life?' Carruthers asked.

'It's from the eighties when they didn't always come right out and talk about people being gay . . . The article just says she showed no interest in getting married or having a family.' Burton frowned. 'It's ironic really. On the one hand, the top men in ballet — men like Balanchine — didn't want female dancers to have boyfriends or think about marriage because it might detract from ballerinas' total devotion to them . . . didn't want them to be independent or think about a life outside ballet . . . expected them to park their brains at the stage door . . . But then on the other hand, they were properly spooked if women didn't conform to the social norm. They had no problem with gay men, but the ballerinas were another story.' She sighed. 'Talk about backward. Thank God, things have moved on and ballet's finally catching up with the twenty-first century.'

'How come it's the bunheads with a screw loose?' Noakes asked. 'What about the blokes?'

Burton was somewhat taken aback at such interest but swiftly rallied.

'Oh, it's not just the female dancers who've suffered,' she said. '*Dancing Times* had an interview with this ballerina who left ballet after a nervous breakdown. When she enquired after some of her former partners to see how they were coping, she got the shock of her life because *fifteen* of them had committed suicide and another was in a psychiatric hospital.'

That sobering statistic brought them up short.

'Ballet's kind of associated with women,' Carruthers observed. 'And anyway, they make better copy . . . so it's *them* you get to hear about.'

Markham suppressed a smile. Unlikely as it might seem, his team was actually bonding over a discussion about ideologies in the performing arts.

Burton, too, was clearly pleased to find them so engaged.

'Balanchine's famous for saying "Ballet is woman",' she continued. A tiny frown. 'He was a dreadful chauvinist and insisted that men were better at just about everything else.' Cue approving smile from Noakes. 'But when it came to dance, he decreed that men were subordinate . . . just good servants.' She smiled approvingly at Carruthers. 'You're right about women being identified with ballet . . . kind of the feminine ideal . . . wafting about all grace and light.'

'An' no one seeing the blisters an' bunions,' added Noakes on whom dancers' swollen, gnarled and bleeding feet had made a great impression during the Baranov investigation.

'True,' she smiled weakly. 'As for women, stories about them *always* get more publicity. I remember one from the *Gazette* a while back when some critic accused a ballerina who was dancing the Sugar Plum Fairy in *The Nutcracker* of having eaten one sugarplum too many.'

Noakes guffawed at this before sheepishly subsiding at Burton's frown.

She continued, 'There's been endless gossip about female dancers and their weight over the years. One American ballerina supposedly celebrated her retirement by driving through the Black Forest eating everything in sight and throwing her old pointe shoes out of her car window.' She smiled, 'As you say, good copy. Also, there's always been that thing with ballerinas of people saying, "Ohhh, that one's having a row with that one because . . ." or "Ohhh, they're so jealous of each other" . . . or "Ohhh, that one's got the first night". Everyone loves a good cat fight apparently.'

Doyle wanted to get back to their prime suspect. 'Kentish didn't *look* screwy,' he mused. 'She reminded me of Florence Nightingale . . . like a nurse or something with how calm she was, those chiffony scarves and the floaty way she moved, wearing her hair in that old-fashioned style like she was in a costume drama.'

Up till this point, Markham had listened quietly as his colleagues batted ideas back and forth, but now he said, 'I agree, Doyle, it's hard to imagine Clara Kentish harbouring such violent impulses.'

He rose and moved across to the window.

The rain had stopped, but the day was still overcast, the sky a bleak dark grey, almost bruised-looking, like the murky landscape of their investigation.

Turning round to face the team, he concluded, 'Given what we've learned about underlying attitudes towards male and female dancers, it seems likely that on top of everything else, Clara suffered from covert prejudice.'

'There were injury problems too,' Burton responded smartly, having clearly mugged up their suspect's biography. 'Clara was always coming down with flu or glandular fever or stomach trouble. And there was a bad knee . . . shredded cartilage or something.' Her colleagues winced. 'Anyway, a truckload of injections and operations. There were all these pleats in her career.'

'Whereas Andrée was strong as an ox and never needed time off.' Markham said wryly.

'Correct,' Burton said. 'She was incredibly robust all her life — at least until the MS. Absolutely dependable . . . management loved that. It was another reason why she eclipsed Clara.'

Markham was impressed by how thoroughly his fellow DI had gone into Clara Kentish's life.

'Very interesting, Kate,' he said. 'It sounds as though Clara somehow lost out at every turn.'

Burton hadn't finished. 'There was the issue of her hair as well.'

Doyle was baffled. 'Her *hair*?'

'She was golden-haired,' Burton informed them. 'Oh, I know she's gone silver with age, but back then she was fair. Apparently, they wanted her to dye her hair black so she conformed to the ideal ballerina image rather than faff about with wigs, but she dug her heels in and said no, attracting even more disapproval.'

There was silence as the team digested Burton's composite.

'Andrée probably elbowed a whole stream of dancers out of the way,' Carruthers concluded, 'but Clara's makeup and the whole culture back then meant *she* was the one particularly badly affected.'

'Exactly,' Burton said with decision. 'The injuries and rivalry with Andrée, plus being *persona non grata* with the people who mattered, would have eaten away at her sanity.'

'But is it *enough*?' Doyle challenged. 'I mean, from what you say ma'am, there's all kinds of reasons why she might have borne a grudge against Mrs Clark . . . and it got worse down the years. But there she was visiting her at Rosemount with the others . . . all kind and caring—'

'She couldn't stay away from Rosemount because she was *obsessed* with Andrée,' Carruthers interrupted. With some acuity he added, 'And it might have given her a perverse satisfaction to watch the progress of Andrée's MS.'

'Plus, she wanted to find out about them memoirs,' Noakes reminded them.

'Yeah, *we* know that, but nobody else sussed her,' Doyle persisted. 'As far as the outside world is concerned, she's just this nice lady making time for an old friend.'

'If we're right about her, then *Kentish* must've been the one who did the poison pen stuff,' Noakes said stubbornly. 'An' that means it were *her* Mrs C meant when she said that about not being scared.'

'There *is* somebody who's sussed Clara Kentish,' Markham said quietly returning to sit behind his desk.

Four pairs of eyes stared at him.

'You're forgetting Mrs Merryweather,' the DI said.

'What about her?' Noakes demanded, baffled.

'As we've established, pretty much everything we've got on Clara Kentish is circumstantial. Not enough for an arrest.' Markham paused to let this sink in. 'So, we need to make Clara show her hand.'

'Using *Merryweather*?' Noakes asked incredulously. '*Hell*, boss, she ain't exactly Mrs Dynamic . . . being in a care home an' all that.'

'But she's all there, Noakes,' Markham replied firmly. 'And I think she can help us to trap Clara.'

Seeing that they were evidently anxious at the prospect of the old lady being used as a decoy, he proceeded to elaborate.

'It came to me when Mrs Merryweather told us about those Blazing Ballet Girls—'

'The ones whose costumes got caught in the gaslights?' Doyle asked faintly, recalling Burton's earlier briefing.

'The very same,' Markham confirmed. 'Mrs Merryweather was clearly fascinated by the story of Emma Livry and those other poor souls and it was obvious from what she said that Clara was equally obsessed with the topic.'

'*So what?*' No one except Noakes ever dared to adopt such a belligerent tone with the guvnor.

'Take it easy, Noakesy,' the DI's eyes were kind, knowing as he did the other's soft spot for the elderly and vulnerable. Markham's tone was as coolly authoritative and controlled as ever, with no hint of nervous tension. 'Mrs Merryweather told us that she had wanted to collaborate with Andrée on a book about the ballet world, only Andrée turned her down. So, what could be more natural than her seeking out Clara . . .'

Burton's expression was intent. 'To talk about the bonfire ballerinas?'

'To discuss what it's like in a theatre behind the scenes and what it might have been like back then in the nineteenth century. The smell of greasepaint . . . miraculous stage effects . . . things that sprang up from nowhere . . . props and costumes . . . wigs, velvet curtains, chandeliers, coloured lights. Mrs Merryweather writes romantic fiction . . . wants to give readers an *immersive* experience, so it makes sense that she'd ask a former ballerina to help with some background colour.'

'When you say, "miraculous effects" and "things that sprang up from nowhere", what d'you mean?' Noakes asked suspiciously. 'Like fire?'

'I mean special effects generally, Noakesy,' the DI replied lightly. 'But there's no doubting Clara seems to have a particular interest in dancers who ended up getting torched for love of their art.'

'What about a picnic?' Doyle said, seemingly out of the blue.

Four pairs of eyes were riveted on him.

Noakes boggled. 'Whaddya mean, *a picnic*?'

The DS looked somewhat self-conscious but forged ahead. 'Merryweather's a romantic novelist, right?'

Nods of agreement.

'Okay, well they're always doing that kind of thing in Jane Austen, aren't they? Al fresco whatsits and outings by candlelight . . .'

Paula's influence again, Markham guessed.

Doyle looked as though he had decided this was a case of in for a penny, in for a pound.

'So, Merryweather could suggest she and Clara meet up at the theatre . . . smuggle a few treats in . . . kind of camp out and soak up the vibes.'

'Like a midnight feast,' Noakes commented sarcastically. 'Very *Malory Towers*.'

'It's the kind of thing Mills and Boon types like Merryweather would be big on, sarge,' Doyle rejoined. 'Which means Clara wouldn't get the wind up . . . wouldn't find it suspicious.'

'Actually, there's something in that,' Burton said consideringly. 'Merryweather could come over all Jean Plaidy and say how about bringing some candles or tealights and, oh I dunno, summoning the ghost of the theatre or something.' Before Noakes could cut in, she continued, 'Wasn't there talk during the Baranov investigation about the theatre being haunted by this janitor who murdered a ballerina after she rejected him?'

'*Jesus*!' Noakes burst out. 'You're worse than *him*.' He indicated Doyle. 'First Enid Blyton an' now the bleeding *Hunchback of Notre Dame*! Kentish'll never fall for it!' Aware of the guvnor's dislike of blasphemy, he amended, 'Sorry boss, but I *ask* you! Talk about poncy an' arty-farty!'

'But that's just it, sarge,' Doyle insisted. 'It's right up their street. Dontcha *see*,' he said earnestly, 'Merryweather and Kentish get off on that kind of thing. All romantic and ethereal and mysterious.' The young DS spoke with newly minted authority. 'Kentish won't find it weird cos that's how folk like them carry on.' He paused then added deliberately. 'If it's all a bit, well, *kinky* and *spacey*, she'll fricking lap it up . . . an illicit séance or something . . . doesn't get spookier than that.'

'You might well be right,' Markham said thoughtfully. Then with more emphasis, 'Yes Doyle, I think you're on to something there.'

'But do you reckon Clara might try to kill Mrs Merryweather, sir?' Burton said steadily, locking eyes with Markham. 'You want to use her as bait?'

'I think that if we can lure Clara to a meeting in Bromgrove Theatre, and Mrs Merryweather lets her tongue run away with her so that Clara feels threatened, then she'll try to engineer some sort of tragic "accident" . . . something fatal.'

'Like *The Wicker Man*,' Noakes suggested witheringly, clearly unconvinced. 'Only ballet-style.'

'Yes, Noakesy,' the DI said meeting the other's eyes. 'Because we're going for broke now.'

'Lemme get this straight,' Noakes frowned, running a pudgy finger round the inside of his smart collar as though it was throttling him. 'Okay, rewind a bit . . . You want Merryweather to carry on like she's mad keen on soaking up ballet stuff for her book so as to get Kentish into the theatre—'

'Which we'll have staked out,' Markham interjected.

'Right,' Noakes continued, narrowing his eyes as he tried to visualise it. 'An' then Merryweather says summat which gives Kentish the heebie-jeebies.'

'Correct.'

'Like *what*, though?' the other demanded. 'Merryweather can't come straight out and say she thinks Kentish is the killer. No way would she have kept schtum about owt like that. She'd have been straight round to the cop shop before you could say "serial killer".' Noakes was adamant. 'No fannying around about second chances or making sure she'd got it right.'

Burton agreed. 'You're right, sarge, it'd be completely out of character for her to let a three-times killer roam around Bromgrove.'

Mollified, Noakes said, 'So what's she going to say then? It's gotta be convincing else Kentish'll smell a rat.'

The team thought hard.

Finally, Carruthers turned to the DI. 'It's like you said before, sir — that about Merryweather letting her tongue run away with her. We get her to witter on about Clara's rivalry with Andrée. She could say she's been reading up about the two of them and it's given her the idea for a book about a pair of ballerinas locked in this deadly rivalry . . . the jealous one stages an accident so that the other can never dance again—'

'Yeah, but that ain't the same as shouting murder,' Noakes said pugnaciously. 'It don' mean she thinks Kentish is a killer.'

Carruthers's voice rang with conviction. 'If we script it cleverly enough, though, Kentish might reckon it's only a matter of time before Merryweather starts thinking along the same lines as Nicholas Gower and works out that *she* could've killed Andrée.'

'Plus, someone talking that way is *bound* to press Kentish's buttons,' Doyle interjected eagerly, 'especially seeing as she's got all these hang-ups . . . Merryweather could even say she's planning a storyline about the killer ballerina being in love with her rival, only she gets knocked back. *Yeah, yeah—*' he raised a hand to forestall Noakes's objection — 'I *know* we don't have any proof that Andrée and Clara ever got it on, but if she's seriously conflicted about Andrée, it might help tip her over the edge.'

'*Conflicted*!' Noakes's piggy eyes bored into his younger colleague. 'You're worse than Shippers, you are.'

Markham smothered a laugh. 'Now you come to mention it, I want Professor Finlayson's input asap.' Then he added grimly, 'Not least as we've zero chance of getting the DCI onside without a very clear strategy.'

'Too right,' came the voice of CID's one-man Greek chorus, 'Sidney'll freak out in case it goes wrong. Imagine the headlines . . . *Ballerina Killer's Final Tragic Victim* . . . an' a big fat piece in the *Gazette* about how our lot shafted an OAP.'

'Thanks for that, Noakesy. Ever the little ray of sunshine,' was Markham's terse response as Burton blenched. But deep inside, the DI felt a surge of energy.

He took a steadying breath. 'Yes,' he said simply. 'I think it might work . . . Carruthers, I like your idea of a scenario which suggests that Mrs Merryweather is sort of nibbling round the edges of thinking Clara's the murderer. She needs to come across as, cognitively speaking, not quite "in the zone", a bit vague and daffy . . . badly shaken by the murders at Rosemount but bright enough to piece things together in the end . . . feeling her way towards it . . . potentially dangerous because she's a blabbermouth.'

Carruthers looked illumined from within, his bloodless physiognomy transformed by pleasure at the DI's approval.

'Presumably we need Kentish to confess, sir,' he said eagerly, 'as opposed to just attacking Merryweather.'

'Correct.'

Carruthers leaned in. 'Well, assuming Doyle's right and this whole thing presses Kentish's buttons so she's on the verge of losing it big style, then if Merryweather pretends to have some kind of lightbulb moment — like she suddenly realises who the murderer is — Kentish will spill her guts. Won't be able to stop herself, er, getting handy with the candles.'

'Ideally, yes,' the DI replied.

Judging from the way Doyle was looking at Carruthers, he was clearly gratified by the way the newcomer appeared keen to share any potential plaudits.

*Maybe we can make this work after all*, Markham thought contemplating his team. *Maybe we're all going to shake down together just fine. Maybe Noakes's departure didn't spell the breakup of his unit.*

Back in the moment, he continued, 'Kate, I want you, Carruthers and Doyle to hook up with Nathan and go through all of this. We need a script and,' he flashed a grin at Noakes, 'a psychological profile that will convince Sidney. Given Mrs Merryweather's age and vulnerability, the operation needs to be watertight.'

The trio were out of his office in a trice, reinvigorated like their boss.

'What about me?' Noakes asked wistfully.

'You and me are going to take a look inside Bromgrove Theatre, Noakes . . . check the lie of the land and work out vantage points.'

* * *

Although the exterior of the little red-brick theatre behind the council offices in Bromgrove town centre was decidedly unprepossessing, its interior was every bit as delightful as Markham remembered, the peacock-blue and gold auditorium resembling some magical confection that belonged to a fairy-tale world of princes and princesses, enchanted palaces and forests, moonstone mists and shimmering visions.

At first, he and Noakes simply sat together on red velvet seats in the dress circle, lost in memories of the Baranov investigation and one horrific onstage discovery in particular.

'You can still feel him here,' Noakes said at length in a hoarse whisper. '*Baranov*. Like he's spying on us from the wings.'

The safety curtain was down and, having requisitioned keys from the doorkeeper with instructions that they wanted the place strictly to themselves, the two men knew they were alone. And yet there was indeed the unnerving sense of a shadowy presence watching them from under hooded lids, just out of sight . . .

'Let's check behind the scenes,' Markham suggested eventually, breaking the spell.

With its twisting passages painted an institutional green and cream, the labyrinthine basement domain accessed from a side door held its unforgettable aroma of dank air mixed with sweat, glue, varnish and the resin the ballerinas used on their pointe shoes. Exploring these nether regions felt decidedly eerie, pipes and rafters rattling in hollow syncopation with the sound of hail coming from outside.

''S'like a morgue down here,' Noakes shuddered as they finally arrived at the open-plan area directly underneath the stage. Involuntarily, his eyes wandered to the rear of the cavernous space with its hampers of props and costumes. 'At least they've blocked off that chuffing door from before . . .'

'Baranov's *gone*, Noakesy,' Markham reminded him firmly as they mounted a narrow spiral staircase up to the stage wings. 'And ghosts can't hurt us,' he said firmly. 'The priority *now* is working out how to mount surveillance.'

'Where's Merryweather going to do her spiel?' Noakes asked as they moved out beneath the proscenium arch onto the stage apron. 'Y'know, the tongue-running-away-with-her malarkey . . . all that stuff about planning a book on deadly rivals an' the rest of it . . .' He squinted into the wings. 'Problem being, up here Kentish will spot anyone moving in from the side.'

'Yes,' Markham murmured thoughtfully, raking back a dark lock with an impatient hand. 'The basement's a better bet. When Mrs Merryweather contacts Clara to arrange a meeting, she can gush about wanting to experience what it's like in the *bowels* of the theatre . . . say she's always wondered about trapdoors and how they manage all the special illusions—'

'Yeah, like that Christmas tree in *Nutbuster* which grows up to the roof an' the little bed that floats round the stage an' the flying sled,' the other said eagerly, causing Markham to recall that his friend had been endearingly entranced as any child by the cunning devices of theatreland.

Noakes experienced a moment of doubt.

'D'you reckon Kentish'll fall for it though, guv?' he asked. 'You're *sure* she won't smell summat fishy?'

'If we can ensure that Mrs Merryweather's initial contact piques Clara's interest at the same time as making her feel somewhat uneasy, then she'll go ahead with the meeting . . . Mrs Merryweather can say one of the healthcare assistants is going to bring her into town and then come back later.' Markham's voice hardened. 'Of course, Clara will have other plans for her in the meantime.'

'You *really* think she'll try to kill her down there?'

'While making it look like a dreadful accident, yes.'

Before they descended the spiral stairs to the lower level, Markham lingered on the apron. Suddenly, he recalled Rosa Maitland's stubborn insistence that someone had viciously shoved her from the wings during the Dance Academy gala performance.

Now he felt certain Clara Kentish had been the hidden aggressor, an upswell of uncontrollable jealousy prompting the older woman to try and ruin the young ballerina's entrance . . . as though reliving her old rivalry with Andrée Clark.

Standing there, he also remembered Doggie Dickerson's characterisation of the ballet world as a veritable swamp of fear and loathing, imbued through and through with envy, malice and spite.

What was it Doggie had said about balletic stamina? Yes, that was it . . . he had said ballerinas possessed 'grasshopper muscles'.

For all her seeming thistledown fragility, Clara Kentish would have had no difficulty dispatching Andrée and Maureen Frost. And in his mind's eye, Markham saw her doubling back across that wildflower meadow to the deadly rendezvous with Nicholas Gower . . .

Aware of Noakes shifting restlessly, he led the way back down to the lower level.

'What'll Kentish use?' Noakes asked peering around.

The dank smell was very strong now. Little wonder the area beneath the stage was known as Hell in theatrical circles, Markham thought to himself.

'*Phew, what a whiff!*' Noakes wrinkled his nose disdainfully. 'Must be all them mouldy old tutus. Smells *rank* . . . like they've skimped on doing the laundry for a while.'

Suddenly Markham felt certain he knew what Clara Kentish would do.

In the corner, next to a hamper overflowing with sequinned costumes, tights and headdresses, were a couple of rickety wooden chairs with a metal fire bucket nearby. Lifting the lid, he spied a few tell-tale cigarette stubs in the grubby yellow sand.

'I'm willing to bet the stagehands have the odd crafty fag down here,' he said, 'even though it's against health and safety.'

Noakes looked alarmed.

'Are we *really* going for all that blazing ballerinas bollocks or whatever the chuff it is floats Kentish's creepy boat?'

'What could be more natural than Mrs Merryweather wanting to come down here by candlelight,' Markham said. 'Like you said, Noakesy,' he continued insinuatingly, 'shades of high jinks in the dorm and all that.'

His friend looked as though he didn't care for that particular narrative. Nonetheless, he watched Markham as though hypnotised.

'Imagine the two of them sitting down here . . . Mrs Merryweather rooting through costumes and props on her lap . . . oohing and aahing over them—'

'Getting high on the pong,' Noakes finished sardonically.

'Enthused by the *romance*,' Markham corrected him. 'Before things start to take a darker turn and she realises her peril.'

'An' then at the end of it, Kentish tries to set fire to her,' came the flat response.

'I'm almost certain that's what will happen provided Mrs Merryweather sows the seed beforehand by talking about the Emma Livry tragedy and we "dress" the set appropriately.' Markham paused. 'Though obviously we'll need to hear what Nathan thinks about the extent of Clara's suggestibility and her propensity towards arson.' He looked around at the hampers of vintage textiles and fabrics. 'There are regulations about non-flammable products in theatres, but I'm willing to bet half of what's in here wouldn't pass the fire safety tests . . .'

'Yeah,' Noakes agreed. 'Bound to be glue an' God knows what else holding them together.' He peered into the gloom. 'Then there's the cardboard masks an' stuff like that.'

'Clara's familiar with all of it,' Markham said slowly. 'I think that had Andrée not succumbed to MS and an increasingly medicalised existence, then her old rival might have sought to finish her off here . . . *immolation* rather than strangulation.' The DI's gaze was remote as he added, 'I think maybe she looked at that miniature toy theatre of Andrée's and fantasised about seeing her down here licked by flames, capering and screaming like a madwoman.'

Noakes shot Markham a sidelong look. When the guvnor travelled into himself like this, there was no saying what he might come out with. It inspired a certain awe in his trusty companion that he sought to conceal by increased gruffness.

'What if Kentish jus' grabs the candles?' Noakes demanded. 'An' makes everything go *Whoosh*,' he gestured expressively, 'before we have a chance to rescue Hetty Wainthrop?'

'Assuming we get the green light from Sidney, if I remember the layout correctly, there's that little physio room just next door . . . The teccies can rig up speakers, so we'll be able to hear everything. I think Carruthers and Doyle are right about Clara needing to unburden herself . . . The minute her confession is in the bag, we move in.'

Noakes grunted in accustomed *on-your-own-head-be-it* fashion.

'It *might* work,' he said finally.

'It's *got* to work,' the DI retorted grimly. 'Clara will figure she's got nothing to lose and she'll spin it as a tragic accident.' Elegant musician's hands spread wide, he exclaimed dramatically, 'She and Mrs Merryweather came down here for a nostalgic chat. They really *shouldn't have*, but it was just for old times' sake . . . they figured there was no great harm in it. Somehow everything happened so fast . . . one minute they were chatting away all nice and cosy, then next thing she knew, the old lady had caught fire . . . she couldn't get close enough to save her . . . dashed out and called *999* . . .'

Noakes shivered.

'It's not jus' Baranov haunting this place,' he said at length. 'There's summat downright *evil* here.'

Markham held up a peremptory hand.

'Whatever curse lies over this place, we're going to *break it*.'

Noakes could only hope that the DI was right.

## 13. BROKEN SPELL

Events moved quickly after that, with the combined efforts of Kate Burton and Nathan Finlayson ensuring DCI Sidney's prompt approval of the plan to snare Clara Kentish.

Linda Merryweather demonstrated a sprightliness that at first took Doyle and Carruthers aback.

'Can't believe she's so, well, *up for it*,' Doyle said as the team assembled in Markham's office on Wednesday morning.

'You're forgetting, Mrs Merryweather's a successful novelist,' Burton pointed out. 'Memorising the dialogue's a cinch. And besides, she wants to avenge the others. Nicholas Gower, in particular, was her friend. If it was Clara who held his head under water like that, then she wants to help us nail her.'

'Merryweather's not totally *sure* though is she, ma'am?' Carruthers ventured.

'I think deep down she knows Clara killed all three of them. Andrée, Maureen and Nicholas. But as for trying to process it . . . well, that's another matter,' Burton replied.

'You're satisfied that Mrs Merryweather's word perfect, Kate?' Markham asked quietly.

'Yes sir. She's making the call to Clara later, arranging to meet at five o'clock . . . *The twilight hour.*' Mock groans greeted this pseudo-romanticism.

'How about the folk at Rosemount?' Carruthers asked. 'Are you going to tell *them* what's going down?'

'No,' Burton told him. 'It's better they don't know . . . then there's no chance of anything leaking. Mrs Merryweather gets dropped off at the side entrance in Jackdaw Lane and Clara whisks her inside,' she grimaced, 'for their girlie adventure.'

'Is the physio room set up?' Markham asked.

'Yes, all good to go, sir. She won't notice a thing.'

'How are we keeping the theatre out of bounds to people from the Dance Academy?' The DI frowned. 'We don't want anyone blundering in on us.'

'Clara will square things with the janitor. Spin it as a sort of clandestine jolly for Mrs Merryweather . . . big ballet fan . . . wants to give the old dear a special treat, blah blah.'

'Does *he* know about it being a stakeout?' Doyle asked.

'No.' Burton was very much in control. 'He just thinks we've been scoping out various locations as part of the investigation . . . no inkling that we're after Clara.' She consulted a clipboard. 'There'll be a static unit posted two streets away, but only the four of us and Noakes inside the theatre. That way, nothing looks odd or out of place.'

'Good,' Markham said. 'Everything has to appear as normal as possible.' Insofar as anything in the peculiar world of ballet could ever be described as normal. 'If we're lucky, Clara will decide to unburden herself and then silence Mrs Merryweather.' Grimly he added, 'She may already have made up her mind the old lady can't leave that theatre alive.'

\* \* \*

The physio room in the theatre basement was cramped, musty and oppressive, but as soon as the team heard voices over the intercom, they knew it was game on.

Linda Merryweather was pitch perfect, spinning her net like a plump, complacent spider, with just the right mix of disingenuous blather and insinuation. Markham's admiration rose as the impromptu 'picnic' proceeded and she touched

all the chords agreed in advance with Nathan Finlayson —
deadly rivals, burning ballerinas, rejection, revenge — drawing the other by imperceptible degrees towards a climax . . .

It came as she said with the over-familiarity of a garru-
lous old woman turned celebrity-hunter, 'Are you sure you're
feeling quite alright, dear? I *hope* I haven't *upset* you running
on like this—'

'*Stop playing games!*'

Clara Kentish's accusatory hiss made them all sit up.

'*What?*' No need for Mrs Merryweather to fake her
alarm. They could hear it in the woman's voice.

Markham raised his forefinger in warning.

*Wait.*

Kentish's voice again. 'You *know*, don't you?'

'Know what?'

'That *I* killed them. That's what you're getting round
to, isn't it . . . ? That you know it was me . . . Andrée Clark,
Maureen Frost, Nicholas Gower. And now,' in a flat, dull
tone, 'I have to kill *you* as well.'

Again, Markham raised a peremptory hand.

*Not yet.*

Linda Merryweather had herself well under command
once more.

'But *why?*' she stuttered with a very convincing imper-
sonation of horror.

'You said it yourself. Andrée *destroyed* me . . . Ballet was
all I had, and she *ruined* it . . .'

'But, my dear, you made it too, a soloist . . .'

Clara Kentish's voice rose almost to a shriek, as though
the other hadn't spoken.

'She always had to play the *star*. Only ever wanted to
strike poses instead of doing the steps and listening to the
music . . . *Poses!*'

Mrs Merryweather murmured something inaudible, but
she might as well not have been there.

'With Andrée it was all about moving as fast as possible
. . . jumping as high as possible . . . raising your leg as high as

possible. So *vulgar* and *flashy*. So *cheap*.' A strained cackle that sounded shockingly harsh in the taut silence. 'She used to taunt me. "*You're* not a swan," she used to say. "You're just a *crane*". Sometimes she'd push me onstage from the wings so that I'd stumble on my entrance.' The ballerina's voice was coming in shallow pants now. 'Everything was *pretence* with her . . . *everything*! Even the curtain calls were fake. She'd pretend she had to be dragged bodily onto the stage because she was so shy and retiring, when all the time she was saying out of the corner of her mouth, "Pull harder, damn you, *pull harder*!"'

Mrs Merryweather gave the signal. 'What are you doing with that candle, Clara? You're frightening me. For God's sake, put it down.'

And now Markham gestured to the team to move.

Glassy-eyed and very pale, but with her trademark beautiful deportment and immaculately coiled hair, Clara Kentish, lighted candle in hand, came into view. Mrs Merryweather sat frozen clutching a pile of fabrics. A folding table next to the elderly lady held the remnants of their 'picnic'.

It was Noakes who spoke first.

'You don' want to be jiggling that about, luv,' he said, the Yorkshire vowels somehow broadening as he held her gaze. 'They're nasty things, fires.'

The sheer ordinariness of it gave her a jolt. Without taking her eyes from his, she slowly bent and placed the candle down on the little table.

'We know how it happened,' Noakes continued, for all the world as though they were discussing the weather or England's chances in the Third Test. 'You'd had enough of it all, luv. All Andrée's movie star carry on . . . Enough of pretending everything were okay when really it were *crap*.'

'You understand,' she whispered. 'Yes, off stage there was nothing . . . it felt like the shadow side of the moon.' A skein of spittle hung from the corner of her mouth down the front of her lilac chiffon scarf, but she barely seemed conscious of the lapse, brushing a hand across her face with clumsy impatience.

'We know you never meant to hurt them other two,' Noakes continued gently.

'They were on to me,' she groaned. 'And I panicked. Maureen spotted me outside down by the lake that morning after . . . after I was in Andrée's room.' Agitatedly, she pleated the folds of her gauzy mauve skirt. 'Maybe if Andrée hadn't laughed at me . . . called me an escaped jumping bean . . . maybe I wouldn't have done it.'

'Maureen planned to come to us, right?' Noakes prompted.

'I came up with some pathetic excuse for why I was there,' she replied mechanically. 'Pretended I was getting ideas for a ballet design, a modern take on *Swan Lake*. She said she believed me but wanted us to tell the police.' Miserably, she added, 'Deep down I don't think she really did believe me. She *wanted to*, alright, but she had doubts. Then in that shed . . . All I can remember is standing there afterwards covered in blood. The rest is a blank.'

'And Nicholas Gower?' Burton fought down a wave of revulsion as she recalled the third death, her lips feeling dry and huge.

'He knew too much about me, my private life, all the history with Andrée . . . *everything*. He would have come to you in the end.'

Click, click.

The dancer drew something from the pocket of her skirt.

The little art deco cigarette lighter.

Suddenly her head jerked back and next minute, her trailing chiffon scarf had ignited, the dancer letting out a demonic scream as she spun in circles like some hideous dervish.

Then Noakes's jacket was round her and she was finally still.

* * *

On a mild Friday afternoon two weeks after the dramatic events in Bromgrove Theatre, the team, along with Noakes and Olivia, were enjoying drinks in their favourite pub the Grapes.

A resolutely old-fashioned hostelry with retro décor and furnishings straight out of the nineteen seventies, it nonetheless had an unpretentious authenticity that contrasted favourably with more chichi establishments.

Markham was surprised and pleased that Olivia had elected to join them.

'How could I not?' was all she said. 'Besides,' with a grin. 'George would only sulk if I didn't toast your success.'

And now, despite a certain stiffness in her manner towards Kate Burton (which the latter put down to awkwardness on account of CID knowing about the split with Markham), she was ensconced with the others in the back parlour, their booth shielding them from any patrons who might be tempted to eavesdrop on the enigmatic inspector. Given how Denise, the beehived landlady, guarded Markham's privacy like a tigress, it would have been a brave customer who dared encroach on their post mortem.

'I think Kentish was in love with Rosa Maitland,' Doyle said, emboldened by his second pint. 'Andrée and that creep of a husband hurt Maitland badly . . . Killing Andrée was payback for that.'

Carruthers, likewise on his second Grolsch and making unexpected headway in his fellow sergeant's good opinion, demurred. 'I know she's gay but isn't it more likely Kentish just felt *maternal* . . . wanted to protect the kid?'

'Yeah, that would've been part of it,' Doyle agreed. 'But there was something about the way she was ranting and raving afterwards about Maitland being so beautiful and unspoilt blah blah . . . It just felt like there *had* to be something else going on.'

'But didn't you say that you thought Kentish might have shoved Maitland during the show at the Dance Academy, sir?' Carruthers asked Markham. 'Surely she wouldn't have done that if she was in love with the girl.'

'It could just have been a sudden outburst of jealousy,' Burton speculated. 'She might even have been reliving what happened with Andrée. Besides, you can be in love with someone and envious at the same time.'

*Uh-oh*, Noakes was wearing his Witchfinder General's face. He was doubtless thinking of his daughter, though Markham had the feeling Natalie Noakes was well able to look after herself in the unlikely event that she ever inspired a sapphic crush. Meanwhile, Olivia's eyes were firmly downcast, but he could sense her choking with mirth as she imagined Muriel's likely reaction to such a scenario.

With a wary glance at Kate Burton, Noakes muttered under his breath, 'For chuff's sake, ain't any of them dancers *normal?*'

Burton knew this was really just a token grumble and there was no offence in it. With commendable restraint, she said mildly, 'I figure, they're pretty much the same as the rest of us, sarge . . . they just take life at a faster pace, that's all.'

Noakes grunted.

To everyone's surprise, Carruthers spoke up. 'You're right about it not being a normal lifestyle, sarge,' he said. 'By the sound of it, stagehands are probably the only "real" people in the place . . . They get to drink, smoke, have a laugh, watch the football, enjoy takeaways and all of that, whereas the dancers just live in some weird world of their own.'

Visibly pleased at being called "sarge" and trying (unsuccessfully) to hide it, Noakes agreed. 'Yeah,' he said. 'One of 'em told me there was this time when Kentish keeled over onstage just after the curtain came down at the end of *Nutbuster*. She were lying on her back, chest going up and down, all sweaty an' soaked through . . . absolutely wiped-out cos of some injury or other. Andrée pestered the boss technician or whatever he's called to whip the curtain back up while Kentish was still laid out flat . . . Wanted to embarrass her and get a cheap laugh.' A grin of satisfaction. 'Sparky told her to bog off.'

'What a mean trick,' Olivia exclaimed indignantly.

Burton chipped in. 'I heard there was some evening performance when Andrée kept them all guessing about whether or not she was going to dance. Then at the very last moment, she told them she couldn't manage it . . . Clara was the understudy and had to hotfoot it out to the theatre—'

Doyle was puzzled. 'That's par for the course if you're the understudy, right?'

'Yes, but Andrée knew Clara had planned a huge spaghetti dinner washed down with a load of Pinot Noir . . . By leaving it so late, Clara was bound to be stuffed and her stomach all over the place.'

Now Doyle was sympathetic. 'Not nice,' he said, 'not nice at all.'

'The backstage lot said she could be kind, though,' Noakes pointed out. 'Really good if some young kid were down in the dumps . . . never forgot birthdays . . . not all hoity toity like some ballerinas.'

'In other words, she was a mixture of good and bad,' Markham said. 'And,' he added quietly, 'she still had a life to live. Just like Maureen Frost and Nicholas Gower.'

'I wonder if we'll ever find out what really went on between Kentish and Maureen Frost,' Carruthers said regretfully. 'I just can't get my head round it.'

Doyle moved on to safer ground. 'C'mon mate,' he said gruffly to Carruthers, 'it's kick-off between Aston Villa and Liverpool at three . . . Chris Carstairs is waiting for us at his place.' As they got to their feet, unseen by Carruthers, he winked at Noakes. A look that seemed to say, no one who liked the Beautiful Game could be all bad. 'What about you, sarge?' he asked. 'Carstairs is thinking of a curry for later.'

'You're alright, mate,' Noakes said. 'The missus is doing chicken in a basket tonight an' apple crumble for afters . . . Then I promised to sit through a film with her an' Nat.' His face displayed the resigned fortitude of a prisoner on Death Row. 'It's on Netflix, some ballet thriller,' his face suggested this was a contradiction in terms, 'called *Tiny Twinkletoes* or some daft bollocks like that.'

'You mean *Tiny Pretty Things*,' Carruthers laughed. 'Cheer up, sarge, it had some decent reviews . . . Quite addictive apparently.'

'Yeah well, this Kentish case has got my lot interested in all that backstage stuff,' Noakes mumbled.

Olivia laughed. 'Like murder and mayhem, you mean.'

A swift glance at Noakes's face as Doyle and Carruthers departed had Burton reaching for her coat. Time to let the Magic Threesome have their catchup, she thought. Once upon a time it hurt to feel excluded, but Nathan had changed all of that. 'I've got to dash too,' she said breezily. 'You've whetted my appetite, sarge,' she added grinning. 'Might give that ballet drama a whirl.'

And with a wave she was gone, Olivia nodding awkwardly at her retreating back.

No sooner were they alone, than Noakes unburdened himself. 'Nat's been dumped,' he told them dejectedly.

Markham noticed that under the table his friend's brawny fists were clenched.

''Course, that's not how *she* tells it,' the other continued. 'So if you see her, don' let on I've told you.'

Vigorous nods greeted this plea.

'I knew he were a wrong 'un the moment I clapped eyes on him,' Noakes lamented.

Which didn't exactly accord with Markham's recollections, since he seemed to remember the proud father being mighty delighted at the prospect of the perma-tanned one hooking the eligible heir to Harmony Spa and a fitness empire. Still, the notion of anyone rejecting his cherished offspring was more than enough to make Noakes do a 360-degree turn.

'What caused the split, George?' Olivia asked gently.

'He's a mummy's boy an' the old witch never took to our Nat,' was the gloomy response. 'Never thought she were good enough for her precious Rick.'

Having come across Rick and Barbara Jordan in the course of a previous investigation, Markham was not surprised to hear that Natalie had fallen foul of this hard-boiled pair. But he was surprised by a sudden upsurge of protectiveness towards Noakes's loud, brash daughter. Essentially she was a decent girl, albeit he had heard her dismissed as being a 'typical chav on the make'. Olivia had once said, paraphrasing a favourite author, that what was good and what was ridiculous were most unfortunately blended in Natalie Noakes and now, catching his ex's eye, he could see she remembered their conversation on the subject only too well.

'The missus is dead worried about her,' Noakes confided, 'cos now she's talking about tying the knot with herself.'

Olivia snorted at this.

'Sorry, George,' she said when she had recovered. 'Fizz going down the wrong way.' Then, faintly, 'What does that mean exactly?'

Noakes looked decidedly queasy as he explained.

'It's a symbolic thingy where you kind of make vows to yourself . . . Nat says it's all about showing you're happy with who you are. It don' mean you're never going to get married, jus' that you're cool with being single, see.' He took a huge gulp of beer as though to oil the wheels. 'Like you're affirming your own self-worth or summat.'

'*This above all: to thine own self be true,*' Olivia murmured.

Markham started, recognising the mysterious words Andrée Clark had quoted to Honor Calthorpe — words he now realised had contained a coded warning about Clara Kentish and her chameleon-like duplicity.

'There's a lot to be said for celebrating your authentic self,' he told Noakes.

'Nat says folk often do it when they're getting over a broken heart . . . with a cake an' bridesmaids an' a wedding dress.' Looking wistful, he added, 'It ain't the real deal, though . . . not like your dad walking you down the aisle.

*Looking like a big meringue.* But Olivia bit her tongue. 'I guess some people might think it's a bit cringe-y,' she observed, choosing her words with care, 'but from a feminist perspective I imagine that kind of ceremony's quite empowering.'

Hardly a cheerleader for the feminist cause, Noakes didn't look as though he considered this to be a plus.

'I s'pose it could be worse,' he acknowledged after a long pause. 'There was some daft bint got herself splashed all over the papers last year when she went and married a *tree*.' He scowled. 'One of the hippie eco lot—'

Olivia couldn't help herself. 'The ones you call *tree-huggers*,' she grinned.

'Yeah, well.' The scowl deepened. 'Anyroad, she changed her surname to Oak or Beech or summat like that . . . to show her *commitment*. Chuffing ridiculous.'

'I remember it now,' Olivia laughed. 'It was on Merseyside, and she changed her name to Elder. Her boyfriend was okay with it.'

'Typical Scousers,' Noakes grunted. 'Mad as a box of frogs.'

Markham looked at him closely.

'It's just a fad, Noakesy,' he said consolingly. 'Don't worry, Natalie will come through it. She's a chip off the old block, remember.'

'Well, the missus don' like it.'

Markham could well imagine that, though it rather tickled him to imagine Muriel's reaction should Daughter Dearest decide to wed a shrub.

'An' that creepy bloke from the bridal shop ain't helping,' his friend gloomed. 'Him an' Nat have been thick as thieves ever since he asked her to help with makeovers.'

'Which shop is that?' Olivia asked curiously.

'The Confetti Club in Bridge Street.' Noakes swigged the last of his beer. 'I reckon Gino had summat to do with her breakup an' all,' he surmised darkly. 'Nowadays it's all "Gino thinks this" an' "Gino thinks that". If you ask me, bleeding Gino's got a sight too much to say for hisself.'

Olivia smiled at him. 'Maybe I'll pop in one day next week,' she said easily. 'Just out of pure nosiness, to see Senor Gino for myself . . . and say hello to Natalie, of course.'

Noakes beamed. 'That'd be *champion*, luv,' he said. 'She thinks the world of you.'

Olivia had a fairly good idea what Natalie thought of her, but no way was she going to destroy Noakes's fond illusions. She had a feeling he fancied the idea of his bridal-fixated daughter playing Cupid and somehow reuniting her with Markham. Much as it diverted her to picture Natalie in the role of 'relationship coach', she knew there was a long way to go on that front.

Still, after Noakes had loped off home, she lingered with Markham in the cosy booth.

'Thanks for that, Liv,' Markham said warmly. 'I think it's a weight off Noakesy's mind.'

'Well, at least I can keep an eye out and see if there's anything to worry about at this Confetti Club place.' After a pause, she added, 'Do you reckon George will stick it out at Rosemount?'

'The place suits him.' Not to mention the subsidised meals. 'I'm going to wangle him some sort of civilian consultancy role too. Make the most of him being in Sidney's good books . . . capitalise on our solving this case . . . just when I was beginning to think we'd never crack it.'

She snuggled back against the leather, realising with a pang just how much she missed being his sounding board.

'It was a strange one,' she agreed. Then, looking him straight in the eyes, she murmured, *'There are girls who do not like real life. When they hear the sharp belches of its engines approaching along the straight road that leads from childhood, through adolescence, to adulthood, they dart into a side turning. When they take their hands away from their eyes, they find themselves in the gallery of the ballet.'*

'That's rather lovely,' he said, feeling that at some level she might have been talking about herself. 'Who said it?'

'Quentin Crisp in *The Naked Civil Servant.*'

He laughed. 'Ah, I can see why you saved it till Noakesy had gone on his merry way.'

She smiled, but there was sadness in her expression.

'It's true, though, isn't it?' she said. 'Ballet's a kind of escapism, a beautiful dream. I think that's how it was for poor

Clara Kentish at any rate . . . until she became obsessed with the idea that her failure to make it to the top was somehow all down to Andrée.' She sipped her prosecco thoughtfully. 'It must've been awful the day her ambition was put on a diet — just like the rest of her — when she realised that Ballerina Land wasn't going to be as straight as she planned, and the straight lines started zigzagging all over the place . . .'

'It was all down to her skewed perception,' Markham pointed out. 'She had a decent enough career as a successful soloist, remember.'

'But somehow she still felt *unchosen*,' Olivia marvelled. 'And then when she stopped dancing and tried to start living, it got even worse.'

'It's a hellishly frightening career really. You put all your energy, time and guts into it, and then it ends each night, and finally for good in just a few years. *Poof*, that's it, no more, no lasting effects, everything just finished. No more glamorous parties and flowers from admirers . . . all gone at a stroke.'

'Unless you're like Andrée and somehow miraculously reinvent yourself,' Olivia retorted. She pulled a face. 'I suppose we should be thankful *we're* able to work into late middle age, whereas for a lot of dancers it's thirty or forty. Somehow for them it's like growing old far too early . . . the body lets them down but mentally they're still totally intact, filled with just the same desire and energy as when they were younger — maybe more so.'

'A concept currently wasted on Doyle,' Markham commented wryly. 'He couldn't really get his head round the idea that folk like Linda Merryweather, in the twilight of their lives, aren't automatically all set for Horlicks and an early night.'

Olivia chuckled. 'He'll learn.' Philosophically, she added, 'No wonder Balanchine was always chanting *Now, now, now*! and asking his dancers what they were waiting for . . . He knew exactly what they were up against.'

'*Carpe diem*, you might say.'

She sighed. 'Clara must have felt that the theatre was heaven one day and then a jail the next.'

Markham regarded her soberly. 'Well, it's been a good preparation for where she'll be spending the next few decades.'

'You don't think she'll get a hospital order?'

'She knew what she was doing, Liv. From that perspective, she was *sane*.' A gulp of his red wine. 'Two of the dead were elderly and one was middle-aged.' His mouth twisted, 'There's more public revulsion . . . more outrage in the media when victims are young. But this was a retirement home, after all. It's not clear whether there was a suicide attempt . . . but even despite her burns, the CPS won't settle for anything less than prison.' Another hasty swallow. 'We still don't have the whole picture, but I doubt she's headed to Rampton.'

'Sidney won't mind so long as Baron Eddy's in the clear,' Olivia remarked with a sour look.

'True, but who can honestly blame him. Besides, nobody wanted Rosemount to pay the price.'

She let it pass, returning to the killer.

'Wasn't there something about Clara hearing voices at the end?'

'Oh, you know how myths and legends grow up round a place, Liv,' he replied cautiously. 'Bromgrove Theatre's always had its fair share of those.'

She knew he was stonewalling.

Sighing, he continued. 'She thought she heard something. That's how she ended up setting fire to herself.'

'What was it she heard?'

'Someone sniffing.'

Olivia stared at him. '*Sniffing*?'

'Yes, Liv. Remember that Russian Orthodox funeral during the Baranov investigation when one of the dancers had hysterics—'

'Because she got it into her head that the corpse had sniffed.'

'Right . . . Well, it was all mixed up with the cult of Balanchine. He was another one who was always sniffing . . . a supercilious little trick he had. At the risk of sounding like

Noakesy, I gather it was something of an affectation amongst Russian émigrés and they all copied it.'

Olivia digested this. 'And Clara was obsessed with Balanchine?'

'I think they all were. A whole generation of teachers and choreographers virtually *ventriloquised* him . . . right down to adopting his mannerisms and training their pets to do ballet tricks.' Quietly he added, 'He had something of a baleful influence by the end.'

'An *obsession*,' she mused. 'So maybe that's why Clara thought Balanchine was there in the theatre . . . Or maybe it could have been *Baranov's* ghost.'

Markham recalled Noakes's fearful whisper that he thought Baranov was spying on them from the wings.

Time to end the morbid speculation.

'Clara was rambling in the ambulance . . . that she knew Balanchine was there because she recognised the sound and he wanted her to go to him. She was talking about the ballet *Coppélia* too.'

'The one with the *doll*.' Olivia breathed. 'D'you reckon that's what was behind the pointing doll at Andrée's bedside?'

'Quite possibly. She and Andrée performed the ballerina role on alternate nights, and it seemed to have a particular significance for her.' Somewhat downcast, he added, 'Clara mentioned the ballet at our first meeting, only I never made the connection with our crime scene. She mentioned a "mechanical toy" rather than a doll, so it went over my head.'

'Don't blame yourself for that, Gil.'

'Anyway,' his tone became brisker, 'the paramedics pumped her full of sedatives and painkillers, so she was pretty much out of it after that scene in the theatre.'

'Sounds like she went round the twist.'

'Arguably yes, but . . . there was a kink there anyway and somehow the ballet magnified it, which is why she never really matured.'

'Maybe it's something to do with dancers being so eager to please . . . always trying to woo an audience. Maybe that's what stops them from growing old naturally and keeps them like children.'

He flashed his rare, charming smile. 'I've missed your insights, Liv.'

'Kate Burton not coming up to scratch then?' But it was said without rancour.

'Kate's gorging on some new guru,' he told her. 'Carruthers is a receptive audience, but I can tell Doyle wishes she'd put a sock in it.'

'Who is it this time?'

'Some writer Nathan's heavily into at the moment. His theory is that killers are just limited, pathetic people and we shouldn't glamorise them as evil because they aren't even that exciting.'

She thought about this. 'The guy might have a point. Somehow it seems wrong the way we fetishise them at the expense of victims.' She caught herself up and reached for his hand. 'Sorry, I don't mean *you*, Gil.' A pause. '*Never you.*'

Her touch sent an electric shock through him. Mistaking his reaction, she timidly tried to withdraw but he retained his grasp of her hand.

They remained like that for some time.

He wanted to ask her what was going on in her life . . . what she was up to with Matthew Sullivan . . . what the future held . . .

But he said nothing, merely allowing the moment to protract into infinity.

The retirement home murders were solved, and a new chapter beckoned.

## THE END

ALSO BY CATHERINE MOLONEY

**THE DI GILBERT MARKHAM SERIES**
Book 1: CRIME IN THE CHOIR
Book 2: CRIME IN THE SCHOOL
Book 3: CRIME IN THE CONVENT
Book 4: CRIME IN THE HOSPITAL
Book 5: CRIME IN THE BALLET
Book 6: CRIME IN THE GALLERY
Book 7: CRIME IN THE HEAT
Book 8: CRIME AT HOME
Book 9: CRIME IN THE BALLROOM
Book 10: CRIME IN THE BOOK CLUB
Book 11: CRIME IN THE COLLEGE
Book 12: CRIME IN THE KITCHEN
Book 13: CRIME IN THE SPA
Book 14: CRIME IN THE CRYPT
Book 15: CRIME IN OXFORD
Book 16: CRIME IN CARTON HALL
Book 17: CRIME IN RETIREMENT

**Thank you for reading this book.**

If you enjoyed it please leave feedback on Amazon or Goodreads, and if there is anything we missed or you have a question about, then please get in touch. We appreciate you choosing our book.

Founded in 2014 in Shoreditch, London, we at Joffe Books pride ourselves on our history of innovative publishing. We were thrilled to be shortlisted for Independent Publisher of the Year at the British Book Awards.

www.joffebooks.com

We're very grateful to eagle-eyed readers who take the time to contact us. Please send any errors you find to corrections@joffebooks.com. We'll get them fixed ASAP.